After three books with the dynamic duo of Peg and Hazel, I feel completely justified in my long-held belief that birds are, in fact, hazardous to your health. And Jen Dodrill proves me right once again in No Egrets, with a twisty mystery that surprised me more than once. (To be fair to our feathered friends, it's not the birds who are dangerous in this series... just the humans who are after them.) —M. Carrie

Peg Howard's adventures are entertaining, interesting, and engaging. She is an empty nester and a widow who finds herself involved in murder investigations. In this third book, she goes from searching for missing egrets to finding a body. Who would have thought bird watching could be dangerous? Peg juggles adult children, her mother-in-law, and potential suitors as she works to discover who dunnit. This is a clean, cozy mystery that values family, friendship, and caring for others. It also keeps you guessing! —Annette T.

This is fun cozy mystery that's full of twists and turns and even some laughs as they search to find the egrets. A little romance makes the story sweet. The previous 2 books compliment this 3rd book but it can also be enjoyed as a standalone read. Clean and is suitable for everyone who wants to relax and read an enjoyable book. —K's Girl

No Egrets

An Empty-nesters Cozy Mystery: Book 3

Jen Dodrill

DEDICATION

Special thanks to my friend, Tonya Sloan, who helped me launch book 2 in the series and won the chance to pick an animal and name it for *No Egrets*. Tonya loves dogs and works with our local dog rescue. She chose a golden retriever mix puppy and named her Lucy.

CHAPTER I

Even at 7:30 p.m., heat hung heavily in the air. Perspiration trickled down my back. This meeting, scheduled to last until nine, stretched before me like an endless road on a moonless night. I shouldn't have attended, and I wouldn't have, except for my mother-in-law's persistent badgering. When she told me to grab my purse, I did. To be fair, she mentioned cookies.

And here we stood, surrounded by the majority of Stone Creek Cove's homeowners, who waited to discuss the problem *du jour*—finding the missing egrets and making the creek a safer place—and no cookies in sight.

"This place has seen better days," I said, looking at the few pieces of decrepit wooden furniture scattered around the room.

Hazel scooted closer to me as more people crowded into the building. "It's been here as long as I've owned my house, Peg, and I've lived here for over forty years. Residents use it for everything from weddings to neighborhood association meetings."

Weddings? Imagining a pristine white gown swishing down the aisle after seeing the number of spider webs on the windows and the dirty, scuffed floor sent shivers up and down my spine. I shook off thoughts of festive nuptials and my own recent proposal. "That's another term for homeowners' association, by the way."

She gave me the stink eye. Other curious neighbors entered, and we shuffled around the left side of the room. About thirty chairs sat in the middle, all of them full. The rest of us lined the sides like random sardines. The scent of hot, sweaty bodies grew.

"Order." A woman of indeterminate age stood at the front of the room and whacked her hand on the rickety podium. Another slam might split it in two. She brushed her stylish gray hair behind her ears, repositioned her bright red cat-eye glasses, and leaned toward the microphone. "I said order. Now shut y'all's mouths."

Having grown up in Northwest Florida and now a resident of Pensacola in general, Stone Creek Cove specifically, the contraction of "you all" was considered perfect English. Northerners who moved to the area adopted the term to avoid being teased. This woman's accent indicated she'd been born into it.

A slim, gray-haired man, sporting round silver spectacles propped on the end of his nose, sat beside the podium. He jumped up and pointed at several women clustered on the right side of the room. "My wife said y'all. That means you too."

Gasps rang out, almost as one voice. The group surged forward and faced off with the African-American couple.

I bent toward my mother-in-law's ear. "Should we leave? We don't want to be tangled up in whatever this is."

"We're here for the birds, remember?" Hazel patted my arm. Her eyes brimmed with excitement.

I made a face but held my tongue. Since I formed the Empty Nesters Birding Group last year, birds consumed my every waking moment. I seemed to live and breathe for our feathered friends, from Hazel's yellow parakeet Roscoe to the rufous hummingbird and the resplendent quetzal. Now, the snowy egrets that used to live in the creek in the middle of the 'hood had vanished. No one knew why or how.

"The woman is Marilyn Croft. She's the head of the association. Derek is her husband." Hazel indicated the man who fussed at the women.

A woman in her late fifties, dressed in stonewashed capris and a graphic T-shirt depicting a '70s rock band, stepped out of the group and stamped her foot. "Derek Croft, you and your wife are not in charge."

Her version of "You're not the boss of me." I bit the inside of my cheek, stifling my giggles.

With a sneer, the man said, "Babs, sit down." His authoritative tone surprised me.

She approached the Crofts and locked eyes with Derek. "Hush. We should vote on this. We must find the birds, and we want better security at the creek."

Derek grabbed her arm as she passed him. "We can't afford that, remember?" he hissed.

She jerked away, a murderous expression on her face. She turned toward the crowd, hands on her hips. "I say we vote."

Marilyn and Derek exchanged glances. "This can't happen," he said in a panicked tone.

Two more women from Babs's group joined her. They linked arms. "Vote, vote. Vote, vote. Vote, vote."

"Hazel," I said. "What is happening?"

She shushed me again, and we waited while Marilyn called for a yay or nay answer on locating the errant egrets and installing lights and security cameras at the creek. Babs insisted on helping her count the responses.

"We have a stalemate." Babs groaned. She raised her arms, palms up. "Come on, people. The birds need us. Let's do this."

Derek stood within a foot of her face. "Just because some birds disappeared doesn't mean we must spend money." He said *birds* as if they were a dirty word.

"Hazel, let's go." I didn't know what was about to happen, but I didn't want to be involved. "These people are a little over the top." Their reactions didn't sit right with me. What would they do next? My mother-in-law didn't budge.

Derek and Babs argued and fussed until Marilyn smacked the podium again.

"Let's appoint someone since we can't agree." She shaded her eyes from the glaring overhead lights and scanned the audience. She jabbed her finger in our direction. "There, them."

And that's how Hazel and I became lead investigators of Stone Creek Cove's missing egrets.

"How did that Marilyn lady know you two?" My daughter, Cynthia, broke off a piece of a chocolate chip cookie and dropped it in her mouth. She joined me on the overstuffed dark blue couch in Hazel's living room.

I bit another chunk of my oatmeal raisin cookie. Lots of shouting took place at the meeting. Some of the words still rang in my ears.

"Ask your grandmother." I'd been promised sweets at the meeting, so when it ended sans cookies, I insisted we drive through our favorite sandwich shop and buy some before we went home. Cynthia happily volunteered to help us consume them.

Hazel sat across from us on a matching loveseat. She heaved a loud sigh. "Our reputation precedes us, I suppose."

Considering how often our names appeared in the news, I agreed. "I think she handpicked us before we got there. How can we get out of it?" I picked out a raisin and chewed it. "Not that I don't care about the missing egrets."

My youngest, Carter, home for the summer from the University of South Alabama, showed me a picture of the beautiful white birds with skinny black legs and yellow feet. I felt sorry for the little things. They mattered to me, but perhaps not as much as to other people.

"I don't think we can. You met Marilyn. She's not the kind of person you want to go up against." Hazel rested a pillow on her lap, smoothing the tassels around its edges. "And what she said at the end? I couldn't believe it."

"What did she say?" Cynthia asked.

"She must not have realized her mic was still on, and she mentioned Babs. She said, 'When is she going to learn not to oppose me?'" I imitated Marilyn's voice.

"Uh-oh," Cynthia said. "How did that go over?"

"Not pleasant." Hazel broke her cookie in half. "Babs Ferguson is a force to be reckoned with. Marilyn is well acquainted with her."

Cynthia sat back, arms crossed, a strong-willed—dare I say bull-dog—expression on her face. "I don't think they can make you take over the homeowners' association."

"Neighborhood," Hazel corrected her. "We don't pay for anything, and no one wanted to, so we call it a neighborhood association. Besides, we only have to locate the birds and set up security."

"Hmm." My daughter shifted in her seat. "Did they spell out what you should do? How are you supposed to find them? It's not like you can put out an APB."

"Remember the letter Grandma Hazel received? The police know about the theft of the birds. That's what started all of this." I explained what else we had to do. "When are we meeting with the Crofts?" I asked Hazel. Perhaps Derek would be open to someone else taking charge.

"Marilyn invited us over for lunch tomorrow to talk about the walkway, security, and the birds." Hazel stood and stretched. "I'm going to bed." She gently snapped her fingers at her gray Weimaraner, Charlie Brown, and blew a kiss to her yellow parakeet, Roscoe. "Night, y'all."

"Let's check out the creek tomorrow before we go to their house," I said.

She grunted in what I assumed meant agreement. CB trotted behind her.

"Bedtime for me too. Goodnight, Cynth. Sleep well." I tossed my napkin in the kitchen trash can.

"Want me to wait up for Carter?" she asked.

"You don't need to." Her brother worked as a busboy at the beach, saving up for textbooks for his upcoming fall semester. "The restaurant doesn't close until after midnight. He won't be home anytime soon." I covered my yawn.

"Okay. I'm staying up for a while." She picked up the remote and clicked on the television. "Will this bother you?"

"No." After hugging her goodnight, I headed for my room, plugged my phone into its charger, and got ready for bed. My cell rang as I got into bed, and I answered without checking the caller ID.

"Hi, Peg."

Oh, boy, it was my boyfriend. Ex-boyfriend? I assumed he wanted an answer to his proposal.

"Hi, Shortie." What else should I say? Ten days ago, he proposed. Two days before that, Marcus kissed me. Or I kissed him. Either way, kissing happened.

And I hadn't talked to either one since.

Shortie cleared his throat. "How are you? How're Hazel and the kids?" His voice, low and husky as usual, carried an edge of hesitation.

This man cared about me, Hazel, and my kids. An original member of the Empty Nesters Birding Group, he stayed by my side through all of the craziness, including when two birders died within months of each other and as another one confessed to murder last month.

Caught off guard by his proposal, I'd avoided him. My previous marriage of thirteen years ended when my husband, Zack, got caught in a riptide and died. My kids, still young then, were now grown-ups. Shortie was my first relationship since Zack. Relationships went through ups and downs, but his reactions to things sometimes bothered me. He'd become possessive in a way I didn't like and hadn't expected from him.

"We're fine. Hazel and I are now in charge of a project for her neighborhood association."

He snorted. "Not surprised by that."

Fair point. "Yeah, some egrets went missing."

"Y'all should open a private eye agency. A bird detective agency. You can call it Two Chicks." He laughed at his joke.

I bristled at the dig in Marcus's direction. When Detective Marcus Sharp and I first met, sparks flew. Then Shortie and I started dating. Marcus tried to run Shortie off, but his arrogant attitude ended up running me off. The handsome detective and I kissed less than two weeks ago. I tried to chalk it up to one friend comforting another since he was in the hospital. But those sparks ignited flames hard to ignore.

"Hazel might be open to your idea, but not me." I banished thoughts of Marcus from my head.

"She and CB can wear one of those old-fashioned detective hats." He chuckled again. "Anyhow, I called to check on you. Any news from your insurance? Can they fix your house?"

"They called yesterday, and the plan is for a contractor to replace the roof after the integrity of the structure is checked. Then I can hire cleaners for the inside." I stretched out my legs. "I still can't believe Owen got involved with Estelle. And he and Gabby tried to burn down my house."

"Yeah. He always seemed like a stand-up guy on our birding trips. Very smart. But I'm glad to hear the news about your house." He paused, and my anxiety soared. "Hey, my timing the other day was bad. I'm sorry."

Sorry he proposed, or sorry when he did it? I wouldn't ask. "Yeah." That's all I could say. I felt raw from loss, and my brain still spun from recent events.

"I'll let you go. Sleep well," he said.

"You too." I ended the call and lay back in my bed. Thoughts of Zack, Shortie, and Marcus floated through my mind. Closing my eyes, I prayed for wisdom and clear thoughts. It had been a while since I experienced either.

CHAPTER 2

THE FOLLOWING DAY, MY oldest child, Chloe, dropped off my first and so far only grandchild, Reese, on the way to her six-week postpartum checkup. I sat on the couch, snuggling him close, and soaking up his sweet newborn scent. Cynthia woke up and, after fifteen minutes, she demanded some "Aunt Cynth time."

"How was Chloe this morning?" She cradled Reese against her.

"A little tired, but she looked content," I said.

"Of course she is with this snuggly little guy." She rubbed noses with him and blew raspberries on his neck. "Mom, I think he smiled. Do babies smile this young?" She continued to baby-talk to Reese.

I turned on the coffeepot. "It might be gas, honey."

She followed me into the kitchen. "No, he adores me. Don't you sweet boy." She nuzzled him again.

"Do you want scrambled eggs?" I asked.

"Sure." She adjusted the baby on her shoulder. "I'm going to the Center later. Dr. Harry is starting a new project."

His previous research at the Bird Rescue and Care Center included overseeing the care of rare resplendent quetzals and protecting their eggs. The quetzals played a role in last month's murders and the arson that almost destroyed my house.

"The birds and their eggs were sent to the aquarium in Texas, right? Invite him over for dinner tonight. He doesn't eat enough." I scooped the food onto a plate and handed it to her, motioning for her to give Reese back.

She passed him over and dug in. She chewed and swallowed before saying, "Yes, they arrived, and Harry thinks they'll be fine. He's hoping they'll continue to reproduce. I'll be sure to ask him over."

"What is his next project?" My voice sing-songed to Reese as I swayed.

"He hasn't told me." She took another bite. "I'm going to talk to him about cheering up his office."

"Take down the black curtains and open the blinds first." Memories of the first time he showed me his dark and forbidding office surfaced. I widened my eyes and pretended to be afraid.

She giggled. "And put away some of those creepy jars that hold whatever they hold." She scrunched up her nose.

Hazel entered the kitchen, CB trotting behind her. "Smells yummy in here." Her eyes lit up when she spotted Reese in my arms. "Hand me my boy."

She cooed and made silly faces. "Aren't you just the handsomest fellow?" CB woofed and nuzzled into her thigh.

"Your dog is jealous," I said. In reality, it might have been me. But I had a plan. "Want some breakfast?" It had worked with Cynthia. Maybe food would entice my mother-in-law, and I'd get my grandson back. My phone rang as I plated Hazel's breakfast. I held up my finger. "He's mine after this."

My BFF greeted me when I answered.

"Hi, Lauree." I held out my cell. Hazel and Cynthia hollered hello, and I returned it to my ear. "How are you?"

"Not too bad. I've only had one treatment. It's experimental, so I'm now a human guinea pig." She let out a short, sharp laugh, devoid of genuine pleasure.

"You're my favorite guinea pig. Tell me how I can help." I hated not living next door to her anymore. Hazel's house was only fifteen minutes away, but after years of being neighbors and best friends, I missed living close enough to help her, John, and the twins during her cancer treatment. I prayed my house would be ready to move back into sooner rather than later.

"The meal train Carter and Cynthia set up has been a tremendous help. Please tell them."

"They'll be glad to hear that." Lauree stayed by my side when Zack died and acted like my kids' second mom. She didn't give up on us or let me stop moving forward. Every day she pushed me. She helped me and the kids stay intact as a family.

"I'm grilling burgers tonight. I'll drop some by tomorrow." I pulled another package of meat from the freezer.

"Yum, John will be happy. We've eaten a lot of chicken casseroles lately." She snickered. "Can't wait to see you. We should plan a beach day too."

My insides twisted remembering our last trip to the beach when she told me about her aggressive breast cancer diagnosis. I shoved the thoughts from my mind and cleared my emotions from my throat. "Sounds fun. Give the twins hugs from me. John too. I'll be over tomorrow."

We said our goodbyes, and I scribbled a sticky note to remind me to take her food. After finding out about her cancer, I vowed to be available for her and her family. I wouldn't let her down.

"You're a good friend, Peg. Don't be so hard on yourself."

Hazel's words and her hand on my shoulder startled me. "What…?" I asked.

Her gentle smile touched me. "She loves you for who you are," she said.

True as that was, I didn't want to fail her like in the past.

"What have y'all decided to do about Mamma Birds?" Hazel asked as she put her plate in the kitchen sink.

"I sent out an email saying we're taking a short summer break. I haven't been away from it this long since I started it after Zack died. I'll get back to blogging soon, and Chloe will be ready to share her experience as a new mom."

Lauree, my former social media manager, took over most of the business duties before her cancer diagnosis. Changes were coming. I'd have to wait and see.

Hazel handed Reese to me. "I'm sure Chloe will do a fine job. Did she remember the stroller? We have the meeting at the Crofts soon."

I nodded, ready to change the subject. "We can check out the walking path and creek before we head there. Wonder if there are any lights already?"

"I can't remember. I'll go get ready."

As I waited for her, tires crunched on the gravel out front. When I peeked out the dining room window, my face flushed. "Detective Marcus is here," I told the baby. Reese and I stood on the front porch while Marcus, one leg in a cast, winced with each step as he balanced on his crutches.

My gut clenched. Because of me, he had a broken leg. Two breaks, actually. He stopped and studied the step up to where we waited.

"Do you need help?"

Without answering my question, he gathered the crutches in one hand, leaned them against the railing, and lowered himself to sit. "Don't want to attempt steps today."

I settled beside him. Reese shifted and stretched as only newborns can.

"Look at him." Marcus grinned and rubbed Reese's tiny foot. "What a beautiful guy."

"He sure is. Want to hold him?"

He held out his hands, and I passed the baby over. My heart warmed as he studied Reese and stroked his head. The baby whimpered. Marcus shifted him to his shoulder like a pro.

"You're good at that."

"Yeah." His eyes clouded. "It's like riding a bike."

Was he thinking of his little girl and wife, who both died in a car accident several years before? I touched his shoulder. "You okay?"

He studied me, his dark brown eyes full of an emotion I couldn't figure out. "Yes."

My raised eyebrow showed my doubt. "How's the leg?"

"Doing fine. I'll be on crutches for several more weeks before I get a walking boot. I'm on desk duty till then." His brows drew together. "Lots of paperwork from your last escapade."

I leaned back on my palms and stretched out my legs. "Don't forget, I didn't want what happened. I'd much rather be safe and sound in my house." I related the news from my insurance company.

"Hope you can move back in before too long." He handed Reese back. "It's hard to hold him and brace my leg at the same time. He's a big fellow."

I laid the baby over my knees and patted his bottom.

There were a lot of apologies going around today. But I owed Marcus one. "I'm sorry." The day Shortie proposed, Marcus arrived at the same time, and I shut the door in both men's faces, not ready to deal with either of them.

Marcus touched my chin, and I turned to face him. "I won't apologize for kissing you, Peg." His thumb grazed my lips.

"I'm not sorry for that."

His eyes darkened, and he leaned toward me.

I held up my palm. "Shortie and I have to talk. You saw what he did."

"You didn't tell him yes, or I wouldn't still be here." He brushed my hair behind my ear.

He made a valid point, but I needed to make decisions. Kissing him wouldn't help. No matter how much I wanted to.

I did enjoy the one kiss we'd shared. Too much. Is it hokey to say it sent tingles through my body? Well, it did. Sparks, too, head to toe. I didn't have that with Shortie. But was being a great kisser the answer to my problems?

Probably not.

Marcus left, and minutes later, Hazel opened the front door. "Are you ready? I told CB he can't come on our w-a-l-k," she said, spelling out the word to avoid igniting the dog's excitement.

She scooped Reese off my lap and settled him into his stroller. Soon we were well on our way to the path. The July heat enveloped us, and I regretted forgetting my sunglasses. We reached the walkway and followed it as it wove beside the creek, birds twittering and tweeting from the trees. Several flew off at our approach. Hazel showed me the egrets' normal nesting area. I left the sidewalk and tiptoed closer.

"You'd better be careful," she said. "It'll be marshy."

I turned, hands on my hips. "Yes, I imagine so."

She pointed to my feet. "Snaky too."

"What?" Just then, something slithered into the bushes near me, and I jumped, windmilling my arms as I attempted to run in the damp grass. When my feet landed, they slipped, and my wild arm movements propelled me backward. I landed with a splash and quickly flipped over onto all fours before pushing up to stand.

Stomping from the water, I made my way up to the walkway. A chill ran through me as I imagined all the creepy crawlies in the creek.

Hazel handed me a baby blanket.

"Thanks." I wiped my face and arms.

"Are you okay? Is your ankle all right?"

I wiggled my foot. In the months since my stress fracture, it had healed well. "It's fine. It's more my heart." I headed toward home, eager for clean, dry clothes.

"Your heart?" Hazel screeched. "What's wrong? Should I call nine-one-one?" She whipped out her cell phone.

"No, I'm joking. You don't have to call anyone." Goosebumps broke out again. "It's the snake."

"You're afraid of snakes? You have seen dead people, Peg. Dying people."

I laughed at Hazel's wide-eyed expression. "True. But snakes? I hate them."

She drew a slithery shape up my back. "I'll have to remember that." Her eyes glittered with glee.

"Come on. I have to change, and Reese needs a bottle—and maybe a change." No more creepy crawlies for me.

CHAPTER 3

AFTER CHANGING OUT OF my wet clothes and finding no critters in them or on my body, my attitude improved. I brushed my hair and found Cynthia in the living room, talking on the phone, with the baby sound asleep on the couch.

"Chloe called. She's on her way here." Cynthia readjusted Reese's blanket.

"Did she mention how her appointment went?" I slipped my feet into my sandals.

"She said the doctor is happy with how she's healed. She's excited to get back to normal living." Cynthia made air quotes. "Hey, I can keep this guy since you and Grandma are leaving. Harry said I could show up at the Center whenever I wanted."

"Yes, please. That'd be helpful."

Hazel entered the room and added some feed to Roscoe's cage, made noises to him, and latched it closed. "You have to stay here again, CB." She stroked the dog's back.

We smothered Reese in kisses before leaving for Derek and Marilyn's. Their house stood among several new builds in the neighborhood. While Hazel's sat low and wide, an older one-story, four-bedroom brick ranch, the Crofts' cream-colored stucco house loomed two stories high. A massive porch stretched across the front, with precisely trimmed shrubs forming a neat line. Waist-high stone pots, brimming with greenery, flanked the dark wooden front door.

"This is beautiful." I touched the leaves of the closest plant.

"It is." Hazel pushed the doorbell. "Marilyn is retired, but she held a high-up role in a tech company at one time. Computer programming, I think. Derek's some kind of contractor."

"Something lucrative for sure." I continued to admire the front of the house. "I wish I had a green thumb."

Derek Croft jerked open the door, a glare on his face. "What do you want?" His frosty voice matched his bright white button-down shirt.

Hazel and I stepped back.

"You invited us for lunch," Hazel said, her eyes narrowing.

"We're supposed to discuss the missing egrets," I added, hoping to prompt his memory.

Marilyn joined us in the doorway. "Remember, dear? We're working with them on the creek situation." She patted his shoulder, and he relaxed.

"Oh, yes, I apologize." His smile didn't reach his eyes. The couple turned, and we followed them inside.

I pulled Hazel back. "You sure we should be here? He sounded mad."

She shrugged me off and continued into the house. We entered a formal living area where Marilyn showed us to our seats on a sofa covered in a patterned brown chenille upholstery. I placed one of the fancy decorative pillows behind my back and reminded myself to sit up straight. Derek joined his wife across from us on a matching loveseat.

Hazel removed her notebook and pen from her purse and flipped to a clean page. "What do you want Peg and me to work on first?"

Marilyn's eyes lit up, delight sparking across her face. "The missing egrets, of course. And better security at the creek. The walkway is crumbling."

"We stopped by the creek on our way over. It definitely needs some work." Hazel jotted notes.

Derek crossed his arms. "It will cost a pretty penny. Security isn't a priority." His mouth pulled down in a scowl.

"Now, dear, we talked about that." Marilyn patted his leg. He shifted away from her and continued to argue.

They went back and forth for a few minutes, almost as if we weren't in the room.

I raised my voice to interrupt their spat and try to refocus the conversation. "Why do you think the egrets are missing?"

Their bickering ended. Marilyn recovered first. "I imagine someone took them." Her statement ended more like a question.

Hazel raised her hand. "If I may, we have some bird experience"—my eyebrow twitched—"and I think it would be hard for someone to steal as many as we had." She twirled her pen in her hand.

Derek stood. "You can search for them if you want to. Go ahead." He flipped his hand. "But we don't have the money to pay for security or to install a new sidewalk." He directed his last sentence at his wife in a growl and tromped out of the room.

Marilyn rose and motioned Hazel and me toward the front door.

"Please excuse my husband." She stopped, her hand on the doorknob. "He hasn't been feeling well."

Her excuse didn't ring true. I wanted more details.

Before I opened my mouth, Hazel said, "While we're alone, I wanted to ask about Babs Ferguson." She stuffed her notebook into her bag. "She was irate last night."

Marilyn's brows drew together into a sharp *V*. "The woman threatened me."

"What?" I didn't hear any threats.

She huffed and crossed her arms. "Yes, when we locked up."

"What did she say?" Hazel and I both asked.

Somewhere in the house, Derek called Marilyn's name. "I ... I need to go. I'm overreacting. No worries." She waved us out of the house and shut the door.

We turned to trudge down their driveway. "Not sure we found out much. They didn't make this any clearer, you have to admit. And those two do not get along."

"I agree. What she said about Babs interested me, though. Come on. Let's check out the creek area again. It'll be cooler in the shade." Hazel took off down the street.

The term "cooler," in Northwest Florida, at least in the summer, lacked definition. Heat and humidity ruled, and we didn't find any shade on our side of the creek. Sweat poured down my face and pooled in my shorts' waistband.

"That's where you fell in." Hazel pointed.

"Snake heaven. Yuck." Sweat beaded on my upper lip, and I wiped it off. I turned, and a piece of white fluff caught my eye. Tucked into the side of the bank sat a small pile of twigs with several white fluffy things in it. Carter once showed me pictures of snowy egrets' nests, and this one looked exactly like them.

I stepped closer, avoiding the grassy area where I'd slipped before. "Here's proof the egrets lived here." Crouching down, I lifted branches of a nearby bush. "That's weird. Hazel, pass me your phone. Mine's at home."

She handed me her cell, and I snapped a picture. I scrambled back up the side of the creek and showed it to her. She zoomed in, a frown covering her face.

"What is that?" she asked.

"Some kind of sticky substance? I didn't touch it, but it appears gummy." I glanced back at the nest. "Think it's from the eggs hatching?"

"I don't think so, but I'm no expert. We can ask Harry."

I refrained from reminding her what she'd just told the Crofts about her expertise. "True. Let's go home. We both need more water too." My stomach growled. "Hey, weren't the Crofts supposed to feed us lunch?"

Hazel texted Harry on our walk home, and by the time we downed water and cooled off, he knocked on the door.

"Hi, there," I said. "Thanks for coming over."

He hugged me. Our friendship had come a long way in a few short months. Getting kidnapped together and running from a burning house sealed it for both of us.

"What do you have?" he asked.

"You'll have to come down to the creek with me."

"Is Cynthia here?" He glanced into the living room. "She's supposed to come by the Center today."

"I'll let her know we'll be back soon. She can go when you do." I knocked on her door and told her my plans with Harry. Returning to the living room, I picked up my phone. "Okay, take me to the creek, and I'll show you what we've found. Hazel,"—I raised my voice—"are you coming with us?"

She peeked around the corner from her room. "Y'all go on without me. I'm going to lie down for a few minutes. It's so hot today."

As Harry drove, I explained what I found. He parked beside the walkway and followed me down the bank, where I showed him the egret's nest. "There's something weird in it. Sticky, I think, but I didn't touch it."

He pulled disposable gloves from his back pocket and slipped them on. "I'll take it back to the center and check it out." He lifted the nest and examined it. "Hmm. I see what you mean."

Since his hands were full, I supported his elbow as we climbed the slick incline up to the walkway.

"Thanks. There's a bag in my trunk if you can grab it." He tipped his chin toward his car.

I found the bag and helped him slide the nest inside. He placed it in the back seat and drove me back to Hazel's.

"I'll call you when I figure out what this is," he said. "Shouldn't take long."

I waved goodbye to the real bird expert.

When the kids were little, Zack and I took them to the Fourth of July fireworks at Pensacola Beach. But in recent years, my family and Lauree's family attended the Blue Wahoo baseball game in downtown Pensacola. When I dropped off the burgers on Friday, Lauree suggested we continue our annual tradition.

"Are you sure you're up to it?" I asked. Her pasty color and drawn face worried me.

"Yes, I want to do this." She reached out and gripped my hand. "Please, Peg."

"Of course. We'll meet you."

The next afternoon, we arrived right before the first pitch. A warm breeze floated off nearby Pensacola Bay, carrying the scent of saltwater and the sound of crying seagulls. John pushed Lauree in her wheelchair, and I bought her a fan with a water mister. It had only been a few weeks since she told me about her cancer. Seeing her in a wheelchair drove home the seriousness of her situation.

We settled into our seats. "Hey, Suzie, what do you like the most about baseball games? When they say, 'Play ball,' the smell of hot dogs, or the scent of fresh-cut grass?" I asked.

"I'm here for the dogs," she said, her eyes sparkling.

"Me too," Stevie said.

The first crack of the bat echoing through the ballpark caught our attention. The ball sailed high, and I held my breath as the center fielder scrambled back, his eyes locked on it. I flinched at the sharp *thwack* as it met his glove and jumped up to yell encouragement.

"Hey, Carter, buy me a hot dog." Cynthia nudged her brother, who groaned but got up when she waved her credit card.

"Anyone else want snacks?" He took our orders and enlisted Stevie to help him carry the food.

While we waited, a vendor made his way through the rows, his cart piled high with stuffed animals and toys. I got his attention and bought a stuffed Blue Wahoo character. I handed it to Lauree, and she clutched it in her arms.

Stevie and Carter returned with the food, and we turned our attention to the game. The players pulled their caps down against the setting sun, rolled up their sleeves, and wiped their faces with team towels. We sipped lemonade and water to stay hydrated. After the third inning, John wheeled Lauree to the top and sat in the shade with her.

The ball soared again, slicing the air toward the right field line. The opposite team's runner on second broke for third, and I hopped up to cheer for the Wahoo's right fielder. He caught the ball in time to tap the runner out. Someone tossed free T-shirts into the audience, and Carter caught one. He ran up the steps to present it to Lauree. Tears filled my eyes at the affection and care he showed.

I followed and offered to help her put it on. She lifted her arms, and I slid it over her head, straightening it at the bottom. "You look good, my friend." I studied her face. "You okay?"

She shifted in the wheelchair. "Just tired." She rubbed her arms.

I sat beside her and held her hand through the rest of the game. To continue the Fourth of July celebration, the local symphony performed when the game ended, followed by the Gulf Breeze High School marching band.

Afterward, with the day's thick humidity clinging to us, the kids joined us at the top of the stadium. During the last moments of daylight, as the bay mirrored the fiery colors of the sunset—soft purples, orange, and glimpses of pink—we snapped several group pictures.

We found our seats when the sky darkened to an inky blue. Around us, people chattered while waiting for the fireworks to begin. The first crackle pierced the night air, and I held my breath for a split second before a blinding burst of color exploded across the sky. We gasped in unison as the colors bloomed and faded, silver sparks floating to earth.

Each round of fireworks seemed bolder than the last, painting the dark above in a red, white, and blue spectacle. The crowd cheered and hollered with patriotic pride. Lauree's massive smile brought tears to my eyes. I blinked them back, thankful for another celebration with her.

The finale began. After a dramatic silence, a single streak of light shot into the air. Then came a series of rapid bursts, one after another. It reminded me of a kaleidoscope I owned as a little girl, full of reds, purples, golds, and blues. The ending came as one last deafening roar, fading into the night. We stood in stunned silence for a heartbeat before erupting into applause. The night might be still now, but the memory of spending time with my family and friends would linger in my heart.

CHAPTER 4

WE BEGAN SERIOUS RESEARCH on Monday. After much discussion, we started our search at the library and decided to expand it if we needed more information. While Hazel drove us to the Pensacola Library on Spring Street, I called Harry, hoping he'd tell us more about the sticky substance on the nest. I put the phone on speaker.

"Some kind of glue, like we thought," he said after we all said our hellos. "I'm not sure why it would be there unless someone trapped the birds to steal them. Why would they do that, though?"

"Would it poison the birds? Could they have died from it?" I asked, wondering why someone would want to kill them.

Hazel shook her head as she listened in on the conversation. "Too many egrets. We would have seen bodies or smelled something."

"I think she's right," Harry said. "That's a lot of birds."

"Any other ideas?" I asked.

"No, not really. I'll keep looking into this."

"Call me when you figure it out," I told him.

"Sure thing. What are you two doing today?" Harry asked.

"We just arrived at the library," Hazel said. "We're searching for more information on the Crofts first."

"Have fun. I'll be in touch soon." He hung up.

Hazel parked her Bug. On this beautiful summer morning, with a clear sky and a soft breeze, I took a moment to appreciate the stillness and quiet before she tugged on my arm.

Once inside the building, we headed for the research area, where we quickly located articles on Derek's company, Croft and Bros. Construction, in the newspaper section. Most of what we read sounded positive, maintaining that he had a spotless reputation.

Then I spotted a picture.

"Hazel, come look at this." I waved her over.

She leaned in, lifting her readers to focus on the tiny print beneath the black-and-white photo. Her mouth hung open. "That's Derek standing next to Estelle."

Estelle Keaton—our nemesis.

"I think they went to the same high school." I checked the date on the paper. "This is from prom at Woodham High School, 1977." She wore a strapless A-line dress, while Derek sported a classic tux.

"The year before she graduated." A puzzled expression flitted across Hazel's face. "They must have been classmates."

"You think they dated? Was that acceptable in the late '70s? Since he isn't white, I mean." I shuffled through some other papers without finding anything else.

"I knew what you meant." She returned to her research. "This is the deep south. It depends on the school, I suppose."

We were quiet on the drive home. Seeing Estelle's picture brought back a slideshow of memories. From being with Anna when she died from a peanut allergy to finding Sylvia stabbed and dying, to last month, my house being set on fire. All because of one woman's jealousy and greed.

Hazel pulled up beside the curb in front of her house. "We should talk to Derek."

"Yes, you're right." I stretched out my fingers on my thighs. I'd balled them into fists, and now my hands hurt. "I need to walk off this irritation. Estelle, again?" I inhaled, held it for four seconds, and blew the breath out. "I can't believe it. Will we never be rid of her?"

"She's like a bad penny," Hazel said.

She parked, and we walked to the other side of the neighborhood where Derek and Marilyn lived in their fancy house. When we reached the driveway, she pulled me to a stop. "He's not a bad guy, is he? Like the old mayor and Owen. Or Estelle?" She patted her chest. "I don't think I'm ready for this."

Her fears were valid. Estelle used people as pawns with no regard for the harm she caused. The first time, she used the former mayor of Pensacola. Then, she got her claws into Owen Walters, one of the original members of the birding group and a retired history professor—a man we trusted. A man whom Hazel had set her sights on.

"I'm not sure we'll ever understand why Owen turned. He blamed it on money, but still." My words trailed off. He seemed like a wonderful man until he pulled a gun on me.

The Crofts' front door opened. "Hi, Peg? Hazel? What can I help you with today?" Derek joined us on the driveway. His polo shirt, tucked into khaki shorts, reeked of "older Florida man" syndrome at least until I spotted his calf-high white socks and slippers.

He reached out a trembling hand. "I'm so sorry I was distracted the other day."

Angry would be more like it, but let him think what he wanted. A strange expression crossed his face. "Are you okay?" I asked.

"No, well, I don't know. My wife is … missing." He abruptly turned and walked into the house. Hazel and I exchanged confused glances before we followed him inside.

"Derek, how long has Marilyn been gone? Have you called the police? How can we help?" I bombarded him with questions as he led us to the formal living room.

He motioned toward the couch. "Sit down, please." He perched on the edge of the loveseat, wringing his hands. "In answer to your questions, no, I haven't called the police. She left last night. I'm not sure what to do." His shoulders slumped.

Hazel leaned forward. "Peg and I, we're like private detectives. Sort of."

I grunted in surprise, and she shot me a stern glare.

"Anyhow, we can help you." She pulled her trusty notebook and pen from her purse. "Tell me everything."

Hazel dragged every last detail from Derek. When he finally shut the door behind us, he looked drained. She clapped her hands. "Another mystery." Her eyes sparkled.

"She might be hurt. You shouldn't be excited." Why did her eagerness surprise me? And why did he suddenly open up to us?

"She's fine." Hazel waved her hand dismissively. "She went shopping or ran away for a few days."

"Wouldn't she have called? She's been gone all night. He said she went for a walk by the creek and didn't come home. Doesn't it strike you as strange?"

"They both strike me as strange." Hazel walked down the driveway.

"What's really odd is he didn't call the police. That would have been the first thing I'd do when she didn't return last night."

"I guess you're right. She wouldn't stay out all night." Hazel picked up the pace. "We should investigate."

"Slow down. It's miserable out. And why do we have to be involved?" Shortie's joke about us opening the Two Chicks Detective Agency flashed through my mind. "You want to go by the creek again, don't you?"

She flashed a toothy grin. I followed her, whining the whole way. She refused my suggestion to call the police. At the creek, we stood, hands on our hips.

"What are we doing again? Nothing's here." I surveyed the marshy area. "Can we leave, please?"

As we left for home, something bright red caught my eye. "Wait, what's that?" I tugged on her arm and indicated the opposite side of the bank.

Hazel squinted. "I can't tell. Want me to go look?"

I never wanted to walk down there again. Snakes could be hiding anywhere. But Hazel was older than me, and I didn't want her to slip and hurt herself.

"I'll do it." I climbed down the other side and approached the red object, thinking it seemed familiar. I lifted more branches, praying no critters or slithery reptiles lurked underneath.

"Hmm. These look like Marilyn's glasses. The ones she wore at the meeting," I said to myself. I moved more branches and reached for them. Another peek farther up the stream revealed more than I wanted to see. Marilyn lay on her back, half in the water, half on the bank. Her brown tank and skin blended with the marshy area, and her black-and-silver hair floated in the water. "Oh, no, no, no, no." Once again, I found myself in a quick scramble up to the walkway.

"What's the matter?" Hazel asked. "More snakes?" She took the glasses from me. "I recognize these."

"You should." My heart pounded in my ears. "They belong to Marilyn. Her body is down there. I think she's dead."

We scurried back to Hazel's, where I called Marcus. Dialing the emergency number while we were at the creek didn't occur to me. When his sedan whipped into the driveway, I hopped in and showed him where to park.

I eyed his crutches. "Not sure how you'll climb down there. The bank is slippery." I explained about my tumble a few days before.

He parked on the side of the road. "Did you go for a swim too?"

"Ha ha, funny man."

Marcus opened his car door and heaved himself out with a grunt. "I called my crime guys. They'll be here soon."

We stood side by side on the walkway, and I showed him where the glasses and Marilyn's body lay. "Last week, I found an egret nest down here with sticky stuff in it. Harry's trying to identify it and help us determine where the egrets went."

Marcus tipped his head, a questioning look crossing his face. He didn't know why Hazel and I visited the creek in the first place. I filled him in on the neighborhood association's letter, skipping the part where Hazel and I were now in charge.

He shifted his cast and leaned on the crutches. Perspiration rolled down his face.

"Let's wait in the car." I helped him in on his side, then got in the passenger seat. "No tissues?"

His lips twitched, and a dimple appeared. "Nah." He bumped the AC up to its maximum setting.

I shoved my hands under my thighs. As I'd discovered when we first met, I was a sucker for dimples.

"Tell me more about the egrets," he said.

After I described them and how the local ones disappeared, he slung his arm across the back of my seat. His hand brushed my shoulder.

"How are you and Hazel tied up in this?" he asked.

"What do you mean?"

"Peg"—a slow smile spread across his face, and he trailed his finger along my collarbone—"I know you, remember. Y'all are in charge or somehow involved." He tugged a strand of my hair.

I crinkled my nose. "We were appointed." I emphasized the word.

He waited, his brown eyes studying me.

"Okay." My face heated up. "We are now in charge of the investigation into the egrets' disappearance for the neighborhood association."

"You can't just move into a house, can you?" A dimple popped out. I shifted my gaze back to the creek in time to see Marcus's team arrive.

CHAPTER 5

MARCUS DROPPED ME OFF at Hazel's on his way to the police station. Before I climbed out of the car, he tugged me to his side and kissed my cheek.

"Keep me informed?" I resisted the impulse to flutter my eyelashes.

His dark brows raised, but he didn't say a word.

"I can't believe I found another dead body." I waited to see if he would comment.

He chuckled and waved me out of his car. Apparently, I was attracted to the strong and silent type.

As Marcus pulled out of the drive, Hazel jerked open the front door. "What else did you find? The ambulance went by. It had Marilyn's body, right? Where's Marcus?" Her blue eyes were alight with curiosity. Charlie Brown waited by her side. His doggie eyes looked equally as interested.

I slammed the door behind me and stomped to the table, slumping into a chair. "Yes."

She sat beside me. "Yes? What's wrong?"

"What am I going to do?" I shoved my hands into my hair. "The dimples. And his lips." Dead silence met my words. It dawned on me where I was and who was in the room. Blood rushed to my cheeks, and I dropped my head to the table with a thunk. "Sorry."

"Wow, Mom, never thought I'd hear anything like that from you." A chuckle accompanied Carter's words.

I rubbed the back of my neck. The kids and Hazel could tell something was up with Shortie, but I never told them about Marcus kissing me. Or me kissing him.

Someone tapped my shoulder. "What?" I groaned.

"Why don't you go shower?" Hazel said in a light tone. "You'll feel much better afterward."

I scooted to my room, gathered clean clothes, and headed for the hall bathroom. Today, of all days, I missed my house, my bedroom, and its ensuite bathroom. It might be a while before I'd be able to face my kids.

I glared at myself in the mirror. "What were you thinking?" I lost my mind. That's all I could say. In the shower, I took extra time and used the last of the hot water. Once dressed, I painted my toenails and buffed my fingernails. After doing all the primping I could, I headed to the kitchen, determined to pretend I'd never uttered those words about Marcus. I needed to grow up and quit acting like a naive teenage girl, especially in front of my children.

I put water in a pot and set it on the stove. "Cynthia?"

"I'm in the living room," she said.

I stuck my head around the corner. "Will you add noodles when the water boils? We're having macaroni and cheese." I went back into the kitchen, removed a bag of marinated chicken from the fridge, and grabbed the tongs from the drawer.

"Sure, Mom." She stopped in front of me and waited until I made eye contact with her. "You're not doing anything wrong. It's okay if you have a relationship with Marcus or Shortie."

"Thanks, honey." I appreciated her words, but I didn't want to discuss romantic relationships with my kids. The more I thought about it, the more I realized my actions were like a middle-school girl—a crush here, a crush there, a crush everywhere.

"She's right, Mom." Carter entered the room. "We're not mad or anything."

Hazel walked up behind him. "Nope, not at all. We're here for you." CB wagged his stubby tail, and from the other room, Roscoe shrieked, "Ta-da!"

"Thanks, y'all. You're sweet." I opened the back door and stepped out onto the deck, relishing the opportunity to avoid their curious gazes and their questions. After I turned on the grill and started cooking the chicken, I leaned against the porch railing.

"Time to think like a grown-up, woman," I said softly to myself. I needed to be intentional in my relationships. I tapped my finger on the railing. Easier said than done. While the food cooked, I surveyed Hazel's small chain-link fenced yard, bordered by several other fenced yards. A typical older neighborhood with similar-style houses. Except the Crofts and a couple of others.

My thoughts shifted to Derek and his reaction to Marilyn's disappearance. He acted so calm, almost detached. Nothing like how I would react—running around in circles and calling the police, demanding help. That's what I did when I learned Zack had been rescued from a riptide. I called Lauree, who stayed by my side even when I found out he died en route to the hospital.

I flipped the chicken with practiced ease and continued rummaging through my thoughts. Why did Derek not call anyone? Did he kill Marilyn?

Please, God, not another murder.

A dead body didn't necessarily mean a crime occurred, but why was her body in the creek? After finding out Derek and Estelle knew each other, I questioned his innocence. At the same time, I didn't want to be mixed up in another investigation.

"No one can make me, either." My words reminded me of what I thought when Babs told Derek and Marilyn a few days ago, "You're not the boss of me." I clicked the tongs at no one in particular. "I'm with Babs."

The door opened behind me. "The mac and cheese is ready," Cynthia said.

"Perfect timing. The chicken is too. Will you bring me a platter?"

The kids helped set the food on the table, and we sat and joined hands. Hazel squeezed mine and prayed, "Thank you, Lord, for this beautiful summer day, this amazing food, and for my family. Guide us in Your way."

"Amen." I squeezed back.

"So, Marcus," Carter said as he passed the bowl of macaroni. "What is he doing?"

"Doing?" I played stupid.

"Yeah, with the dead lady." He grabbed a chicken thigh off the plate.

"Carter," Cynthia fussed. "That's a horrible thing to say. But yeah, Mom, what did he say?"

"How did you find out she died?" I narrowed my eyes at my mother-in-law, who shrugged and batted her eyelashes.

"Who killed her?" Carter wouldn't stop.

"No idea." I threw my hands up in the air. Luckily for CB, he sat close enough that the piece of chicken that flew off my fork landed beside him. He scooped it up and swallowed. "Uh-oh."

We all waited for what would happen next. He smiled at us, and then he burped. Confusion passed over his sweet, doggy face. He jumped up and ran for his water bowl, lapping with vigor.

"Poor fellow." Hazel took a bite of her food. "It's spicy tonight."

"Sure is. This marinade is yummy, Cynth." I praised my daughter. "Those culinary courses are paying off already."

"Thanks, I've enjoyed what I've learned so far. Way different than doing paperwork in the Navy." She scooped up a spoonful of cheesy noodles.

Through the dining room window, I spotted Harry's car pulling into the driveway. When he knocked, Carter opened the front door, and Harry followed him into the room.

"Hey, are you hungry?" I pushed back my chair. What a silly question to ask a single man. He'd eaten dinner with us a few days before. This might become a regular occurrence.

He pulled out a chair. "Yes, please. Whatever you're having smells good." CB sat beside him and laid his head on Harry's leg. "Um, what has he been into? His face is all wet." He grimaced and grabbed a napkin to dry off his cargo shorts.

Carter elbowed him. "Wait till you try the chicken. My sister added some hot spices. CB didn't enjoy his sample."

Harry dug into his plate with gusto. We waited for any reaction, but he ate without breaking a sweat.

Cynthia leaned over and caught his eye. "You okay?"

"Oh, yes. I love it. My daddy used to cook like this." He shoveled another bite into his mouth, chewed, and swallowed. "Peg, I came over to tell you what I think is on the nest." He emphasized his words with his fork. "What it might be."

"What is it? Do you think it killed Marilyn?"

"What?" He choked on his food.

While he caught his breath, I told him about how we found Marilyn's body.

He gave a half-laugh, half-sigh. "Always with the dead people." He stopped at my frustrated expression. "Well, back to the nests. It's like a sticky pad. Reminds me of what is used on mouse traps."

"Why would it be in an egret nest?" Hazel asked.

"They're all missing?" he asked.

Hazel nodded.

"Someone trapped and stole them, I assume. Relocated them. But why?" He took another bite of his chicken. "Snowy egrets do move, but they must feel safe in that area if they're nesting by the creek. I'm not sure why else they'd be gone."

"They have been here for a long time." Hazel's words confirmed Harry's statement. "Carter, where is the letter from the neighborhood association?"

While he retrieved it from the kitchen, I filled Harry in on how she and I were now in charge of investigating the missing birds. He lifted his water glass to me. I raised mine and clinked his.

"What are we celebrating?" I asked.

"Another thing you can add to your resume." His lips twitched, and a dimple appeared briefly.

His dimple didn't affect me like Marcus's. Harry was like another one of my kids. Carter returned with the letter and handed it to Harry, who read it aloud.

"To the residents of Stone Creek Cove. Please be advised that we are in contact with the police about a recent theft. The snowy egret colony in our neighborhood creek is missing. If you know of anyone involved in this, contact us or the police. They have suggested we install security cameras on each side of the creek and along the walking trail. Be advised—we will not put up with losing our egrets."

He laid the paper on the table. "Sounds serious and a bit intimidating. So now you two"—he wagged his finger between Hazel and me—"are in charge of finding the birds and installing cameras?"

I crossed my arms. "I suppose so. But I'm not excited about it."

"I can tell." His eyes twinkled.

"There's something else we have to do," Hazel said.

"What's that?" Harry scraped his plate clean.

Hazel sat up straight. "Figure out why there's a dead body, of course."

CHAPTER 6

THE NEXT DAY, I woke before anyone else. I brewed a pot of coffee, poured mine over ice in a travel cup, and secured the top. I shut the front door behind me and set off for the creek. Something one of the Crofts said tried to come forward in my mind, but I couldn't make my hamster-wheel brain stop long enough to figure it out. My phone buzzed as I arrived at my destination.

"Hey, Hazel. Did I wake you when I left?"

"No, CB needed to potty, and I smelled the coffee. Where'd you go?" she asked.

I told her where to find me and sipped my iced drink while I waited. Less than five minutes later, she walked around the corner, her own travel mug in hand.

"What are you up to, Peg?"

"Thinking about what Harry told us last night. The sticky pads would be sturdy enough to hold down a small egret." I studied the creek, as birds and butterflies fluttered from tree to bush. "No one would have noticed them down here. They would blend, and the whitish part would resemble feathers or fluff from plants. But who put them here?"

"Do we need to go talk to Derek again?" she asked.

"Yep. I have so many questions."

By the time we reached his house, my shirt clung to my back. "This heat. It's worse than ever." I fanned my face.

Hazel nodded and wiped her brow. She knocked, and Derek answered right away.

"You two again?" He exhaled sharply.

He wasn't excited to see us. "May we come in?" I asked.

"More questions, huh?" He turned, and we followed him inside.

"Before we talk, can I get some water?" I asked.

At his nod, I made my way down the hall to the kitchen. The high-end appliances and décor blended with the house's style. I found glasses and filled them with ice and water. I passed them out and settled onto the sofa beside Hazel.

She sipped and set her drink on a coaster on the glass-topped coffee table. "So, Derek, any word on Marilyn?"

His quizzical expression tore at me.

"Her death, she means." I raised my hands. "Have you heard what happened?"

"Not yet. I called the detective. Marcus somebody. But he didn't have more information." He rubbed his palms on his pants and stared at the floor.

Hazel tapped the table to get his attention. "Did Marilyn have enemies? What about Babs?"

Leave it to her to ask the hard questions. I still wasn't sure I wanted to pursue this at all.

Derek sat back in his chair, a puzzled crease between his brows. "What do you mean? What would she have to do with it? Babs is ... Babs."

Did he think his wife just happened to die at the creek? That it was an accident? "How did Marilyn die?" I asked.

"I suppose she slipped." He waved his hand in the air. "She was a little older than me. Shouldn't have been walking down there."

Why didn't he express more interest or concern? He already spoke about her in past tense. I changed tactics. "You and Estelle Keaton. How do you know each other?"

A quick frown flashed across his face. He shifted in his chair. "Who?"

My detecting senses tingled. Hazel drew a deep breath and raised her finger. "Derek," she said in a commanding tone, "tell us about your construction company."

"What a useless conversation," Hazel said when we left Derek's.

"Not really. Did you notice how he avoided the question about Estelle? His body language screamed he was hiding information." I stopped for a moment just outside Hazel's front door. "He acted odd before we discovered his wife's body. Something's up."

"I agree. And we did learn more about his company, I suppose." She unlocked her door, and we headed for the kitchen. CB greeted us with a nuzzle and a soft woof.

I wet a paper towel and mopped the sweat off my face. "He admitted they're surveying down by the creek. Think Marcus has discovered that?" I handed her a dampened towel and refilled the dog's water bowl.

"He also assured us it was legal, and they would stay environmentally friendly. He denied responsibility for the missing egrets without using those words." She reached down for CB's food bowl.

"You're right, and we didn't ask him that. He is charming once he gets on a subject he cares about."

She rose, dog bowl in hand, and studied me for a long moment. "What did you say?"

"He cares about his company."

"But not his wife." She pursed her lips, eyes narrowed, brows drawn together. "Hmm."

Hazel left shortly afterward for a hair appointment. I considered where to turn next in the investigation. I still couldn't decide how involved I wanted to be. Harry called, and I explained what we learned about Derek's company.

"If they're surveying at the creek, it would be easy for them to lay the pads up and down the bank," I said. "What if they left one behind by accident?"

"No cameras in the area?" he asked.

"That's one of the things we're supposed to do for the association. But none now. You won't believe what else I found," I said.

Harry whistled long and low when he heard about the photograph of Derek beside Estelle. "Those Keatons have caused a lot of problems."

"It's only her now since she killed her husband. But she's always been the mastermind." Her husband, Roger, a bad guy in his own right, held a reputation in Pensacola as someone you didn't want to mess with. At some point, his wife adopted her own evil ways. "The picture I found was dated 1977. Looked like she and Derek went to prom together."

"I'll come over. Let's revisit Croft. Last month, Owen got tangled up with Estelle. She's a busy lady."

Harry stopped by the house and gave me a ride to Derek's. My neighbor opened up to Harry in a way men often do with each other. While they chatted, I considered the five Ws and the H—Who, What, When, Where, Why, and How.

"Derek," I interrupted their conversation. "I have a question."

He tipped his head. "Yes?"

"Who is surveying the creek?"

"My company." He shifted in his chair. "I told you that. You and your friend."

"My mother-in-law. Right." I stood. "May I get myself a glass of water?"

"Sure." His mouth said yes, but his eyes flashed a warning.

In the kitchen, I spotted Marilyn's purse, a high-end summer bag, bright pink with a fancy bow, and stuffed to the brim. Inside, I found her wallet, two packages of gum, mints, a protein bar, a bag of makeup, her car keys, and several pens. Nothing stuck out, so I flipped through her wallet, and a sticky note fell on the floor.

I reached for it as footsteps sounded in the hallway. Derek entered the doorway, and I stuffed the paper in my back pocket.

"Did you find a drink?" he asked.

I pushed the purse away from me on the counter, hoping everything was in its proper place. "I forgot where your glasses are." Would he believe me, considering I found them a few hours before?

"I'll help you. You go join your friend." He waved me out of the room.

I scurried back into the living room and scooched as close to Harry as possible. "Her car keys were still in her purse."

"Didn't he say she walked to the creek?" He smirked.

"True." I snapped my fingers. "Thought I found important information."

Harry grinned. "It's possible he's on the up and up." He shook his head. "Although he feels ..."

"Not quite right?"

"Yeah."

Derek entered with two glasses of water. "Here you go." He handed one to each of us and took a seat.

After Harry's comment, I didn't want to drink anything Derek gave me. I pretended to sip and set my glass on the coffee table. Harry held his but didn't drink.

Derek clapped his hands together. "So, what else can I help you with?"

I racked my brain. He explained his company was in the middle of conducting a survey at the creek and insisted they were eco-friendly. "But he didn't say why."

"What?" Harry asked.

"Why?" I directed my question to Derek.

A look of annoyance crossed his face. "Excuse me?"

"Why is your company surveying? Your wife appointed Hazel and me to have security cameras and lights installed along the creek and walkway. Why would we do that if you're surveying the area? What is your company's role in this?"

"Oh, well …" He pursed his lips. "Well, it's a project. Yes, a project." He sat back, seemingly satisfied with his answer.

Harry turned to me, one eyebrow cocked. Did Derek not keep up with what his company did?

"A project?" I asked. Did it endanger the egrets?

"Right. Yep." He smacked his hands on his thighs and stood. "I have plans today. I'll need y'all to leave now."

Harry and I followed him to the door, and Derek locked it behind us.

"Well," I said.

"Yeah." Harry hurried to his car. "Let's check out this creek some more."

Oh, no. Snakes might be involved. I volunteered to send Hazel, citing her advanced detection skills. We parked at the creek, and I hurried to the house to tell my mother-in-law that Harry required her help. While I walked, I thought back to our short chat with Derek. The question that had burrowed into my brain finally emerged.

His company wouldn't survey the area. Surveyors would do that. Too fine a point? I didn't have enough information yet.

Hazel left, excited to help Harry. I stayed behind, hoping to organize my thoughts. I found my cell and pulled up Shortie's number.

"He's at work. He won't want to discuss this. He's busy." I punched the call button. If I didn't do it now, I wouldn't do it at all.

"Peg?"

His voice settled my racing thoughts. "Hey, I have a question." I curled up on the loveseat.

"Oh." His tone changed from a friendly greeting to a guarded one.

I laid out all the information about the egrets and the Crofts. Silence reigned when I finished.

I checked my phone screen to ensure we were still connected. "Shortie? Are you there?"

"Another one, huh?" He muttered something under his breath, and the line went silent for a beat.

"What?"

"Dead body, mysteries, questions. You can't leave this alone, can you? Even after what happened last time." The irritation in his voice came through loud and clear. "That was just last month."

I imagined him shaking his head, a frown crossing his handsome face. "Oh, okay. Sorry I asked. I wanted to bounce some ideas off you." I didn't know where to turn. Marcus couldn't discuss it with me. As a police officer, he wouldn't consider anything besides the strict rules he followed.

"Call Harry. He might help."

"Really? You're still going there? That's one of the reasons ..." I stopped. We needed to have this discussion in person. He deserved it. "Can we meet? For dinner? We need to talk."

"Sure. Text me the time and place. Gotta go." He clicked off.

Well. He was angry. I couldn't blame him. Before I changed my mind, I messaged him with the information and got ready to leave. Helping Harry and Hazel, as long as I didn't run across any snakes, sounded easier than tonight's dinner meeting with Shortie.

CHAPTER 7

WHAT DO YOU WEAR to dinner with the man who proposed to
you, and you shut the door in his face? I initiated tonight's date and
already regretted it. My stomach flipped each time I considered what
I might say. A knock on my bedroom door interrupted my confusing
thoughts.

I grabbed a shirt off my bed and slipped it on. "Yes?"

"Mom?" Cynthia stuck her head around the door frame. "Want me
to start dinner?"

Oh, how I wanted to stay home. "You guys are on your own
tonight." I smoothed the silky fabric over my hips.

She stepped into my room. "Where are you going?" She stared at
the pile of discarded dresses and outfits on my bed. "What are you
doing?"

Fair question. I sank onto the bed. "I invited Shortie out to dinner
tonight."

"Okay." One eyebrow arched. "Why?"

The kids guessed something was happening between Shortie and me, but I never divulged the details. "I need to talk to him."

"Will you accept his proposal or what?"

So much for secrets. "Who told you about that?"

"Calm down, Mom." She held her palm toward me. "I figured it out from everything you haven't said."

"You did?" I always thought that was a "Mom" power.

"Yep." She buffed her knuckles on her shoulder, her mouth up-turned in a grin. "Like mother, like daughter?"

I raised a detective without knowing it. "I'm very proud of you, dear." I motioned toward my top and capris. "I'm going semi-casual to dinner. What do you think?"

She hugged me. "You always look great. What are you going to tell him?"

I had no idea.

As soon as I climbed into my car, my top clung to my back, and my curls drooped. I cranked the air to high and rolled down all four windows. I backed up onto the street. Before putting the car in drive, I paused to whisper a prayer for guidance and wisdom and the right words to say to Shortie. The best words. If I let my feelings guide me, everything would get messed up.

"God, please show me Your will. I care about Shortie, but is it love? Is it enough for a lifetime?" God's will was the defining factor for me.

A dark-colored car zoomed around me and stopped in front of my vehicle. It backed up until it almost touched my car. Movement in my rearview mirror showed a black sedan parking behind me, close to my bumper. My heart skipped a beat. The hair on the back of my neck rose. I put my car in park and grabbed my cell, searching for Marcus's number. I pushed the call button and set it on the seat beside me.

The rear passenger door of the car in front of me opened. Sweat dripped into my eyes. Marcus's voice came through my phone. "I don't have my speaker on, so I hope you can hear me. Someone has blocked my car. I'm in front of Hazel's. They're coming to talk to me." I rushed to tell him the information and prayed he understood.

A man dressed in a black suit, a pristine white shirt open at the collar, and black, wrap-around sunglasses approached. He stopped at my open window and raised his glasses. His ice-cold blue eyes sent fear skittering through me.

"Can I help you?" I asked, somehow keeping my voice steady.

"Peg Howard?" His voice held a slight accent.

"Mm-hmm. Can I help you?" I repeated.

He opened my door. "Come with me."

"I don't think so." I attempted to close the door.

He pulled harder without breaking a sweat. "I insist."

I threw my body toward the passenger seat. Was I being kidnapped in broad daylight with no one around? Cynthia and Hazel both thought I left to meet Shortie. Carter was at work. My cell smashed against my hip, and I snatched it up, slipping it into the waistband of my capris. "I don't want to come with you. Who are you?" I raised my voice and prayed Marcus would hear me.

The passenger door opened, and someone else grabbed me under my arms and dragged me out of the car. My hip bumped over the console, and I bit back a scream. The person kept a firm grip on my upper arm. He marched me to the vehicle in front of mine and shoved me into the back seat. The door slammed shut. Everything in me screamed to kick, holler, and run, but I froze.

"No need to buckle," the driver of the car said.

I eyed the door. It didn't have inside door handles. I couldn't escape if I wanted to.

The man in the front passenger seat turned around to me. "Ms. Howard …"

"Mrs." The automatic correction popped out before I could stop it.

He exhaled, jaw tightening as irritation flickered across his face. "Mrs. Howard, thank you for meeting with me."

I didn't answer that, considering I had no say in this meeting. "I'm on my way somewhere. They're waiting on me." My cell phone dug into my back, but I ignored it, hoping they wouldn't find it on me. *Please don't ring.*

"Right." He nodded. "Mr. Jackson has been informed of your delay."

They knew Shortie? And about our plans? "Who *are* you?" From what I saw of the driver, he also wore wrap-around shades, wore his dark brown hair short, and sported a midnight-black suit. He didn't say a word after instructing me not to buckle up. Beyond baffled, I blurted, "What do you want with me?"

The man stared with eyes so dark they were almost black. "I'm friends with a … friend of yours."

My brain grabbed onto every fact and nuance it could. His accent might be South American. I scanned the interior for the make of the car, but found nothing. "Oh?"

"Yes. She has a message for you." His gaze never left my face.

She. Estelle Keaton. It must be her.

He closed his eyes briefly. "She told me you were stubborn." His jaw muscle twitched again. "She says to stay away. You've done enough." He leaned between the seats. "Do. You. Understand?"

Sure, but I didn't like his bossy tone. "I have questions."

"Ah, she spoke the truth about you. You, Mrs. Howard, don't ask questions. This is not a question-and-answer matter." He motioned with his hand, and the back door opened. Once again, one of the brutes dragged me out and forced me into my car.

My would-be kidnapper leaned close, his breath foul. "No more interference." He shook my arm. "Got it?"

"Yes." I glared my hardest glare.

He slammed the car door. The two dark sedans sped away. Something vibrated against my back, and I pulled my phone out of my waistband.

"Hello?" I gritted my teeth to keep from screaming.

"Peg? Are you all right?" Marcus asked, his voice strained.

"I guess so?" My arm hurt from getting jerked in and out of cars, and my hip throbbed. "Are you coming?" My breath hitched.

"On my way."

The shakes set in. My body buzzed, and dizziness hit me. I leaned against the headrest and closed my eyes, but couldn't get my emotions to stop spinning. What happened? Some mobster confronted me? Who had I talked to? Someone acquainted with Estelle for sure.

I drew in several deep breaths and tried to relax. The dead bodies—Roger, Kurt, Anna, Sylvia—haunted me. What if I were next? I licked my lips and attempted to force down the nausea. I reached for an old water bottle tucked in the center console. Someone rapped on the side of my car, and I screamed.

The door opened, and Marcus pulled me out and into his arms, shifting his crutches for balance. "Shh. You're okay. I'm here." He rubbed my back while I held onto him and cried.

"They dragged me out and pushed me into a car." My words came out in a slow, clipped manner. The world tilted again. "Can you hand me my water?"

He reached past me and grabbed the bottle. I drank a few sips.

"What did they say?" He kept a tight grip on me.

"He knows Estelle. He didn't say her name, but everything else he said implied it was her. He spoke with an accent, and a couple of men were with him." I moved closer into his arms. His warmth and fresh scent comforted me. "They said I have to stop. That she said to stay away." My nose dripped, and I wiped it with the shoulder of my shirt.

"Okay." He kept an arm snug around me while he fished his cell phone from his pants pocket. "I'm going to call for help. Gotta report this."

"Are you sure? These guys ... they weren't playing around." A whimper popped out, and I covered my mouth.

He kissed my temple. "It's okay, honey. We have to find them. I've got you."

My legs trembled. I followed him to the passenger side of his police cruiser and got in. Marcus placed his crutches in the back of the car and shifted into the driver's seat. He finished his call and asked me, "Where were you going tonight?"

"To meet Shortie for dinner. To talk to him in person."

"Where is he?" he asked.

"The man said they informed him of my delay." I told him the name of the restaurant.

Marcus blew out a sharp breath. "He hasn't called?" Sarcasm and anger filled his words.

I checked my cell. "No, he hasn't, but I'm not late yet. Should I call him?"

Marcus's left eyebrow twitched. "Might not want to ask me." Sirens sounded, and several police cars pulled up beside us. He gripped my hand. "Is anyone home? You can wait in the house if you want."

"Hazel and Cynthia are in there." The front door opened, and the two women hurried out.

Hazel beelined it for Marcus's car, and I opened the cruiser's door.

"Peg, what's happening? I thought you'd left. Why is Marcus here?"

Cynthia joined her grandmother on the sidewalk. "Mom, are you all right? Why are the police here?"

I climbed out. "Let's go inside, and I'll fill you in." I watched Marcus as he worked. He glanced up, saw me, and winked. Heat filled me, a warmth I needed at that moment. With him there, everything would be okay. He would help keep me safe. But I had work to do and bad guys to find. "Get your notebook, Hazel." Estelle Keaton was out there somewhere—no more waiting.

CHAPTER 8

HAZEL RETRIEVED HER NOTEBOOK and joined Cynthia and me at the table. Cynthia shifted in her chair. "Mom, weren't you supposed to have dinner with Shortie? Why didn't you leave? Why are Marcus and his police buddies here?"

Hazel patted Cynthia's hand. "We'll get there, dear." She flipped through the pages of her notebook until she found a blank one. "Tell us what happened, Peg."

I explained what occurred after I went out to my car. "Marcus is checking into it all."

Hazel's hand trembled as she held the pen above her notebook.

"Calm down." I leaned over and rubbed her back in slow circles. "I'm okay."

Cynthia shot me a worried glance. Sometimes I forgot Hazel's age. The stress of the last few years—at least the last year since she'd lived with me—had continued to increase.

Hazel's shoulders sagged. "This mystery-solving stuff might not be for old birds like me." CB sat beside her and laid his head on her lap.

I side-arm hugged her. "The other day, Shortie suggested we open a private detective agency and call it Two Chicks." I chuckled at the memory.

She stroked the dog's soft ear. "Hmm, that does sound fun. As long as there are no dead bodies." Her lips tipped up in a smile, and CB added a bark of approval. Suddenly, Hazel whacked the table with her spiral notepad. "Shortie hasn't called you?"

"No, not yet. The guy said someone told him I would be late." I checked again for a missed call. "He's probably waiting on me." I wanted to joke about the situation, but shouldn't he have at least texted me?

Hazel, mouth pursed in frustration, clicked her pen several times. "I don't understand that man." She voiced my exact concerns. "What am I supposed to write?"

"Chronological order makes sense." Cynthia sat back, hands behind her head. "What happened first?"

"The neighborhood association meeting." Hazel wrote and added the date. "Six days ago. We haven't even checked into lights or security cameras yet."

"Write that on a separate note too. We need security here at the house." Through the front blinds, I spotted police cruisers leaving. Marcus walked up the driveway. I held the door open as he made his way inside. "Want something to drink?"

He wiped sweat off his forehead. "Yeah, ice water or sweet tea, please." He spotted Cynthia and Hazel, and CB nudged his hand. Marcus rubbed the dog's ears. "Evening, y'all."

Hazel stood. "What are you doing about all of this, Marcus? Or should I say, Detective Sharp?"

She was still salty about last month when he corrected her on his official title. He grinned and pulled out her chair.

"Sit down, please. I'll fill you in." He propped his crutches in the corner and sat beside her. "Hazel, I'm sorry if I hurt your feelings." He patted her hand. "I'm taking this all seriously."

Her face softened at his apology. "Thank you. I'm worried about my daughter-in-law. How did this happen?"

"I'm concerned too. And I don't know yet. That's what we must find out." He directed his next question to me. "Who knew you and Shortie were going out?"

I thought back. "No one. I called him and texted him the time and place."

Marcus took out his notepad and wrote something. "I'll check into it. Somehow, someone found out your plans."

My cell phone rang, and Shortie's name appeared. I handed a glass to Marcus and raised the phone.

"Go ahead and answer that. We'll wait." Marcus sat back, his arms crossed.

I headed for the couch and answered the call.

"Peg, where are you? Are you coming?" Shortie asked, his tone curt.

"Didn't someone tell you I'd be late?" I curled up on the couch with my feet tucked under me. Roscoe perked up in his cage but stayed silent.

"Yes, some man came to my table and informed me you were held up. What did he mean? Did you know him?"

"No, I don't. Describe him for me." I hoped Shortie could fill in some of the blanks.

He paused. "He spoke with an accent. Possibly Hispanic? Dark hair, trim beard, shorter than me."

Most men were shorter than him. "Did he appear threatening?"

"No, not at all. What's happening?" He sounded concerned now. "Are you okay?"

I told him what the men did to me and assured him of my safety. "Marcus is here too."

"He is, huh? You're sure you're all right? You don't need me?" he asked.

"Yes, I'm okay. I'm sorry we didn't have a chance to meet up tonight. I wanted us to talk."

"Me too. I'll come by if you want," he said.

Marcus walked into the room and held his hand out, palm up.

I held my cell away from my ear. "I'll be right there." To Shortie, I said, "I'm okay. I'm sure. You don't have to stop by." I hung up and stood. "You're pretty agile on those." I gestured to his crutches. "Thank you for being here tonight."

Marcus stepped closer, his gaze fixed on me. "I'm always here for you."

"Peg, are you coming?" Hazel's strident tone broke the link between Marcus and me.

"Do you have to go?" I asked him.

He caught my hand and pulled me to him. "Not yet." He dipped his head and brushed a kiss across my lips.

"Oh, oh, my." I hadn't expected a kiss.

He grinned. "Thought you didn't want to kiss me until you talked to Shortie?" His eyes danced with mirth.

"Peg?" Hazel hollered again and once more broke the spell.

"We should go help," I said, grateful for the interruption. Marcus, crutches under his arms, followed me to the dining room. He let go of my hand at the last moment.

"How far did you get?" I sat beside my mother-in-law.

Hazel shoved the notebook my way. The high points were listed by date, starting with the neighborhood meeting, followed by my discovery of Marilyn's body, and the picture of Derek Croft with Estelle.

"Pass me the pen?" She handed it over, and I added a summary of the night's events.

We had all the information down, but where did we go from there? The four of us sat in silence for several minutes.

Marcus pushed away from the table. "I have things to do at the station." He squeezed my shoulder. "Walk me out?"

Once outside, he held my hand until we reached his cruiser. The sun had set, but the air hung heavy. Sweat trickled down my back.

"You should go inside," he said. "I'll send someone over tomorrow to install security lights and cameras."

"Thanks." I squeezed his hand. "For everything. It's such a beautiful night. I'm going to take a few minutes for myself and enjoy it."

He winked and climbed into his sedan. "I'll stay right here until you're in the house. Take all the time you need." He closed his car door.

I turned around, closed my eyes, and breathed deeply. The fresh scent of honeysuckle brought memories of summers when my kids would pick the flowers, and the tiny drops of sweet nectar would drip onto their tongues. Critters scurried in the woods beside the house. My shoulders relaxed, and my jaw unclenched. I opened my eyes. The fear from earlier wasn't gone, but I thanked God for His peace and headed inside. I locked the front door and waited for Marcus to drive away.

Hazel and Cynthia still sat at the table. They both looked frustrated.

"What's going on?" I asked.

"Absolutely nothing." Hazel clicked the pen.

I joined them, and we stared at the notepad.

Hazel tossed the pen down. "I used to enjoy this sleuthing. What happened?"

I reached out for her hand, convinced that Owen's deception had influenced her feelings. "You've been through a lot. Anything else going on?"

Tears filled her eyes. "No. Just, you know, Lauree and Owen." She reached for a napkin and blew her nose. "And you getting carjacked."

A chuckle popped out. "I wouldn't call it a carjacking."

She glared. "Fine. Add in your house burning down." She leaned back and let out a deep breath. "I need a vacation."

"One, my house did not burn down. And two, a vacation sounds amazing." I handed her the pen and flipped to a clean page in her notebook. "Go ahead. Where would you want to go?"

We spent the next half hour kicking around vacation ideas. Cynthia suggested the Bahamas, I voted for Scotland, and Hazel wanted a cruise to Alaska.

Hazel yawned, sparking reciprocal yawns from Cynthia and me. While I prepared the coffee for the following day, CB sat up and barked. He ran to the front door, continuing to woof.

"Someone's out there," I said. "Cynthia, call nine-one-one. I'm going to look. It's too early for Carter to be home."

Hazel grabbed my arm. "No, you can't do that! What if those men came back?" Her words came out in a whisper-screech. "Don't forget what happened a couple of hours ago."

"I haven't." I peeked through the peephole but didn't spot anyone. Before she could stop me, I jerked open the door. "Who's here?" My words came out in what I thought of as my threatening voice.

CB wagged his tail and yipped. I looked down to find a tiny, golden puppy curled up in a white wicker basket.

"What in the world?" I scooped up the basket. "It's a puppy? Who left this?" When did they leave it?

"Aww, hand it to me." Cynthia set down her cell phone. "I haven't called nine-one-one yet. I want to hold him." She motioned with her hands and scooped up the little guy. "What a sweet boy. A lab or retriever, I think, with this short fur." She checked his underside. "Oh, wait, this is a girl." She burrowed her face into the doggie's fur while the puppy licked her hands and face. "Why would someone leave us a dog?"

"Marcus left a little while ago." I held onto the basket. "When did someone drop her here?" And, most importantly, why?

"Well, she's ours now." Cynthia kissed the puppy on its head. "I'm going to name her Lucy."

CHAPTER 9

THE NEXT DAY CAME way too early. Lucy whined and yapped for what felt like the whole night. I washed my face with cold water, hoping I'd wake up some. After I dressed, I headed for the kitchen. It would take an entire pot of coffee for the day. Maybe two. While the coffee brewed, I opened the blinds. Hazel's notebook sat on the dining table, still turned to the page where we brainstormed vacation ideas.

I wanted to help my mother-in-law out of her funk. Shortie's private investigator idea floated through my mind. Hazel would enjoy it, but I wondered if I wanted to commit to something else. Sure, we'd solved several mysteries, but did I want that life? Would it be healthy for either of us? Thinking about the mysterious men who "carjacked" me the day before, I decided the whole thing was a bad idea.

I sat down and flipped to a clean page in the notebook. At the top, I wrote "Two Chicks Detective Agency" and underneath "Two Chicks Private Investigators." I added, "Two Chicks PIs." I pushed the pen and paper away.

"Time for breakfast. This is not the time to open a detective agency." I poured myself a cup of coffee.

Hazel joined me in the kitchen, CB on her heels. "What did you say? Oh, coffee. I want some." Her face brightened. She poured a mugful and added a spoonful of sugar.

"Didn't sleep well?" I asked.

"The puppy never slept." She stirred the liquid in her cup and took a sip. "Nope. More." She tipped in extra sweetener and tried again. "Oh, that's yummy." She walked into the dining room. "What's on the agenda today?"

I pulled out a seat and joined her at the table. "I think we need to figure out who left Lucy and why. There has to be a reason, don't you think? And what do we do with her? She's cute and all, but do we need another dog in the house?"

CB barked.

"Yes, you like her now but wait till she chews on your tail or steals your toys," I said. He barked again. "Hazel, do something with your dog."

She chuckled and pulled her notebook toward her. "What is all this?" She indicated what I'd written.

"Remember, Shortie suggested we open a PI business." I shrugged, attempting to portray indifference. This wasn't the day, time, or place to think of starting any kind of business. "Nothing we should do, though."

She traced the names with her finger. "Cute ideas."

I sat back, arms crossed. "The dog is cute too."

"Point made." She rose. "I'll toast some bagels for breakfast."

Cynthia stumbled from her room, Lucy in her arms. "Open the door, quick!" She hustled to the front lawn and set the puppy down.

"Did you sleep at all last night?" I asked from the doorway.

She shook her head and yawned. Once Lucy finished her business, the two of them came back inside. She put the puppy on the floor, and Lucy toddled to CB. The older dog lay still, allowing her to check him out. When she tugged on his ear with her sharp, little teeth, he let out a slight growl, got up, and left the room.

Cynthia scooped her up. "He doesn't want to play, Lucy." The tiny dog curled up in her lap. "Now you're quiet." She ruffled the puppy's sleek golden fur. "Mom, do you think they make doggie melatonin?"

I chuckled. "I doubt it. You'll take her to a vet soon?"

"I'll call today," she said.

Hazel set bagels on the table along with a container of flavored cream cheese and three plates. We ate in silence, enjoying the bark-free time.

"I thought we'd go to Derek's construction company office and ask questions today." Hazel brushed crumbs off her hands. "He said they were surveying, but why? He never explained."

"No, he didn't. He blew us off. You're on puppy duty?" I asked Cynthia.

She hugged Lucy. "Yes, no problem." She yawned again. "We might both take a nap."

"What really needs to happen is to find out why someone left her." I propped an elbow on the table and rested my chin in my palm.

Cynthia raised her eyebrows. "With the way things happen to you two, we might want to."

Hazel and I dressed and left for the Croft and Brothers' office, located in downtown Pensacola on South Alcaniz Street. It sat almost opposite Old Christ Church. I managed to snag a parking spot on the street.

"How does he afford rent here?" Hazel asked as she unbuckled and climbed out of my car. "These places go for well over half a million. Sometimes more."

I joined her on the sidewalk and studied the building. "Quite the upscale office for a construction company."

The one-story, shotgun-style house had a wide front porch supported by slender columns painted a crisp white to contrast with the mint green of the house. A porch swing hanging in one corner swung in the breeze. I opened the picket fence gate, and we climbed the steps to the front door.

"You know why they call it a shotgun house, right?" she asked.

"Yep, it was popular in the South. Each room leads to the next without the need for hallways. Before air conditioning, the front and back doors could be opened to allow the breeze to flow through the house in the summer." The other reason it was called shotgun-style is a bullet fired through the front door would travel straight to the back without hitting a wall.

"The architecture came from Haiti. And West Africa before that." Hazel turned the doorknob. "It's my favorite style of house."

We entered the office. Walls painted in coordinating soft pastels and white wicker furniture gave it a tropical feel. No one sat at the receptionist's desk. I hollered "Hello" down the hall. No one responded.

"This is gorgeous," Hazel said as she roamed the room. "So relaxing. I wonder who decorated for them?"

I rifled through the pamphlets stacked on the unmanned front desk. One stack proved to be about the old church across the street. "Christ Church is one of the oldest surviving churches in Florida."

"Yep." She sat on the wicker loveseat and picked up an architecture magazine. "I used to be a tour guide down here."

"You did? You never told me." I scooted in beside her. "What other secrets do you have?"

She chuckled. "None. I didn't keep it from you. It never came up." She pointed to a trifold brochure in my hand. "What's that?"

As I unfolded it, the front door flew open and slammed into the wall.

"Ugh, I hope that didn't leave a mark." A well-proportioned, middle-aged woman dressed head-to-toe in high-fashion, brand-named clothes sailed into the room. "Ladies!" She halted and stared. "I didn't know anyone was here. So sorry."

She hurried to the desk, tucked her bright white handbag into a drawer, and perched on the seat, back straight and hands clasped in front of her. "Now, how can I help you?" She eyed the top of the desk and straightened the pamphlets.

Hazel spoke up. "We are here to investigate Marilyn Croft's murder."

Her words must have startled the receptionist. Her hand flew to her throat.

"Her ... what?" Her voice lost its modulated tone, and the word came out as a screech.

"Yes, honey. Did they not tell you Mrs. Croft is dead?" Hazel rounded the desk and patted the lady's shoulder. My mother-in-law looked at me, eyes wide, in some kind of communication. But I didn't understand it. She jerked her head to the side three times.

I stood. "Can I get you a drink?" I made a face at Hazel and shrugged.

She closed her eyes.

"Sure, can I have three fingers of ..." the woman said.

"Find her some water, Peg." Hazel made the big eye face again, her eyebrows rising high on her forehead.

I came to an empty office first. File boxes overflowed with paperwork, and an old, scarred desk sat against the farthest wall, an unplugged bronze lamp on top of it. Deep red wallpaper hung in strips. Next, I passed a small bathroom. A peek inside showed it hadn't been updated. Broken pink tiles lined the wall above the tub, and the top of the toilet leaned against the tiny cabinet. Finally, I reached the kitchen.

A mini refrigerator sitting on top of one of the counters held bottled water. Beside it were several bottles of a pricey brand of bourbon. I grabbed a water and returned to the front of the office. "Here you go." I handed her the bottle and sat.

Hazel cocked her head.

"I don't have any idea what you're telling me," I hissed.

She tilted her head back and stared at the ceiling. "May I use your bathroom?" she asked the receptionist.

The woman unscrewed the bottle. "Of course."

Hazel trekked down the hall on her own exploration.

"So," I said. "Are you in charge of Croft and Bros.?"

"Brothers." She pulled out her purse and rifled through it. She filled in her smudged lip color, looking in a compact mirror, lipstick in hand. When she finished, she checked her face, ran the tip of her index finger under each eye, snapped the compact closed, returned everything to her purse, and put it away.

"Croft and Brothers. Right. So?"

Her dark brown eyes studied me, starting at my feet and working their way up. I resisted fluffing my hair—my favorite feature—and waited for her assessment. One of her well-plucked eyebrows twitched.

"I fill in occasionally." She rearranged the pens and calendar, her hands fluttering over each item. "You're sure it was Marilyn?"

"Yes. I found her." The memory shook me. "On Monday."

"Two days ago. And he never told me," she said in a quiet tone as if she were thinking to herself.

What did she mean by that?

CHAPTER 10

HAZEL BUSTLED BACK INTO the room and stopped beside the woman. "What is your name, dear?" she asked.

"Elizabeth Sarconni." She tucked a lock of her auburn hair behind her ear.

Hazel stuck out her hand. "Nice to meet you." After Elizabeth shook it, Hazel grabbed my arm and dragged me to the door. "Ready?"

She was burning to tell me something. We stepped onto the front porch and closed the door behind us. She blurted, "Tiny houses. Vacation rentals. That's what Derek is up to." Her voice filled with disgust.

"What?" I pulled my arm away and followed her to the car. "Hold up. What are you talking about?"

She patted her purse. "I've got all the proof in here. Come on, let's go home."

I rounded the back of my car and paused before opening my door. "Dear Lord, please help me with this woman." I climbed in and buckled. "Amen."

"Huh?" Hazel said. She flipped down the visor and fluffed her hair. "Amen to what?" She tipped her head to the side. "Do you like my new haircut? Is it too short?" She stared at me. "Why aren't you driving?"

"Hazel, I love you. But please tell me what you mean by tiny houses and vacation rentals." I started the car and flipped the air conditioning to high. "And yes, your hair is pretty." I didn't see a change, but I wouldn't tell her that.

She dug in her purse and pulled out several pieces of paper. "I found these in the room beside the bathroom. Did you check in there?"

"No, I stopped at the kitchen. What's up with all the liquor?" I shifted into drive and traveled down Alcaniz back toward I-110.

"I found an oversized closet area with a fax machine and printer. These were in the tray." She glanced through the paperwork. "They say Derek's company has been hired to build tiny homes."

"He is in the construction business."

"Yes, but that's not the problem." She shook one piece of paper my way. "This says he's building in Stone Creek Cove. He can't do that!"

I turned off Alcaniz and drove to the closest burger joint. "Let's get a milkshake. Bring all that with you."

While we drank our shakes—chocolate mocha for me and strawberry for Hazel, who said it sounded healthier—we read through what she found. A letter from Croft and Bros. Construction to a realty company based in Colorado outlined all of the details. Derek's company would build the tiny, one-room houses, and High Mountain Realty would oversee the rentals.

"And look at this. Right here." Hazel poked the third piece of paper. "Right in the middle of the neighborhood. What a creep."

I pulled the letter closer and read the details. "Oh, Hazel. Not right in the middle." I closed my eyes. "He's building *over* the creek."

Hazel sputtered, shrugged, and stammered for several minutes. We left the fast-food restaurant. When I reached the exit for I-10, she said, "Turn around."

"I am not turning around. We're going home."

"Peg, I'm going to strangle the man. He is behind all of this." She huffed and burrowed into her seat, arms crossed like a petulant child. "That's not very Christian of me, is it?"

"You're mad. I understand." We reached Scenic Highway, and I turned left at the light and headed for Stone Creek Cove. "Besides strangling him, what else can we do today?"

She checked her watch. "It's not even eleven yet. How about we pay a visit to Babs Ferguson?"

"Where does she live?" I pulled into Hazel's driveway and parked.

She unbuckled. "I have a directory. We'll find out."

While Hazel checked for the address, I joined Cynthia and Lucy on the couch. The puppy, full of energy, bounced beside Cynthia. She had dark circles under her eyes.

"Mom, can you take care of her while I shower? I haven't had a minute to do anything," Cynthia said.

My lips twitched. She reminded me of Chloe with Reese. "Being a dog mommy is hard work." I picked up the puppy. "Come on, little one. We'll go play out back."

Lucy romped in the grass until she panted. I ran the outside faucet for a minute, and when the water cooled, I let her sip out of my hand. She ran under the stream and shook her little body, spraying water all over my legs.

Cynthia opened the back door and joined us, her hair wrapped in a towel. She took it off and handed it to me. "I think you need this." She grinned at Lucy, who nipped at her toes.

"She's full of energy."

"She is." A rueful smile crossed her face. "I'm beat."

"If she plays a bit more, she'll be tired enough to nap, and you can too. I'd watch her, but Grandma Hazel and I are going to visit Babs."

"Who's that?" Cynthia tossed a stick, and Lucy raced after it.

"She's the one Marilyn said threatened her. She also isn't afraid of Derek." I reminded Cynthia of how Babs acted at the neighborhood association meeting.

Hazel joined us in the backyard. Charlie Brown followed her, but stayed on the porch, his eyes tracking the puppy's every move. A soft breeze ruffled through the trees and bushes in the yard, providing some relief from the heat. The smell of honeysuckle reached me, and I breathed deeply.

"I love the scent," Cynthia said, closing her eyes.

"Remember when you and Chloe picked all of Ms. Lauree's bushes?" I chuckled, thinking about her reaction.

"Oh, she was mad." Cynthia laughed, and Lucy yipped. "She never got angry at us, but that time she did. I thought we'd never get to watch TV again."

"Your dad made me drop the punishment after two days. He said we were the ones being punished." I grinned. He'd been so adamant about it.

Hazel put her arm around Cynthia. "Remember all of this when your baby"—she pointed to Lucy—"misbehaves. Pick a consequence you can live with."

Cynthia snuggled the puppy to her chest. "She'll be perfect, won't you, little girl?" She rubbed noses with Lucy while Hazel and I exchanged smirks.

"Did you make her an appointment with the vet?" I asked.

"I'll call them this afternoon."

"I wonder who left her." Hazel shook her head. "It doesn't make sense."

"No, but I'm glad she's here." Cynthia rubbed Lucy's fur. "No matter what, I'm keeping her." Her fierce feelings for the puppy showed on her face.

"Hazel, did you find Babs's address?" I asked.

"Sure did. You ready?"

Babs lived several streets away. The weatherwoman predicted the day would be one of the hottest of the week, so I drove.

I pulled into Babs's driveway and switched off the car. "Is she home?"

"I did a 'ding dong ditch.'" Hazel made air quotes.

"You did a what?" We approached the front door.

She rang the doorbell. "I called her and hung up when she answered."

That wasn't what the expression meant, but I didn't explain because Babs opened the door. "Why'd you call and hang up?" she asked.

I pinched my lips together to stifle my laughter.

Hazel stepped back. "Oh, sorry, I didn't mean to call you."

Adding lying to her resume wouldn't help the situation. I leaned around Hazel. "Sorry, we wanted to speak with you. She checked to make sure you were home."

Babs let us inside. "Ah, I see. You're a ding dong ditcher."

Again with that. I couldn't change the two women's minds, so I held my tongue. Babs left us in the living room while she went in search of water bottles.

Her home was a serene and relaxing space, decorated in soothing colors. Kind of a contrast to Babs herself, at least what I'd learned of her so far.

She returned and passed out the water. "It's so hot out."

Discussing the weather wasn't a bad place to start. Hazel began with intense, personal questions after talking about the heat and the quiet hurricane season.

She pulled her notebook out of her purse. "Do you mind if I ask about your relationship with the Crofts?"

Babs shifted in her chair. "Relationship? I mean, I heard Marilyn is dead."

Obviously, she didn't know my mother-in-law well. Hazel retrieved her pen and set her pocketbook aside. "She is. We found her." She flipped to a clean page. "What I want to ask is about you and Marilyn."

"You found her?" Babs's eyes bugged out.

"I did." I shrugged.

Hazel clicked her pen. "About what Marilyn said at the end of the meeting." Her brows knit in curiosity.

"The end of the ..." The woman's words trailed off.

"The meeting. Yes." Hazel's steely-eyed gaze never left Babs's face. "She said, and I quote, 'When is she going to learn not to oppose me?'"

"Oh, right." Babs made a face. "So, Derek and I were ... friends back in the day."

Hazel scribbled that down.

"Like friends friends, or like ..." I cocked my eyebrow.

Babs's shoulders drooped. "We had an affair, okay?"

Hazel turned to me, a question in her eyes. I nodded. She gave up the information too fast.

"What did Marilyn do when she found out?" Hazel asked.

Babs stood and paced the small room. "She was angry, of course. Derek told her." She stopped and stared at us. "Please don't think badly of me. I worked for Derek for a while. It ..." Her cheeks flushed. "Happened."

"Worked for him?" I asked. It didn't matter what we thought of her. This was a new development in the case.

"Yeah, at the place downtown. It needed fixing when he first moved in there. I helped him." Her eyes glimmered. "We had fun."

"You two fixed it up and decorated it?" Hazel asked.

"I did the decorating." She thumbed at her chest. "Derek has zero sense of style. But that's my business." She walked out of the room. "Hang on a minute," she called behind her.

Hazel and I exchanged confused glances.

Babs came back and handed me a business card. "See, I am an interior designer."

I passed the card to Hazel. "But you only did the front room."

Babs slumped into her seat. "Right. That's how far we got before Marilyn figured out what was happening."

Chapter II

"What did Marilyn do? Did she find you together?" Hazel tucked the business card into her purse and added the new information to her notebook.

Babs scoffed as she sat. "Oh, she was mad." Her lips tipped up into a grin. "What's funny is she's the one who hired me."

"Oh?" I asked. "Why is it funny?"

She waved her hand in front of herself. "Look at me. I'm nothing like Marilyn. She's proper and put together. Nails and toes done, lipstick always on. Or rather, she used to be." She paused a moment as if paying respect to the dead. "Me? I'm an old-school Florida girl. I weighed about the same as she did then, but I loved my shorts, T-shirts, and flip-flops. Hair up in a ponytail, and not the pretty, stylish kind girls wear these days. I'm sure she thought I was safe."

I sipped from my water bottle. "Safe. That's an interesting word. Why would you say that?"

She laughed. "Derek had a reputation."

"I didn't know about any of this," Hazel said.

Babs waved a hand. "You weren't part of our group—the married but no children group. We did stuff together. Dinner, plays downtown, that kind of thing."

"So, this happened a long time ago?" I asked.

"Some of it, yes." Babs squinted in thought. "But me and Derek? Not too many years back."

"Hmm. Any more questions for her?" I asked Hazel.

She said no, and we left after thanking Babs for the information and the water.

"Let's run by the creek," Hazel said.

I switched directions and parked beside the walkway where I found the nest. "Wonder if Marcus has the report on how Marilyn died?"

"Why don't you call him? The nests had the sticky stuff, and the egrets are gone. We found out about Babs and Derek. We also discovered his plans for this area. Now to put the pieces together and find out who killed Marilyn and why, don't you think?"

"Yep. I have no idea how to do that."

The side of her mouth crinkled. "Me either. Make the call."

I called Marcus and put my phone on speaker.

"Hey, Peg, how are you? Do you miss me?" His arrogance, front and center, didn't irritate me for once.

My face flamed. Hazel chuckled, and I gave her the stink eye. "Actually, I want to ask what you've learned about Marilyn. We might have information to add to the story."

Tapping on a keyboard sounded over the speaker. "Hang on … okay, here we go. No, nothing yet."

Hazel and I exchanged glances. "You're sure?"

"Yep." A chair squeaked. I imagined him leaning back, hands behind his head. My mouth went dry at the thought. If he smiled in my imagination, I was done for.

I pushed thoughts of his handsome face from my mind. "We talked to Babs today."

"Babs? Who is Babs?"

Hazel pumped her arm in victory. "Yes."

"Come over and we can fill you in." I ended the call and grinned. "We are one step ahead of Detective Sharp." Hazel and I high-fived.

All was quiet inside Hazel's house. Charlie Brown lay sprawled out on the couch, and Lucy and Cynthia were nowhere in sight. I scribbled a note for Marcus to come in when he arrived, stuck it on the front door, and stretched out in the recliner.

"Take a nap while you can," I said to Hazel. "If the dog is asleep, we need to take advantage of it." My eyes closed before I finished talking. No puppy yipping. No one kidnapping me. Peace and quiet. Heavenly.

A noise woke me. I opened my eyes and held still. Had I been snoring? Lucy wasn't barking, and the house felt quiet. I turned my head and spotted a man's back as he limped toward the kitchen. After lowering the foot of the recliner and wincing at the final thunk, I shifted off it and stood. I grabbed a book off a side table for protection and raised it to clunk him on his head when he turned.

"Marcus?" The name came out as a scream, and the whole house woke up. CB flew off the couch, barking and jumping on both of us. Roscoe squawked "Ta-da" over and over. From Cynthia's room, Lucy barked and scratched at her door. Hazel ran out of her bedroom, creases on her face and hair sticking in all directions.

"What's going on?" she shouted.

"Peg, it's me." Marcus held out his palms as if to calm me.

Cynthia jerked her door open. Lucy ran out, sniffed Marcus's cast, and pottied on the floor.

I laid the book on the kitchen counter and patted my chest. "You scared ten years off me. What are you doing here?"

Cynthia grabbed several kitchen towels and cleaned up the puppy's accident. CB licked Marcus's hand. Hazel told Roscoe to hush, mumbled about how her life had never been crazier, and shuffled back to her room.

My daughter took Lucy outside to finish her business. CB followed them. I turned to Marcus, hands on my hips. "Why are you here?"

His lips twitched. "You invited me to come over. Said you'd tell me about Babs. Remember?" He tipped his head. "And don't leave your door unlocked with a note saying, 'Come in.' You were just carjacked."

"I didn't think of that." I made a face.

He pinched the bridge of his nose. "Come on, let's get something to drink before we talk." He gestured to my hair. "Might want to fix that too."

After a few minutes in the bathroom, my hair in place and my teeth brushed, I joined him on the loveseat. He held a glass of sweet tea. Another waited on the coffee table for me.

"Thank you." I lifted my glass.

He tapped his against mine. "You're welcome. Where did the puppy come from?"

"We don't know." I explained about finding Lucy on the doorstep.

"Doesn't make sense." He rubbed the stubble on his chin. "We need to find out who left her. Now tell me about this Babs person."

I filled him in and added what Babs told Hazel and me. "We forgot to ask her for her alibi." I snapped my fingers. "We can go back and ask."

Marcus patted my leg. "I'll take care of it. You've done everything you need to do."

"Did I tell you Hazel and I went downtown to Derek's office?"

He pulled his notebook out of his shirt pocket. "Do you have a pen? I can't find mine."

I retrieved one from my purse and handed it to him.

He pointed with the pen. "Give me Babs's address and Derek's office address." He added the information to his notebook.

Cynthia and the dogs came inside. Both canines headed for the water bowls, and Cynthia grabbed my glass of tea. She drank half of it and set it down. "Thanks."

"Can you do me a favor?" I asked.

She nodded.

"Will you sneak into Grandma Hazel's room and bring me her purse?"

While she went to do that, I refilled our glasses. "Have you eaten lunch? Want a PBJ?"

"Sure," Marcus said. He limped into the kitchen and leaned his crutches against a counter, shuffling out of my way when I needed to find the peanut butter. He watched me prepare our sandwiches. "I don't make you nervous, do I?" he asked.

I stopped what I was doing. "No, why do you ask?"

"Most people are nervous when the police are with them."

I bit the inside of my cheek to keep from giggling. I pointed with the knife. "I don't think of you as a policeman."

He lowered my knife hand. "What do you think of me as?" He cupped my cheek in his palm.

My mind went blank, and my body responded to his touch. "Um, well, not a cop," I stammered.

He bent his head to kiss me. I closed my eyes and moved in toward him. His lips touched mine. I stepped closer, wrapping my arms around his waist, enjoying his warm, masculine scent. His strong arms embraced me.

"Those PBJs sure look yummy," Hazel said.

"They're my favorite," Cynthia said.

Charlie Brown added a woof.

I groaned and leaned my forehead against Marcus's. "You see what I have to put up with?"

His lips tipped up. "I think you like it."

"Y'all want a sandwich, I take it?" I asked my daughter and my mother-in-law.

Cynthia grabbed the two I'd already made. "Thanks. You can go back to kissing."

Hazel laughed and followed her to the table. Heat filled my cheeks, but I made two more PBJs, and Marcus and I joined them. CB sat beside him, waiting for a taste.

"He loves peanut butter," Hazel said. "You can give him some if you want."

Marcus tossed him a piece of his lunch, then folded his sandwich and stuffed the last of it in his mouth. After he chewed and swallowed, he stood and grabbed his crutches. "Got to go." He patted his shirt pocket, which held his notebook. "Thanks for the info, Peg. See you soon." He winked and left.

"Nice of him to stop by." Hazel pulled off some crust and gave it to CB.

Through the blinds, I watched him make his way out to his cruiser.

"That was quite the kiss." Cynthia snickered.

I joined them at the table, pulled off a chunk of my crust, and threw it at her.

"What did he want?" Hazel asked.

Cynthia snickered again but stopped when I glared at her.

"I told him about Babs and Derek's office." I finished my sandwich and wiped my hands on my napkin.

"He didn't bring up Marilyn?" Hazel asked.

How to answer this? "I forgot to ask?" My sentence came out as a question.

Cynthia stacked our plates and took them to the kitchen. "He distracted her, Grandma."

"Ha ha, funny girl." I cleared the table.

"Hey, Mom?" Cynthia said. "What about Shortie? Did you ever talk to him?"

CHAPTER 12

Shortie. I hadn't thought about him all day. Less than twenty-four hours before, Estelle's goons derailed my attempt to meet him for dinner. Marcus consumed my emotions and thoughts, but now, my muscles tensed, and a sharp pang shot through my stomach as memories of being dragged out of my car raced through my mind.

"Mom?" Cynthia wiped her hands on a dish towel and hurried to me. "You okay? You got really pale."

Hazel held my hand. "Peg?"

"I'm all right." My chest tightened as a cold unease crept up my spine. "Just remembering last night and how they threatened me."

Cynthia pulled her chair beside mine. "I'm sorry, I wasn't thinking."

"It's not your fault, honey." I drew in a deep breath and blew it out. "I'll be all right." I checked my phone. "I'm going to call Shortie and set up another time to meet with him."

"How about some water before that?" Hazel waved Cynthia toward the kitchen. "Take your time. You've been through a lot, Peg."

Cynthia hustled back to the table, a glass of ice-cold water in her hand. "Drink, Mom."

I did what they told me to and gave myself a minute to calm down. Shortie and I needed to talk. Things were moving too fast with Marcus. Already, I'd broken my stipulation to resolve my relationship with Shortie before kissing Marcus. I couldn't blame anyone but me, and I wouldn't take the easy way out and blame it on hormones. As a grown woman, I knew what had to be done.

I pushed up from the table. "I'm going to my room for this."

"Let us know what he says," Cynthia said with a sympathetic expression. "I'm sure he'll understand."

I hoped so. On my way out of the room, I grabbed Lucy's basket.

"Mind if I use this? It'll be great to throw my keys into."

Cynthia shook her head. "Lucy mainly sleeps with me." She wrinkled her nose.

In my room, I piled my pillows against my bed's headboard and got comfy. This conversation needed to happen, even if I hadn't decided what to say. I reached down for my favorite plush blanket and laid it over my legs. It might be the hottest month on record, but I kept my bedroom chilly. Plus, tucking the blanket around me delayed the inevitable. Finally, I punched Shortie's number on my cell and held it to my ear, hoping to get his voicemail. I scolded myself for my cowardice.

He answered, "Peg?"

"Hey, is this a bad time?" I scrunched the blanket in my fist.

"No, I have a few minutes. What's up?" he asked.

My brain went blank. Did I want to have this kind of conversation right now? "We never got to have dinner."

"Yeah." He exhaled sharply. "How are you anyhow? I'm sure what happened scared you."

It was scary, but Marcus made things better. I couldn't tell Shortie that. "I'm doing okay. You want to try again for dinner?"

"Sure. This time I'll pick you up. Seven tomorrow night?"

He didn't seem at all affected by what happened to me the night before. "Yes, tomorrow, I'll be ready at seven. Can we go to our favorite place at the beach?"

After he agreed, I punched the off button and set down my phone. It irritated me how Shortie ignored what I went through. To be fair, I hadn't told him everything, like I did with Marcus. Frustration filled me.

And the desire to make better decisions, to act my age and not like some hormone-riddled teenager.

It wasn't right to kiss one man while another waited for an answer to his proposal. I knew better. I prayed for wisdom and added a prayer for Shortie. Who knew how this would go? How it should go? I was clueless, and God understood. He knew me better than I did.

I wanted a break from solving mysteries, checking alibis, and finding criminals. I decided to use the rest of the day to work on my blog on my new laptop.

Mamma Birds' readership held steady, but it begged for care. I took some time to answer my faithful followers' questions and comments. The blog, part of my healing after Zack died, allowed me to talk to other adults and moms who might not be young widows but were in the thick of raising their kids. It became an outlet to share some of my healing journey.

I needed to talk to Lauree and ask how involved she wanted to be—could be—as she went through her cancer treatment. Dread filled me as I dialed her number. I explained the reason for my call and waited through a long pause.

"Peg, I'm not sure." Her heavy sigh came through the line. I pictured my friend at the baseball game and fireworks a few days ago. Her face then had revealed the pain she felt. Now, she explained about the bone-deep fatigue. "It's like nothing I've ever experienced. Imagine the worst flu you've ever had and multiply it by … oh, I don't know … a hundred."

The line went quiet. For too long.

"Peg, I don't think this treatment's going to help."

The sorrow in her voice and my fears about her cancer overwhelmed me. How could she make it through this? I wanted to be there for her. Hold her up when she didn't have the energy. I drew inspiration from how she helped me when Zack passed away.

I chewed on my lip and blinked back tears. She and I both knew God was with her and would carry her through, but this didn't seem the right time to remind her. "I love you, Lauree. I'm here for whatever you need. We may not see the outcome, but whatever happens, I'm here. God's here. We're going to cling to that." I prayed aloud for her.

She sniffled. "Thank you. Can you come over soon? I want to spend time with you," she said, her voice thick with tears.

"Does tomorrow morning work?" I wiped tears from my cheeks while batting away dire thoughts about how I needed to spend time with her before the end. That kind of thinking wouldn't help either of us.

We made plans for the next day and ended our call. I turned back to my blog—all my responsibility now. Six weeks postpartum, Chloe still hadn't written anything for her new mom's section. I would call and discuss it with her, but the rest of the work—social media, financial, interaction with readers, creating new content—fell on my shoulders.

Did I still want it? Lauree took on more of it because of my other commitments and her desire to work more hours. My sticking point was financial. Mamma Birds supported the kids and me for years. Could I let it go, or sell it?

I pulled out a three-by-five card and wrote bullet points for my questions. On another index card, I arranged the points in sections: financial, emotional, and time constraints. Finally, I wrote out a complete list of tasks I needed to do and how often they had to be completed. Laying them all in front of me, I bowed my head and prayed that God would guide me and give me wisdom and insight.

Wisdom seemed to be a common prayer request of mine.

Nerves hit me when I headed for Lauree's the next day. I swung through our favorite coffee shop for some sugar-laden java and lemon pound cake without knowing if she had an appetite. All I understood about breast cancer and cancer treatment came from stories I heard or read—none of those involved my best friend.

I pulled into her driveway and avoided looking at my house, which sat empty, waiting for people to fix it so I could move home. How I wished they were hard at work right now.

Lauree waited on her front porch, sitting in a rocking chair, wrapped in a blanket. My car's outside temperature display read ninety-five at only ten in the morning. After I passed her a coffee, I sat in the rocker beside her and shook the bag of cake slices.

"Your favorite. Want some?"

"Sure, put a piece on the table." She indicated the small, round, wrought-iron table between us.

We rocked in silence for a few minutes. She sipped her drink and picked a tiny bite of pound cake off the napkin. Sweat dripped down the side of my face.

"I'm sure you're discouraged," I said. "How's John?" Question after question ran through my mind, but today didn't seem to be the right day to ask them.

She wrinkled her nose. "He's inside. He's taken a leave of absence. He hovers. It's making me crazy." Her lips tipped up in a shallow grin. "He means well, but ..."

"Oh, yeah, I can imagine." I tried to put myself in his place, but the fear almost crushed me. I changed the subject. "How about the meal train? Do you want us to put the word out again?"

She nodded and shifted in her chair. "Yes, please. It's so helpful." She pulled her blanket closer. "Tell me what you've been up to. I want to talk about anything besides cancer."

"Are you ready? It's a lot." I chuckled. "You won't be alarmed if I tell you I found another dead body?"

She faked a gasp and pressed her hand to her throat, her eyes wide. "No way, you did not."

"Ha ha. Yes, I sure did." I sipped my hot coffee, wishing I'd ordered it iced.

"It might come as a shock, but I'm not surprised at this point. When did that happen?"

As I talked, her eyes widened. By the time I finished, her face was frozen in disbelief. She reached out her hand. "Who are you, and where is my friend?"

We laughed together. I grabbed her hand. "I'm as shocked by all of this as you are. I thought after last month and the craziness with Owen"—I thumbed toward my house—"that Hazel and I were done solving mysteries. This isn't what I want to do. Did I tell you what

Shortie suggested?" I filled her in about his Two Chicks Detective Agency idea.

"What I'm curious about is who you're going to pick." Her eyes twinkled.

I crossed my arms in mock anger. "Shortie and I have a dinner date tonight." I rose and held out my shirt, hoping for a cool breeze. "We have to go inside. I'm dying out here." The second the words left my mouth, I froze. "Oh, Lauree, I'm sorry ..."

She pushed herself up to stand, wrapping her blanket around her shoulders. "You of all people cannot become this." She waved her hand up and down in front of me. "Do not baby me. Be my friend. The one you've always been. Please."

I blinked back my tears and gave her a sharp nod. "Got it. You gonna get the door for me, woman?"

Chapter 13

When I arrived home from Lauree's, I went straight to work cleaning the house from top to bottom until the bathrooms sparkled, all the beds had clean sheets, and the windows were spot-free. I was on a roll, working out my emotions and concerns for my friend and her family. And I was panicking.

What should I tell Shortie? His proposal played in my mind. Shortly before he proposed, I realized that he and I had fallen into a relationship. I didn't make a conscious decision to date. At least I didn't think so. It wasn't a formal thing. He liked me, I liked him. Not much thought went into it on either of our parts.

And neither of us ever said those three little words. Considering I'd been married before, I was pretty sure they were important words.

What would my answer have been if Marcus hadn't shown up right after Shortie asked me to marry him? I didn't know. I had trouble picturing myself answering him at all.

Speaking of Marcus, how serious was he about a relationship with me? Or me with him, for that matter. Shouldn't I be more concerned with how *I* felt and what *I* wanted?

What if he wanted more children? What if he wanted me to quit solving murders? What if I had to kick out my kids, sell the house, and move to Europe?

My brain spun out of control. For a fleeting moment, I considered joining a convent.

Finally, I went in search of Hazel.

"Knock, knock." Her bedroom door stood ajar, and I pushed it further. "Can I come in?"

"Sure." She turned from where she sat at her desk. "What's up?"

I perched on the edge of her bed next to where CB lay. I shrugged, not sure where to start.

"How was Lauree this morning?"

"She's weak and has horrible fatigue. She fell asleep on the couch while John and I talked. He thinks this new treatment will help her. I'm not sure." I shrugged again. "I want to believe, but it's difficult."

"Walking by faith isn't always fun. It can be, but not in the deep darkness. I've been where you are."

Her husband, Arthur, Zack's dad, died from a rare, aggressive cancer. "Art went fast, didn't he?"

"He did." Her words were soft. "I wish you could've met him. He would have loved you."

"Me too. Zack showed me pictures of him."

"Carter looks like him." Her face brightened. "Art's been gone for over thirty years, but I think about him every day."

I didn't know that. She never mentioned him. I opened my mouth to ask her what she thought about Marcus and Shortie, but she turned toward her laptop.

"Enough reminiscing. I want to show you this." She tapped the computer screen.

I leaned closer. She'd created a spreadsheet with the murders we'd already solved, suspects included, as well as the names of everyone in our birding group. One name stood out.

"We haven't talked to Carmen in almost a month. I'm surprised she hasn't called," I said. She'd been part of the original group, like Shortie and Owen. More real estate agent and less birder, she was still a vital part of our little band of birders.

"She dropped off my radar with all that's gone on. Think she heard what happened with Owen? The story made the news all over this area." Hazel picked up her cell. "I'm going to call her."

Carmen's phone rang four times before it switched to voicemail. Hazel left a short message and asked her to call back.

"Surely she hasn't gone to the dark side." My joke fell flat. "No way she'd do that." I sat cross-legged on Hazel's bed. CB scootched over and laid his head on my thigh.

My mother-in-law turned back to her spreadsheet. She highlighted Carmen's name. "Only until we talk to her. Take a look at the thread Estelle left."

Last fall, Estelle got her claws into Pensacola's mayor and used him as her puppet to kill people, both of whom were in my birding group. Earlier this summer, Estelle killed her husband and used her great-niece, Gabby, along with our former friend Owen, to burn down my house, among other things. Estelle threatened Chloe when Reese was born, and one of her minions drugged Cynthia. Estelle's name showed up throughout the spreadsheet.

"All along, we've seen her black sedan with the women's veteran 'BrdsAliv' plate." Hazel tapped her fingers on her desk. "Two months ago, the news said the Keatons were back in the area. Besides hearing from Owen how she instructed him and Gabby on what to do, and Harry saying the Keatons set him up with the quetzals, we haven't seen Estelle. She's gone dark."

I clapped at her words. "You're learning the lingo again." CB woofed and laid his head back down. "She's probably hiding since she's a suspect, but I feel her presence. I'm sure she sent those guys who dragged me from my car and threatened me. The man who told me she said to stay away didn't say her name, but who else would it be?" I rubbed the goosebumps breaking out up and down my arms.

Hazel held up her hand. "The birds went missing." Her thumb went up. "Derek knows Estelle. They went to prom together." Her index finger went out. When she raised her third finger, she said, "Marilyn died. And you were carjacked." She raised her ring finger.

I leaned forward and lifted her pinky. "We met Babs."

"True." She nodded. "Estelle is in there, Peg. She has to be. She's been involved with bird ... stuff each time."

"Yep, she killed Sylvia over the rufous hummingbird." The sight of Sylvia dying would never leave me.

"And Kurt died because of the quetzals," she said.

We both grimaced, remembering when we found his body in Harry's inner office.

"Why would she care about the egrets in a small neighborhood in Pensacola? It doesn't make sense. Means, motive, and opportunity. That's what we need to think about. Who are our suspects?"

She glanced at her laptop. "Derek is involved for sure. He's got this idea of building tiny homes over the creek. He had to have played a part in removing the egrets."

"I agree. He gives me the creeps for so many reasons. And he and Estelle have some kind of past relationship." I tapped my fingers on my leg. "What about Babs? If we consider motive, she'd have a good one for killing Marilyn."

"Her affair with Derek took place a while ago, though." Hazel groaned when she stretched. "All that's left is Estelle."

"And her goons. We can't forget about them," I said.

"True. Derek had the motive, means, and opportunity." She saved her work and closed the laptop. "His motive could be greed. Like with Owen." She snarled Owen's name.

"Did Babs have a motive to kill Marilyn? Or to get rid of the birds? She was kind of pushy about having someone investigate the missing egrets and making the creek a safer place. Unless it was a ruse." I shifted on the bed. "When we talked with her, she didn't seem to know about Derek's plans to build tiny homes and rent them."

Hazel stood. CB jumped off the bed and padded to her side. "All that's left is our original problem child, Estelle." She motioned for me to follow. "I want a snack. We'll have to wait for Marcus to tell us more about how Marilyn died. Then we can go after Estelle."

I never asked Hazel about the men in my life. By the time I began to dress for my date, she, Cynthia, and Carter were eating dinner, both dogs sitting nearby, anticipating dropped food. Lucy was less well-behaved than CB. She tugged on his ears and tail until he put his big doggie paw on her head and growled. She calmed down after that.

I smoothed my black tunic top over my white capris and sat at the table to slip on my sparkly red sandals.

"Mom, you look pretty," Cynthia said. "Hot date?" She winked.

"Shortie's picking me up in a few minutes." I checked the time. "Any minute now, actually." I peered out the blinds at the empty driveway.

"What will you tell him?" Hazel asked.

I shrugged. "I meant to talk to you about that earlier, but you distracted me talking about Estelle."

She took a bite of her salad. "You'd rather talk about mysterious stuff anyhow," she mumbled.

She had a point. I rechecked the time.

"Mom, sit." Carter pointed to a chair. "You're hovering. Makes me nervous."

I sat beside him. After a minute, he set his hand on my knee. "Quit tapping your foot."

Deep breath in and out. "Sorry, honey." I plastered on a fake smile and picked a piece of dog fur off my top.

"Why are you nervous, Mom?" Cynthia asked. "Shortie's your friend. You'll figure it all out."

I was thankful she believed in me. I pictured a scale—Shortie on one side, Marcus on the other. What to do, what to do.

"Peg," Hazel said. "Have you prayed about this?"

"Yes," I said.

She tipped her head. "So, let God tell you. It doesn't have to be tonight. You don't have to make a permanent decision. Not right now."

Her words caught me off guard and reminded me of the truth. Relief coursed through my body. My shoulders relaxed, and my mind cleared. Sure, I prayed, but had I stopped to listen for an answer?

A knock sounded, and I rose to open the door. "Thanks, Hazel." Her words set me at ease.

CHAPTER 14

CARMEN STOOD BEFORE ME on the front porch dressed in cream-colored linen slacks, a silky sleeveless top, and gold sandals. Her makeup and hair were picture-perfect as always.

"Peg!" She opened her arms and hugged me, squeezing me tight.

I'd been expecting Shortie, not a hug from Carmen. I returned her embrace and stepped back, gesturing for her to enter. "Hazel, look who's here."

Hazel greeted her. "Where have you been?" My mother-in-law wasn't known for her tact or warm, fuzzy greetings.

Carmen waved hello to Cynthia and Carter. "I've been out of town for a few weeks helping my mother move into assisted living."

I pulled out a chair for her to join us at the table and introduced her to the dogs. Lucy curled up on her feet and let out a big puppy sigh. "You're the dog-whisperer," I said, hoping the puppy wouldn't chew up what appeared to be an expensive pair of sandals.

She leaned over and stroked Lucy's soft fur. "She's a sweetie. I've always had labs. She looks like one. When did you get her?"

"You don't think she's a retriever?" Cynthia asked.

"No, she's probably a mix, but she has some lab features." Carmen and Cynthia talked about raising puppies for a few minutes before Carmen asked again when we got Lucy.

"It's a strange story," I said. Cynthia told her about how the puppy showed up on our front porch.

Carmen's eyes narrowed. "You don't think that's odd?"

"Of course we do, but we have no way to find out who left her." I switched topics. "Did you hear what happened with Owen?"

Tears filled her eyes, and Carter passed her a napkin. "Thank you." She blotted her eyes and wiped her nose. "I saw the story in the newspaper when I got back. And your house. That's where I went first. Your neighbor told me you were here." She grimaced. "I'm so, so sorry, Peg. It must have been awful."

"It was." I paused. "You talked to Lauree?"

She nodded. "I remembered her from our first meeting of the birding group. That seems like so long ago. Is she sick?" She paused. "Is your home salvageable?"

I explained about Lauree's cancer. "The insurance says they can fix my house. They're supposed to replace the roof, and it needs a thorough cleaning." I wondered about telling her the rest. "Owen did it. Started the fire. He and a young woman named Gabby."

Carmen closed her eyes. "Why? What in the world possessed him? I thought he was such a decent man."

"Greed," Hazel snapped. "Pure greed. That man ..." Her fists clenched.

Carter gave his grandmother a side hug. "It's okay, Grandma. Calm down."

She patted his hand, took a deep breath, and released it slowly. "Thanks, sweetie." She looked at Carmen. "It was all about Estelle again. She got to him. Can you believe it?"

"The police haven't found her?" Carmen sat back in her seat and crossed her legs.

"No, they haven't. She's back and causing trouble again. At least we think so." I filled her in on all that happened recently, starting with the neighborhood association meeting and the missing egrets.

When I finished, she stared at me. "You two sure find trouble, don't you?"

Cynthia laughed. "That's one way to put it. Mom, where is Shortie?" She checked the time on her phone. "It's after seven thirty."

Carmen perked up. "Shortie? What's happening with him, Peg?" She wiggled her eyebrows, her eyes twinkling.

Hazel leaned toward her. "We don't know. No one does. Not even her." She stuck out her thumb my way. "He proposed, did you hear that?"

"What?" Carmen shrieked.

Lucy jumped up and barked. CB raised his head and added his own deep response. From the living room, Roscoe called out, "Ta-da!"

Carmen picked up Lucy. "When's the wedding. Wait, you said she doesn't know what's happening with him?" She narrowed her eyes and huffed. "Peg, he's a wonderful man. There aren't too many of them left." She ruffled the puppy's fur. "Remember Owen."

"I'll never forget him." Hazel sneered. "I always thought you liked him?"

Carmen tipped her head, a question in her eyes. "Well, yes. As a friend. You thought it was more?"

Hazel blew out a breath. "I did. I'm sorry."

"Don't apologize. Apparently, he fooled us all." She turned to me. "Shortie is a good guy, though."

"Yes, he is. We have a few things to work out." I checked my phone, but it showed no missed calls or texts. I called him, and his cell rang several times before switching to voicemail. I left a short message asking where he was and ended the call. "Wonder why he's not here yet?" He always did what he said he would. His steadiness was one of the things I liked about him.

Carmen studied me. "You didn't say yes when he proposed?"

"She shut the door in his face. His and Marcus's," Cynthia said.

"Marcus too?" Carmen tsked. "I don't know what to say, Peg."

"Yeah, I get that a lot." Time to change the subject. "You're a real estate agent. From what we've found out, a contractor in this neighborhood wants to build tiny houses. And erect them over a creek where the egrets went missing. Is that legal?"

She thought for a minute. "Well, I am not sure he could do that. Besides having the area surveyed, code enforcement and the Florida Fish and Wildlife Conservation Commission would also be involved. And the subdivision's covenant would need to be checked for any restrictions on what can be built."

"Huh. I wasn't aware of that," I said.

"Me either," Hazel said.

Carmen passed Lucy to Cynthia and retrieved her cell from her purse. "Let me ask my boss. Do you mind if I give him this information?"

Hazel and I both shrugged. "Sure. We're not protecting anyone." I gave her Derek's name.

While Carmen spoke to her boss, I dished supper for myself. Shortie disappointed me. He'd never failed to show up without telling me. My imagined scales tipped in Marcus's favor.

Carmen scribbled notes in Hazel's notebook. She hung up. "This should not be happening." She pointed to what she'd written. "It looks like plans are underway that aren't eco-friendly. Someone's hiding the truth. And the birds—who has them? Where would they even be kept? Or ... were they killed?"

I had the same questions. "Can we talk to this code-enforcing guy?" I took a bite of my food. "Do you want some dinner?"

"No thanks." She checked her notes and gave me the Code Enforcement Office phone number.

"I'll call them in the morning," I said.

"Do you have access to the covenant for the neighborhood?" she asked.

Hazel shrugged. "I might have them in my papers from when we bought the house. I'll have to see."

We had our tasks for the next day. Carmen suggested we also check with the Fish and Wildlife people. I doubted Marcus knew this information but suspected the police wouldn't care if Derek's construction company illegally built in the subdivision. At least not yet. Right now, they were focused on Marilyn's death.

Carmen left, and the kids cleaned up from dinner. Hazel and I sat at the table, kicking around suspects and thinking up places where someone could hide egrets. Derek assured us his company's actions were on par with environmental laws. But what Carmen said implied the opposite. Someone must know the truth.

When I woke the following day, I heard voices from the living room. Hoping it was Shortie, I rushed out to find Hazel sitting on the couch, talking on her phone.

"Who is that?" I asked.

She pointed to her cell and bumped up the speaker volume. "Code enforcement," she mouthed.

I perched on the loveseat opposite her and listened.

"Ma'am, I can't find any violations by Croft and Brothers Construction Company. Not in your neighborhood anyhow," said a woman with a heavy southern accent.

"Does the company have other violations?" Hazel asked. "In Pensacola."

The woman clicked her tongue. "I suppose I can check for that. It will take a while." She drew out the word 'suppose,' indicating how much of a chore it would be.

Hazel looked at me, and I nodded. "Yes, please. It's a lot, but I appreciate your work. Can I leave my number, and you can call me back when you've had time to check?"

The woman agreed. Hazel recited her number before she hung up. "Well, what an interesting conversation."

"Have you made coffee yet?" I wandered into the kitchen. Seeing the pot mostly full, I poured myself a mug before sitting and enjoying the aroma of the hot java.

"I had a thought after she said Derek's company has no violations in Stone Creek Cove. What if ..." She raised a hand. "Hear me out now. What if Estelle tampered with their records to cover up Derek's activities?"

"Hmm. That's possible. She'd know some way to get it done. But she's wanted for questioning in Roger's death, remember? Wouldn't whoever she dealt with at code enforcement have turned her in?"

"Maybe?"

"Think Derek changed the records?" I sipped my coffee.

CB padded down the hall from Hazel's room and curled up by her feet. She rubbed his back. "Who else could have done it? Had knowledge of computers like that?"

We sat in silence for several minutes.

"Hazel? Remember when we first went to the Crofts' house?" I asked.

She nodded.

"Do you remember what you said Marilyn did before she retired?"

Her eyes grew large. "Yes."

"She was a computer programmer," we said at the same time.

CHAPTER 15

"Let's suppose Marilyn did alter records at code enforcement. She needed to have an 'in,' right? Someone who let her into their programming system or whatever that's called."

"I'd think so." I tapped my nails against my coffee cup. Roscoe chirped several times, and Hazel rose to give him some seed.

She settled back on the couch. "How about we go back to Derek's office downtown and ask Elizabeth more questions. She said something when we met her that I didn't understand."

"The comment about how he hadn't told her Marilyn died?"

"Yeah. It sounded personal. She seemed to know him well, but how well? Remember Babs's comment that he had multiple affairs." She stood. "I'll get dressed. Holler when you're ready." CB followed her out of the room.

As I picked out clothes for the day, I tried Shortie's number again. It went to voicemail, just like before. This wasn't typical behavior for him. He'd been distant since I shut the door in his face, and I understood why. I pulled back too. But for him to make plans and then ignore me was unlike him.

I wavered between worry and anger. Should I ask Marcus to check on him? I didn't want to. Hazel interrupted my thoughts when she knocked on my door and said she would be in her car. I pulled on tan capris and a lightweight floral top and grabbed my purse. I'd try Shortie again later and hope he answered. If he didn't, I'd figure out the next step.

Cynthia and Lucy met me in the kitchen. "Where are you going, Mom?"

"Back to Derek's office. Why are you two up so early?" I filled a travel mug with iced coffee.

"This little one," she snuggled Lucy, "has her first veterinarian's appointment."

I patted the puppy. "Be a sweet girl. Let your mom sleep tonight." I kissed Cynthia on the cheek and left.

Hazel parallel parked around the corner from Derek's building. When I got out of her Bug, a soft breeze from Pensacola Bay lifted my curls. I tipped my face toward the sun, enjoying its warmth. The shade from the live oaks in Seville Square Park helped keep the area slightly cooler.

"Come on," Hazel said. "You can get a tan later."

"Let's pick up lunch and eat in the gazebo." I pointed to the park. "Skip all the drama. Someone else can agonize over missing birds and a dead woman."

Hazel cocked an eyebrow. I shrugged. "Just a thought."

I followed her toward the Croft and Bros. office. I paused on the sidewalk, listening to loud voices coming from inside the building. Hazel opened the fence gate, and we climbed the steps to the porch.

The front door stood open, and through the screen door, I saw Elizabeth shouting at someone, but I couldn't tell who.

I pulled Hazel to the side, away from the door and window. "We shouldn't go in there." A crash came from inside the office, followed by more yelling. "Should we call the cops?"

Hazel huddled behind me. "I think so. They sound angry." Another thud sounded, and she jumped.

Elizabeth and a man continued to fuss at each other, arguing about paperwork and unpaid bills. She lowered her voice, and I leaned forward, straining to hear what they talked about.

"She called him Finch, I think." I listened more and turned to Hazel. "And he did something and doesn't care but wants to be paid."

The man yelled again, and we heard another thump. I reached for the latch to open the screen door. "I'll ask her if she wants me to contact the police."

The door screeched when I opened it, but a loud, sharp crack drowned out the sound. I let go of the latch. Hazel grabbed my shoulder and tugged me back to the corner of the porch.

"That was a gun." Her voice trembled.

"Yes, it was." I wrapped my shaking hands around myself.

We waited for more noise, but nothing came. Then the screen door banged open, and a man ran down the steps, jumped over the short fence, and took off down the street. The person wore khaki shorts and brown boots. Right before he rounded the corner, he glanced over his shoulder and yelled, "I ain't got no regrets, 'Lizbeth."

Elizabeth shouted, "Go on and run away, Finch. That's what you always do. Just like your momma."

"She might be hurt. Call nine-one-one." She jerked open the screen door and hustled inside.

I reached for her arm. "What if more people are in there?" She eluded my grasp. I followed, stepping into the lobby and scooting to the side and out of the way of the door.

Hazel knelt beside Elizabeth, who lay flat on the floor. She patted the receptionist's cheek. "Are you okay?"

I called the emergency number and explained where we were, and that one woman had been injured. Elizabeth pushed herself up and shook her head. Hazel rubbed her back.

"Take your time. The EMTs are on their way," she said.

Elizabeth shifted her legs underneath her and stood, holding onto the corner of her desk. "Why?" She leaned down and picked up a handgun.

"Are you all right?" I didn't see any blood. "We thought you were hurt. We heard a gun go off."

"Pfft." She waved her free hand. "I'm fine. Just wanted to scare him." A disgusted expression crossed her face.

"Someone ran out and jumped the fence."

She set the gun on her desk. "Yep. He's like that. Always running away." She repeated the words from earlier. "I didn't hit him. He's fine."

I wanted her to move the gun. If nothing else, to point it in the other direction.

Sirens sounded in the distance.

"You called the police?" She scoffed, her face contorted into a grimace. "Why'd you do that?"

Hazel and I exchanged glances.

"We thought you'd been shot. That you were dead or dying You were lying on the floor." I didn't understand this woman.

"I tripped when I fired the gun. Otherwise, he might be dead. He got lucky." Elizabeth rubbed her arm. "I hit my elbow on the way down." She smoothed her bright green and pink paisley dress. "Tell them they can leave. Nothing happened here."

An ambulance and a police cruiser parked in front of the office.

"It doesn't work like that," Hazel said. "She's in for a rude awakening," she whispered to me.

I agreed. The police entered to talk to Elizabeth. She played it off as if a homeless person barged in off the street, but Hazel and I knew she lied. We could tell from the argument she and the man had that they knew each other. When the officer took us aside for our statements, we both told him our side of the story.

"They argued about unpaid bills," I said.

The EMTs approached to check her out.

"I'm fine. I didn't do anything," she said. "No one got hurt." She kept repeating the words, but the police officer handcuffed her.

"Call Derek," she said as she ducked her head and sat in the back of the cruiser.

The police and EMTs left. Hazel and I stood on the front porch steps of the office.

"What do we do now?"

Hazel locked the office door and pulled it shut. "Call Derek like she asked?"

We walked back to her Bug. "Why is this our responsibility? We came here to ask her questions, not be caught up in this." I buckled my seatbelt. "I'll call Croft, but then it's in his hands."

Derek spluttered and fumed when he heard what happened. I reminded him I was only the messenger. When Hazel pulled into her driveway, Derek waited on her porch.

I got out of the car. "You didn't have to come over here. I told you everything already."

Derek held out his arms, blocking our way into the house. "Why were you at my office? You're not going inside yet. You have questions to answer."

Who did this man think he was? "Me? Your receptionist tried to shoot someone. You need to go take care of her." I wanted to ask how close they were but held my tongue.

"Nuh-uh." His lip curled. "She said you called the cops, and it was a misunderstanding."

"Of course, I called them. She tried to shoot someone." I emphasized each word.

He stepped toward me. "As a matter of fact, I want to come inside and search your place. I bet you have information I need." He raised his arms higher to intimidate us.

I scrabbled in my purse for my cell phone. "You've lost your mind. What in the world would I have?" The man was delusional. I prepared to dial 911.

"How do you and Estelle Keaton know each other?" Hazel interrupted our back and forth.

He froze.

"What are you doing?" I asked her. She'd lost her mind.

"Wait and see." She waved Derek aside. "Don't block me from my home, or I'll call the police." She sauntered inside, and I scurried in after her.

She slammed the door and threw the lock before wiping her hands together. "See? I caught him off guard, and we got in the house."

My mother-in-law. She was something else.

Chapter 16

Derek turned in circles in the front yard, shaking his fist when he spotted me at the window. He and his receptionist were in trouble. He should go to the police station and hire a lawyer.

Hazel drew me away from the window. "He's all bluster and nothing to back it up. He can figure out what to do."

"This moves him up on my suspect list. He has more motivation besides money. He's personally involved in all that's happened. And with Elizabeth, I think." I grabbed a large plastic cup, filled it with ice and water, handed it to Hazel, and did the same with another cup for myself.

"Thanks." Hazel headed for the living room. She turned the overhead fan to high and sat on the loveseat, the ice-cold cup pressed against her forehead, her feet propped up beside her.

I settled on the sofa, enjoying the cool air conditioning and the breeze from the fan. "I feel like we're stalled in this investigation."

Hazel hummed.

"What does"—I imitated her humming—"mean?"

She motioned to me with her cup. "I knew you were in. Calling it an investigation." She did a happy dance in her seat.

I wrinkled my nose. "Pretty sure I've been in. Anyhow. Moving on. Derek is a suspect for me. At least for removing or killing the egrets to build his tiny homes. Code enforcement may not know, but I do." CB curled up on the floor, and I rubbed his back with my foot. "How Derek thinks anyone in the subdivision would approve tiny homes being built here is another matter. Did you ever find the covenant?"

"No." She gestured with her cup again. "Don't forget Babs. There's more to her than we think. She definitely didn't like Marilyn. Motivation right there."

It's a big step from not liking someone to murder, but I didn't say that. "Estelle?" I shifted on the couch. "It always comes back to her, doesn't it?"

Somehow, we needed to find Estelle Keaton. Pensacola wasn't that big. I considered several ways to set a trap for her, but would they work? "We should call High Mountain Realty. That's who Derek made the agreement with about the tiny homes. We can ask someone there more questions."

Hazel pulled her cell from her back pocket. "I'm too tired to go find the paperwork, but I can find the number online."

While she looked, Cynthia and Lucy came inside.

"Hey, Mom, Grandma." She unhooked Lucy's leash, and the puppy toddled to the couch.

I picked her up and cuddled her, stroking her soft fur and inhaling fresh puppy smell. "Where have you two been? Is Derek still outside?"

Cynthia joined me on the couch, grabbed my water, and drank half of it. "No one's out there. I took Lucy to the vet, and she's healthy, like I thought." She rubbed her hand down the puppy's side and told us Lucy's weight like any proud parent. "We stopped by the

Center. Harry enjoyed Lucy. He took her out back, and she chased the pelicans. I don't think they liked her. Harry sure did, though."

That didn't surprise me. When we first met Harry, he'd acted uptight, but deep down, he was a softie for birds of all kinds, even Roscoe, and he adored CB and now Lucy.

Lucy yipped and struggled in my arms. I set her on the floor, where she nudged CB with her nose, her tail wagging set on high. "He's an old guy, Luce. Give him a break," I said.

CB opened one eye, groaned, and stretched out his leg. Lucy took that as a sign to keep playing.

"I'm not supervising the puppy." I spotted the basket on the hearth. "Why did you bring it out of my room?"

"She likes to sleep in it." Cynthia covered her eyes. "Whatever helps her sleep, I'll do it."

"Don't blame you. It's her size too," I said.

"I found the number." Hazel waved her cell phone at us. "Calling them now." She turned on the phone's speaker so we all could hear.

I leaned closer to Cynthia and told her what her grandmother was up to.

The phone rang several times before someone answered. "High Mountain Realty, this is Adam. How may I help you?"

Hazel explained why she called, and Adam redirected her to an agent.

"This is Kitty Lynch. What can I do for you today?" Her silky voice and exaggerated Southern accent gave me the giggles.

Hazel glared at me and introduced herself. I sipped my water, attempting to control my laughter. When Hazel mentioned Derek and where we lived, Kitty interrupted.

"Y'all live in Pensacola? I miss Florida." Her accent drew out all of her words. "If you're acquainted with Derek, you've met Babs, too, right? And Marilyn?"

My giggles stopped. "What?" I mouthed.

"Babs?" Hazel asked.

"Yes, my dear old friend Babs Ferguson. We all went to school together." The word came out as "togetha." "We went on dinner dates when we were grown-ups. Went to plays and things." She tittered. "Derek was quite the man back in the day. I really liked him. He knew how to have fun. How's Marilyn?"

"She's dead," Hazel blurted.

"What?" Kitty's shriek made both dogs bark, and Roscoe screeched, "Ta-da!"

Hazel apologized for all the noise. Cynthia calmed the dogs while I shushed the bird.

Kitty sniffled and talked for a few minutes about Marilyn and how she couldn't believe she was dead. Hazel waited until the woman slowed down.

"We have a couple of questions," she said. "I found paperwork showing Derek and High Mountain Realty have a deal where he'll build tiny homes here in our subdivision. Then you will rent them. Can you confirm that information?"

"Yes, ma'am." Kitty blew her nose in a loud honk, the first thing she'd done that wasn't cute and delicate.

"You're the realtor who will handle the rentals?" I asked.

"Yes." She paused. "Babs is involved too. Derek didn't tell you?" Tapping of computer keys came through the line. "What did you say your name is again? Does Derek know you called?" Her sweet Southern accent disappeared, replaced with hard syllables and a harsh tone.

"Thanks for your help." Hazel hung up.

"Babs, huh?" I dragged my hand down my face. "Did not see that one coming."

Hazel shifted off the couch, pushing herself up. She groaned.

"You okay?" I asked.

"I'm stiff today." She straightened up, rubbing her lower back with her knuckles. "Let's go talk to Babs." She stifled a moan.

Now I worried. She never complained about being stiff or hurting. "Do you need to rest?"

Her gaze whipped to me so fast, my head spun. "Peg. I am not old. Just a little uncomfortable," she said through gritted teeth.

Cynthia glanced my way, her eyebrows raised.

I held up my hand. "Got it." I toed CB. "Come on, big dog. Let's go potty." Cynthia and Lucy followed us out back. While the dogs took care of business, Cynthia and I discussed her grandmother.

"I'll make dinner tonight," she said.

"Thanks. I'll keep the visit to Babs brief. I think things have been too much for Grandma lately."

Cynthia nodded. "You're right. Any news from Shortie?"

I pulled my phone out of my pocket. "He hasn't called or texted. Maybe I should talk with Kim?"

Shortie's daughter, Kim, worked as a lifeguard at the University of West Florida pool. Cynthia checked the time. "I can run by there while y'all go to Babs's. I remember her from school."

What else could we do? Shortie and the egrets were missing, Marilyn was dead, and no one had a clue where Estelle was holed up. Hazel's pain was flaring, and Babs was now a suspect. All my plates were spinning, and I feared one would tip and set off a massive crash.

No car sat in the driveway at Babs's house. "No ding-dong-ditch this time?" I teased Hazel. She gave me the stink eye.

"Will you go knock?" she asked.

My concern for her grew, but she'd made it clear she didn't want me to ask. Now that I was aware, I'd keep an eye on her. At Babs's front door, I knocked several times with no answer. I tried to peer in the front window, but heavy drapes blocked my view.

"Looks like she's not home," I said when I got back in the car. I held my hair off my neck while the A/C blew on full blast.

"I called her, and she didn't answer," Hazel said.

"What do we do?"

"While you were knocking on the door, I remembered Babs and Kitty both mentioned how they all hung out together and went to parties. Babs said the group was for people who didn't have kids."

"And?" I didn't understand her point.

"Estelle. She and Roger didn't have children together. But Roger had a daughter."

"Charlene." We met her months ago when her mother was killed. Charlene's father, Roger Keaton, was Pensacola's notorious bad guy. "How can she help?"

Hazel massaged her hands. "She might have some pictures of Estelle. Yearbooks? I don't know." She grimaced.

I rummaged through my purse until I found a pouch of over-the-counter pain relievers. I shook two into my hand and passed them to her. "Here."

"Thanks." She swallowed the capsules and closed her eyes. "It hasn't been this bad in a long time."

"Arthritis?"

She nodded. "Usually, it's manageable. I'm not sure what's changed."

I started the car. "Stress? It'll make lots of things worse."

"True." She held out her phone. "I'll call Charlene while you drive. Maybe we can go to her place now."

My mother-in-law would make it happen. She had that way about her.

CHAPTER 17

"Hi, Charlene, this is Hazel Howard. Remember, we met last year when your mother ... um, when she died." Hazel stumbled over her words. "You remember me? Oh, good." A big smile lit her face. "Well, my daughter-in-law wondered if we could stop by to ask some questions."

"Way to throw me under the bus." I pulled into Hazel's driveway and waited for Charlene's response.

"Yes, Peg found your mom." She listened for a minute. "Yes, she started the Empty Nesters Birding Group." She paused. "Right, and that led to your mom's murder ..."

Charlene's voice sounded through the line reminding me of Lucy's puppy yips.

"So, would now be a good time to run by?" Hazel persisted.

Charlene's response came through loud and clear. She explained with emphasis why she didn't want us to visit today. Hazel's shoulders sank.

"Yes, I understand. Tomorrow. Thank you. We'll come over then." She clicked off the call. "She's busy today. Said tomorrow. I'm not sure she wants to see us at all." She palmed her forehead. "No one understands."

I turned off my car and unbuckled my seatbelt. "Understands what?" The air—dense and damp—smacked me in the face when I opened the car door.

Hazel followed me to the front porch. "The importance of this investigation. We have to find the birds. We don't know why Marilyn died, or where Shortie ..." She stopped short, staring at the door. "What's that?" She pointed.

My gaze, focused on finding the key to the house, followed her finger. A piece of lined paper, obviously jerked out of a notebook, judging by its jagged side, was taped to the door. The words, "We got her 2," were printed in large block letters in red crayon.

"Oh, oh, no, they don't." I shoved the key in the lock and pushed my way inside. "Cynthia? Are you here? Cynthia?" I threw my purse on the dining table and ran to her room. CB trotted out of Hazel's room, barking at me. Roscoe piped up and screeched, "Ta-da!" I shoved Cynthia's door open and found her and the puppy curled up on her bed. Sound asleep.

"Oh, my." I bent over, hands on my knees, and tried to breathe through my panic. Hazel bustled in behind me.

"It's not her. Okay. Thank you, God." She inhaled and forced the air out.

Cynthia rolled over and opened her eyes. "Why are you two in my room?" She yawned. "Mom, take CB out. Don't wake the puppy." Her eyes pleaded with me. Lucy continued to snooze as only puppies can.

I waved my hand. "You're good. Go back to sleep." Thankfulness flooded my body as I pulled her door shut. "Hazel?" I turned to find my mother-in-law, phone in her hand.

"We have to check with Chloe." Eyes wide and face pale, Hazel made the call.

Chloe answered and assured us she and Reese were fine. He'd just woken from a nap, and she was holding him. Hazel played off the call as a check-in. When she hung up, we stared at each other.

"Oh, boy, I need to sit down." She plodded out to the couch.

"What does the note mean?" I paced. "Trust me, I'm grateful they didn't mean my girls, but who else could it refer to?"

"Plus, they said they had her also. Like they have two people." Hazel pursed her lips. "Shortie and Babs are the only people we haven't heard from or can't get hold of." Her mouth dropped open. "You don't think they have them, do you?"

I collapsed on the couch. "They might. But who are they? Who has Shortie? Why would they take him?"

I called Marcus, explaining the note and informing him that my girls were safe. He and his team arrived at the house within thirty minutes. A female police officer "bagged and tagged" the note, and Hazel sat with one of the other officers and told him about our trip to Babs's.

I listened for a minute before following Marcus out to the back deck.

"You've gotten better with the crutches," I said.

"Kinda needed to." He leaned them against the railing and sat in one of the chairs. "Okay, it's been two days since you talked to Shortie?" He took out his notebook and pen. All business—no flashing dimples or twinkling winks today.

I nodded, thankful that he took this seriously. "He hasn't answered any calls or texts since." Shade covered this part of the backyard, but the temperature soared. I fanned my face.

After several more questions, Hazel joined us outside. "I'm finished. But I remembered Cynthia planned to check with Kim. Did you ask her?"

I left her to explain Kim's relationship to Shortie and went to Cynthia's room. I knocked and opened her door again. Lucy perked up and yipped.

"Mom?" Cynthia groaned.

"I'm sorry, honey. Did you find Kim? Has she heard from her dad?"

She sat up in bed and brushed her hands through her hair. "No, she hasn't talked to him since the beginning of the week. She called him while I was there, but it went to voicemail. I left my number in case she hears from him."

Lucy tripped across the bed, and I picked her up. "Thanks. I'll take this little girl out to potty."

"Thank you." Cynthia collapsed back on the bed. "Do I have time for a shower?"

"Sure. Marcus and two of his team are here right now."

She jumped out of bed and peeked out of her door. "Do I want to know why?"

I chuckled. "Go ahead and shower. I'll keep this munchkin busy and fill you in when you finish."

Lucy nipped my thumb. I hurried through the house and opened the back door. CB slipped out behind me. He nudged Marcus's hand before joining Lucy in the grass. I repeated Cynthia's conversation with Kim to Marcus. He added the information and tucked his note-book into his pocket.

"We'll check on Shortie and Babs and try to find both. And figure out why they're missing." He rose and kissed my forehead. "Please be careful. Time to let the police do their thing." He grabbed his crutches and told the dogs goodbye. Hazel followed him inside.

I let the dogs play. The sun began its descent, and I found a better strip of shade to stand in while they raced up and down the backyard. CB finally tired of playing and joined me. He flopped onto the grass, his tongue lolling. Lucy toddled over and tugged on his ears. His go-to now was to set his big paw across her back until she stopped pestering him. After a minute, she got the message and settled beside him.

I lowered myself to the ground beside them. Lucy scooted over to me, and I cradled her in my arms, enjoying her puppy snuffles. For the first time in days, quiet reigned. Concern nibbled at me, so with my eyes closed, I whispered prayers of thanks for my family's safety and prayers for direction and help in finding Shortie and Babs. If that's who the note referred to, and I felt sure it was.

Cynthia joined me. Lucy reached for her from my arms. "Just like a real baby," I said, passing the pup over.

Cynthia snuggled her and kissed her little forehead. "Keeps me up like a baby." She sang a silly tune. "Oh, I forgot to tell you." She put Lucy down and tugged a piece of paper from her shorts' pocket. "I started a load of laundry today and found this note."

I smoothed it out. "I found this at Marilyn's the other day. It fell out of her purse. I forgot to look at it."

Cynthia leaned over my shoulder. "I think it's a phone number." She pointed. "It doesn't have dashes, but it's the right amount of numbers."

"Not a password?"

"Try calling it first." She scooped up the puppy and stood. "I'm going in to cool off."

CB and I followed her. Hazel set glasses of iced tea on the coffee table for us. I joined her on the couch, and the dogs trotted off to the kitchen for their water bowls.

Cynthia drank her tea and curled up on the loveseat. I explained about the note and put the numbers into Hazel's phone. It rang several times before an answering machine picked up.

"You've reached me," said a woman. "Leave a message."

My mouth dropped open. "Did you hear that?"

"No," Hazel said. "Call them again and put it on speaker."

I pressed the call button and set the phone to speaker mode. "It wasn't a them. Listen."

When the woman spoke, Hazel's face paled.

"Who is it? Mom? Grandma?" Cynthia asked.

"I think I know who has Shortie and Babs." My legs trembled. If I was right, both of them were in great danger.

"Who? Who has them?" she asked.

"Estelle Keaton," Hazel and I said together.

"Ta-da," Roscoe called from his cage.

CHAPTER 18

I FORCED MYSELF TO breathe normally as I considered all the things that could happen to Babs and Shortie. Hazel reached out and took my hand.

"Can you feel that?" she asked. Her hand shook so hard the sensation traveled up my arm.

"Yes." My stomach lurched. "What do we do now?"

Cynthia jumped up and fanned us with a magazine. "You need to calm down, for now. Mom, Grandma? Look at me."

We both obeyed her command.

"Take a deep breath. Okay, blow it out." She continued fanning. "Another. There you go."

Hazel dropped my hand. "Thank you, dear." She wiped her brow.

Cynthia left the room for a minute, returning with Hazel's notebook and pen.

"I can't do it right now," Hazel said.

"It's okay, I will." Cynthia flipped to the last list we made. "These are Ms. Carmen's notes about code enforcement from yesterday."

"Yeah, Hazel, you called the lady this morning."

"She's checking on Derek's company to find out if they have violations anywhere." Hazel's exhaustion showed in her voice. "It doesn't matter though. I think Marilyn changed the records to get approval for Derek to build in the subdivision."

"Why do you think that?" I asked, not fully following her train of thought. "Marilyn, I mean. She's dead, so obviously she didn't benefit from it."

Hazel scoffed. "Well, she wouldn't have known ahead of time that she would be killed."

Cynthia returned to the loveseat. "You two. The things you talk about." Lucy scampered over to her. "It's late. I'm going to bed. We can talk about this tomorrow." She tucked the puppy under her arm.

"I can't sleep yet." I twirled my finger at my head. "Too much happening in my brain."

"I'll make us some decaf coffee." Hazel hugged Cynthia and took the notebook from her, passing it to me. "We might need this."

I flipped through what we'd written in the last week or two. Before Carmen's notes were Hazel's from when we met with Babs. Too many people were in the mix, and they globbed together in my head like a ball of slime.

Derek, Marilyn, Babs, Elizabeth from Derek's office, some guy named Finch ... I leaned back and hollered to Hazel in the kitchen. "Did we ever find out who Finch was?"

She came around the corner, the coffeepot full of water in her hand. "No, we didn't."

Elizabeth argued with him right before she shot at him. "He said he didn't have any regrets."

Hazel came closer. "No regrets? That's what Carter said when I first got the notice from the neighborhood association. Remember?"

That's right. "No regrets. No egrets." I chewed on my lower lip. "Hazel, what are the odds this Finch guy is related to Estelle and has something to do with the missing birds?"

The next morning, Hazel and I sat at the table with her notebook and started back at the beginning.

"It all began with the letter from the neighborhood association," I said.

"No, the egrets went missing first." Hazel tapped her pen on her notebook. "We have lists upon lists of what to do and look for in here." Her forehead furrowed.

"Why do you think Elizabeth argued with Finch about unpaid bills?" I asked. "Let's go talk to her and ask some of these questions. Do you think they're open on Saturday?"

Hazel used her phone to confirm they had weekend hours. Before we left, I grabbed the basket Lucy arrived in and dusted it out. The night before, Carter brought home blueberry muffins. I picked out the best-looking ones, wrapped them in a decorative dish towel, and nestled them in the basket. "These are to apologize for her getting sent to jail," I said.

Hazel volunteered to drive. Several miles down the road, her cell rang, and I answered it to find the Code Enforcement Officer on the other end.

"Mrs. Howard, I know it's a Saturday, and normally I would wait for Monday, but I thought you needed to hear what I found when I checked into Derek Croft and his company a little more. Like you asked." Her last words were said with a bit of snark.

I hit the speaker button. "Yes? Thank you. What did you find?"

"No violations for Croft and Brothers Construction. Not any-where." She paused. "I shouldn't say this, but that's odd, and that's why I called you today. It doesn't make sense."

"What do you mean?" Did she have helpful information? Evidence that would lead us in a new direction?

"It's unlikely there were never any warnings or at least notes of some conversations. It's almost like the company's records have been wiped clean." Her voice held suspicion.

Hazel and I exchanged glances.

"Thank you so much for doing this," I said, ready to end the call before her doubts went any further. "I appreciate it."

When I hung up, Hazel said, "I'm glad she called, even though it's the weekend. And she corroborated what we thought."

Somehow, Marilyn accessed the records system and cleaned it up for Derek's company. Why? Could we prove she did it?

Hazel parked her Bug a block away from Croft and Bros.' office. "Let's get some questions answered."

She hustled up the street. I retrieved the muffins and trailed behind, not as eager to talk to Derek's receptionist. The front door was locked when we arrived.

"We got here early." I checked the time. "We can wait in the gazebo in the square."

We made our way across the street and to the middle of the park. Massive oak trees provided shade, and sunlight filtered through the leaves and branches, casting dappled shadows on the ground.

"Did you know this park was originally a Spanish outpost?" Hazel asked.

"No, when?"

"Mid 1700s."

We climbed the steps into the gazebo and leaned on one of the railings.

"Give me the Seville Square tour, Ms. Former Tour Guide." I waved for her to perform.

Hazel brushed down the front of her shirt and stood up straight. "Today, ladies and gentlemen, I'd like to tell you about the land on which you stand. At first, an outpost known as San Miguel, this area was converted into a public square in 1764 and named after Seville, Spain. The structure here has been updated to its current status and is now used for weddings and some of the annual festivals here in Pensacola."

A small crowd gathered. Hazel never missed a beat. She continued to describe several of the surrounding buildings, adding in random tidbits of history here and there. Finally, she pointed out Old Christ Church to the visitors.

"Tours begin at eleven." She told them where to go to enter the church. She came to me and whispered, "While I was talking, Elizabeth entered Derek's office. Let's go."

We made our way to the building. I paused at the bottom of the steps leading up to the front door. "Any idea what to ask her?"

"Let's see what she says first," Hazel said.

I held the door, gesturing for her to go before me. She smirked. "Coward."

I didn't want to be the first face Elizabeth saw. It had only been a day since our last escapade with her, and I wouldn't be surprised if she was still a little salty about it. When we entered the room, she sat at the desk, sipping coffee and scrolling through her phone, not a hair out of place. Her dress of the day was a sleeveless, bright orange shift with a lime-and-white swirl pattern. She'd painted her nails in a matching orange. I couldn't see her toes, but I assumed they were the same color.

Her smile changed into a grimace when she spotted us. "Why are you two here?"

Hazel pulled a chair close to the desk and sat. She motioned me to do the same. "Elizabeth, how are you, dear?" Hazel beamed. "We were so worried about you yesterday. I'm thankful that mean Finch boy didn't hurt you." The sticky sweetness of her words made my teeth hurt.

Elizabeth ate it up, and her expression shifted. "Thank you, Mrs. …"

"Howard. I'm Hazel, and that's Peg." She thumbed in my direction. "I'm sorry we didn't have a chance for proper introductions before. Were the police kind to you? I can't believe what happened with that man. You called him Finch? What kind of parent names their son that?"

Elizabeth beamed. She brushed back her hair. "I wasn't there long. Derek took his sweet time, but a friend helped me out."

I handed over the towel filled with the muffins. "I thought you'd like these."

"Thank you!" Her smile turned even brighter.

Hazel wiggled her fingers between us, below the top of the desk where the woman couldn't see.

"You okay?" I asked her out of the corner of my mouth.

Hazel huffed. "Didn't you need a restroom? Remember?" She spoke through gritted teeth.

"Sure, um, yes." I stood. "May I use your bathroom?"

Elizabeth gave her permission. I passed her and turned around to face Hazel. She had a job for me, and I needed to read her mind and accomplish the goal. I caught her eye and raised my hands in a "now what" gesture.

She glared before coughing into her fist. It sounded like she said, "Finch." I gave her a thumbs-up and left to search for information on the mystery man.

The day before, I checked the bathroom and kitchen and saw nothing of paperwork importance in either. After peering into the small room with the printer, I headed for the empty office. Boxes overflowed with books, used notepads full of scribbles, and some photographs. It seemed that when Derek opened the office, he never fully unpacked.

Several framed pictures caught my attention. One showed Derek at a construction site, and a couple were of him standing beside Marilyn at what appeared to be fancy dinners, judging by his suit and her dress. I checked the other boxes but didn't find anything helpful.

The last box I found was small and held loose photos. The one on top showed a ribbon-cutting ceremony for his office. Marilyn stood at the front and center of the top step. Derek and another man were on the step below her. They each held parts of the large scissors, and Derek grasped a section of the newly cut ribbon in his other hand. Excited smiles filled both men's faces. But Marilyn wasn't looking at whoever snapped the picture. She glared at someone off to the side, her face mottled red with anger.

I stepped out of the room and peered around the corner into the front office. "Elizabeth, do you have a magnifying glass?"

Hazel shot me a "What are you up to now?" look. I ignored her.

Elizabeth rifled through her desk drawer, pulled out a small magnifying glass, and handed it to me.

"Thanks." I headed back to the room.

"What are you doing?" she asked.

"Oh, nothing. I'll be right back."

I picked up the photo and held the magnifier over the other face. "Hazel?" I cleared my throat, attempting to control the fear running through my body. "You'd better come here."

CHAPTER 19

HAZEL ASSESSED THE SITUATION in record time. She tucked the photo into her purse, grabbed my arm, and hurried us out of the office. She made excuses to Elizabeth as we rushed past her desk. Before we left, I stopped in my tracks, jerking Hazel to a halt.

Elizabeth glanced up, a curious look in her eyes. "What? What do you need now?"

"Finch." I narrowed my eyes. "What exactly did he mean by 'I have no regrets?'"

Her mouth drew to the side in a smirk. "He didn't say regrets." Her expression indicated what she thought of my intelligence. "He said egrets." She emphasized the "E" at the beginning of the word and waved her hand. "He did a job for Derek."

"What did he do?"

Hazel tugged my arm. "Come on, let's go," she hissed.

I dug my toes in. "Uh-uh. Elizabeth, what's Finch's last name?"

"Keaton. His dad is Roger Keaton. Or was, since he's dead." She shrugged.

"I knew it," I said under my breath.

"How'd you know?" Hazel asked. She started her Bug and pulled into the light mid-morning traffic. "What made you think that?"

How to explain my muddled thoughts? If Finch was related to Estelle, what hold did she have over him? I shifted in my seat and faced her.

"I just took a chance. Marilyn glared at Estelle in the picture. Everything always comes back to Estelle. She was the one behind Sylvia's death—and Anna's. She's greedy and competitive."

I paused momentarily to pull my thoughts together. "I'm having trouble figuring out her motivation this time. What value do egrets hold for her? Or is it the real estate deal Derek made? Is this Kitty lady from Mountain High Realty involved?"

I shrugged. "Finch has to tie back to Estelle. Somehow. I didn't expect him to be Roger's son, though."

"Do you think Charlene knows?" Hazel asked. "She's never mentioned a brother to us."

"Aren't we supposed to go to her place today?"

Hazel checked her watch. "Yep, in about thirty minutes."

I plugged Charlene's address into my map app and directed Hazel. "She lives in a condo right before the bridge to Pensacola Beach." We spent the drive batting ideas back and forth.

Hazel went through Gulf Breeze, took a right on Pensacola Beach Road, and a left into the Sailfish Point Condos. The sign out front claimed they were all two-bedroom, two-bathroom units with a view of the bay. Three stories high, with gray stucco and darker shingles, the building featured a garage at the bottom level. It was an attractive area and fit in with the beach feel.

"I've always wanted to live out here. How fun to wake up with Pensacola Bay right in front of you. Look through there." I pointed. "You can see the Gulf."

"And you'd have a front row seat to the Blue Angels when they practice or have a show," Hazel said.

We got out of her Bug and approached Charlene's building. Our shoes crunched on the gravel lot. The scents I loved hit me—sand, salt water, and tar. The sun warmed my face, and I wished for a chance to go to the beach, maybe drive by the Pensacola Island cross out there. "What are we asking her?"

Hazel knocked on her door. "We're going to wing it. Get it? Birds, egrets, wings?" She chuckled at her own joke.

Charlene opened the door and held it for us to enter, preventing me from responding to Hazel's corny words. Her condo was bright and full of sunshine. A sliding glass door led off the living area onto a deck. The open floor plan, decorated in pale shades of blues and tans, fit in with the beach view.

"This is beautiful," I said. "How long have you lived here?"

She tipped her head. "Oh, five years, I think? It's my favorite place. It's out of the rat race of Pensacola, although beach traffic this time of year is pretty heavy. And when the Blue Angels fly, I shop several days beforehand and then stay home. It's almost impossible to get out if you want to."

"What's their summer schedule?" Hazel asked.

"They'll be here next weekend." Charlene's eyes brightened with excitement. "I sit on the deck the whole time. It's amazing."

"And hot, I'm sure." I fanned myself.

She grinned. "I have an overhead fan and carry one of those misting water bottles. It's worth it all." She gestured to the couch. "Y'all have a seat. Want anything to drink?"

Hazel and I asked for sweet tea, and once she'd passed out our glasses, we all sat. Charlene smoothed her teal blue tunic over her white capris and crossed her legs. "What did you want to talk to me about?"

Hazel leaned forward and patted her knee. "I'm so sorry about your father."

Charlene's eyes darkened. "That woman killed him. I never liked her. She was responsible for my mother's death too." She clenched her hands. "My father was not a good person. At least in the eyes of most of Pensacola. But he was my dad, you know?"

I held back my opinions of her father. Months ago, her mother died because of Estelle Keaton. Then Estelle killed her father. But, like she said, a dad is a dad.

"We are investigating some missing birds." Hazel pulled a piece of paper from her purse. "Here, read this." She showed it to me before she passed it over.

Charlene skimmed the neighborhood association letter. The one that started everything. When she finished, she set it down. "What do egrets have to do with me?"

"Everything," Hazel and I said together.

Getting Charlene to understand the pattern Estelle designed took a while. From the first death in the birding group to now, with Shortie and Babs missing, Estelle's hand showed on it all. Different emotions crossed Charlene's face as she listened. She'd experienced a lot of changes in such a short time.

"I'd be ecstatic to catch Estelle." Her voice grew husky. "Or see the police do it." She rose to refill our glasses.

"Charlene, dear," Hazel called after her. "Do you know Finch? We think he's your half-brother?" She ended in a question. In the kitchen, a glass broke, and Charlene yelped.

"Are you okay?" I asked.

"Yes, yes," she said. "Please stay in there while I clean up this mess."

Hazel made a face, her eyebrow twitching. "Guess that was the wrong thing to say."

Why did Finch make Charlene nervous? What kind of relationship did they have? After several minutes, Charlene rejoined us. She carried fresh glasses of iced tea and set them on the coffee table in front of us.

"I'm sorry to take so long." She rubbed at a spot on her capris. "Glass and tea went everywhere."

"My question startled you," Hazel said. "Please tell us about Finch. We think he's somehow involved in Shortie and Babs's disappearance. You remember Shortie, don't you?"

"Sure, he's your boyfriend, right, Peg?" she said.

How should I answer that? Charlene didn't need all the details about my relationship issues. "Yeah."

"I know Babs too," Charlene said. "She's kind of loud? A bit ... overbearing?"

She expertly described Babs. "Yes, that's her. How did you meet her?"

"When I stayed with my dad—this was when I was much younger and before he married Estelle—he would have big dinner parties. Some of his"—she paused and clicked her tongue—"business associates, I suppose you'd call them. I met all kinds of people, including Babs."

"What about Derek and Marilyn Croft? Did you know Kitty?" I asked.

Charlene nodded. "They were part of Dad's group."

Were they her dad's business associates? He'd been involved in some nefarious dealings.

"We're trying to figure out how all of this works together," I said.

"Did Estelle attend the parties?" Hazel asked.

Charlene thought for a minute. "Near the end. She got her claws into my dad and didn't let go." A disgusted expression filled her eyes.

"But she's not Finch's mother?" I asked.

She gazed out the glass door. "I don't think so. I remember him being there when I was about ten. Dad never really explained him. Who he was or where he came from. I accepted it. Kind of strange, huh?" She shook her head. "Dad was such a different man with me, but I wasn't supposed to question things." Charlene glanced at Hazel and me. "I have no idea who Finch's mother is."

We chatted for a few more minutes and left. Charlene had no other information as far as we could tell.

"How can we find out more about Finch?" Hazel asked as we walked to her car.

"Look him up online?" I glanced up and saw her Bug sat crooked. "Uh-oh. What's wrong with your car?"

When we got closer, it was apparent both tires on the passenger side were flat. I bent over and examined them.

"These have been slashed, Hazel. You can see." I showed her the marks. "Someone did this on purpose."

"Who would know where we are?" she asked.

Good question. I called Tom since he and Chloe lived only ten minutes up the road. He helped me find someone to tow the Bug and replace the tires. In the meantime, Hazel and I rode with Tom back to his house.

"Is Reese awake?" Hazel asked.

"He was when I left," Tom said. "You never know with a newborn."

Spoken like a true dad. Reese, at only seven weeks old, was constantly changing. I couldn't wait to hold him. The hard part would be finagling him away from his great-grandmother. We arrived at Tom and Chloe's, and as we walked to the door, I said, "Hazel, why don't you show Tom your spreadsheet. Maybe he can help make sense of what Estelle's done. We might get a better idea of what's going on."

"Yes, can you help?" she asked him before explaining what she'd included on the spreadsheet. When Chloe handed Reese to me, Hazel stopped and narrowed her eyes. "I'm on to you, missy." She shook her finger. "That baby's mine next. Don't you forget."

After several hours of enjoying Reese and chatting with Tom and Chloe, the tire shop called to say Hazel's Bug was ready. I kissed the baby, hugged my daughter and son-in-law, and promised to visit them in the next few days. Tom dropped us off at the shop. Hazel paid for the tires, and we headed back to Pensacola. As we pulled into Hazel's driveway, my cell phone rang.

"Hello?" I said.

No one responded, but birds tweeted in the background of the call. A raspy voice came on the line. "Peg?"

I froze. "Shortie? Shortie, is that you?"

"Yeah." His voice sounded strained, as though it hurt him to speak.

"Are you all right? Where are you? What happened?"

"Just got a minute." He moaned. "She got me. She ..." A sharp crack rang out, and the line went dead.

Chapter 20

"Oh, Hazel. Oh, no. She has him. Estelle has Shortie. I think she shot him." I stared at my phone. "I need to call nine-one-one." I tucked my head down, wrapped my arms around myself, and rocked back and forth in my seat.

"Dear Lord, please keep him safe." I couldn't catch my breath. My chest tightened, and my lips tingled. When I opened my eyes, everything looked fuzzy. I squeezed them shut.

Hazel touched my back, and I jerked away. Her fingers felt like fire through my shirt.

"Peg, stay here. I'm leaving the air conditioning on. Be right back," she said.

After what felt like hours, my car door opened, and someone placed a cool towel on the back of my neck. I flinched and then relaxed into it. Someone put a water bottle in my hand.

"Drink," Cynthia said, her tone light and quiet. "I already took the top off."

I sipped, attempting to control my breathing.

"Mom, open your eyes," she said.

"I can't."

"Mom, open your eyes," she repeated.

I did what she said. She crouched beside me.

"Okay, good. Breathe with me." She drew several deep breaths before I joined in. "Now, tell me four things you see."

"My knees, my shoes." I sat up straighter. "The hood of the car." I met her gaze. "Your beautiful face." My eyes filled with tears.

"You're okay, Mom." Her voice stayed calm, and she continued to reassure me. Behind her, Hazel paced the driveway, her cell phone glued to her ear. I couldn't hear her, but I worried about the expression on her face.

"What's Grandma Hazel doing?" Panic fluttered in my stomach, and I gripped the water bottle so tight the plastic crinkled. "Is Shortie all right? I don't think he is. Someone shot him." My words ended in a wail.

Cynthia rubbed my back. "Look at me." She touched my cheek to steer my gaze back to her. "You're safe. Grandma is safe. She's checking on him. Let's not worry yet."

"Yet." I tried to smile and failed. "You're funny." The tears came, and I couldn't stop them. "It was horrible. I think they shot him. Why would anyone hurt him?"

She grabbed my hands and opened my tight fists. She rubbed my fingers. "We don't know for sure."

I squeezed my eyes shut and sniffled—one deep breath, then another. "Okay, I got it. I'll pray and not be afraid." Saying the words out loud helped me settle.

She sat back on her heels. "Whew, Mom. You scared me."

"I'm sorry, honey." I turned to the side and put my feet on the driveway. "I think I can get out now." She held my arm as I walked into the house.

My legs shook like jelly by the time we reached the sofa. I plopped onto it. Cynthia passed me the water bottle and encouraged me to continue drinking from it. A deep fatigue hit, and my body sank into the couch. I remembered how she guided me in deep breathing and attempted several on my own.

Hazel came inside and headed to her room before I could question her. She'd share any news once she found a minute. As bad as I felt, I imagined she was upset too. I pushed myself to a better sitting position and placed my water bottle on the coffee table.

After a few minutes, my head stopped spinning. I rubbed my chest, remembering the tight feeling. Shortie's voice flashed through my mind. I drew several more deep breaths and waited for the next round of panic to end.

Lucy trotted into the room and sniffed my shoes. I picked her up and let her snuggle and wriggle in my arms. She nipped my fingers and licked my cheek—one big slurp from chin to forehead.

"Thanks." I set her on the floor and dried my face with the corner of my shirt.

"She's comforting you," Cynthia said. "Come here, girl. Let's go outside." Lucy ran for the back door. CB, who'd been asleep in front of the hearth, perked up and woofed.

"Go on, silly fellow," I said. He rose and ambled outside.

Hazel joined me on the sofa. "How are you?" She patted my leg.

"Better, I think. I keep remembering his voice." I waved toward the front door. "Sorry about all that."

"Pfft. No, do not apologize." She squeezed my hand and didn't let go. "I can't imagine how you felt hearing him. I only heard your side

...” Her fingers twitched. “Anyhow, I called Marcus. He's on his way, so you don't have to go to the station. He'll want your phone. I hope he can get information from the number Shortie used to call you.”

“Okay.” I leaned my head against the couch's headrest and closed my eyes. “Tell me when he's here.” My body melted into the sofa. In the background, I heard the dogs come in, clattering and chatting in the kitchen, and someone knocked on the front door. That startled me out of my doze. Hazel let Marcus in. He hurried over as fast as his crutches allowed and sat on the couch beside me.

“Peg?” He caressed my cheek, peering into my eyes. Worry lines puckered his forehead and pulled his brows together. “How are you?”

I leaned into his palm, enjoying his warm touch. “I'm okay. I am. But Shortie ...”

He drew me into his arms and held me close. In the kitchen, Hazel and Cynthia bustled about. I glanced behind me. The day flew by with so many crazy events. Now it was dark out.

“Did Hazel tell you we talked to Charlene?” I asked. “And about Finch?” I had so many things to catch him up on.

“Peg, relax. We can talk in a bit.” He kissed the top of my head and pulled me closer.

Cynthia entered, steam rising from the two bowls in her hands. “Clear a space for these, please.”

Marcus did as she asked, and she set them down. He checked his watch. “I can't stay long. I need to get your statement, Peg, and head to the station.”

“I know. Just give me a few minutes.”

“Chicken noodle soup, Mom.” Cynthia pushed my bowl closer. “Comfort food. Grandma is making sandwiches too.”

“Thank you, honey. Y'all going to eat with us?” I asked.

She nodded. “Be right back.”

We slurped the soup and dipped grilled cheese sandwiches into the broth. Lucy sat at my feet.

"She's waiting for you to give her a bite." Cynthia laughed. "Little beggar."

"Can she lick the bowl?" I asked.

"Just a little and only yours. She doesn't need people food."

I finished my supper and set the bowl down. Lucy's ears and snout ended up covered in leftover chicken broth. I picked her up and used my napkin to clean her face as she struggled to get back down and find more people to beg from.

When I set her on the floor, she scurried over to Cynthia and yipped.

Marcus placed his bowl on the coffee table. "That hit the spot. Thank you." Lucy tried to jump up on the table but couldn't quite make it. He petted her head. "You need to learn from CB. He's got the skills."

Charlie Brown had his front paws on the kitchen counter, his head tilted and tongue out, attempting to snag a piece of bread.

"Hazel, you need to get your boy," I said.

She scolded him, and he ran into the living room, a sad expression on his face. Marcus called him over and held his bowl while CB licked it. Hazel made a face, but Marcus defended the dog.

"Lucy got some. He deserves some too." When CB cleaned the bowl, Marcus picked up mine and somehow, even on his crutches, carried both bowls into the kitchen. He rinsed them, put them in the dishwasher, and cleaned up the counters.

Hazel's expression softened. "He's a keeper, Peg."

I smiled. Marcus had become a true friend, and if I was honest with myself, he was turning into much more than that. Shortie's gravelly voice returned to me. "He said, 'She got me.'"

Cynthia leaned forward. "What?"

"Shortie. He didn't say much. I asked if it was him, and he told me she 'got' him."

Marcus stood at the entrance to the room, drying his hands on a kitchen towel. "That's all he said?"

"Yes." I closed my eyes. "I heard a loud, sharp crack." I imitated the sound. "After that," I gulped, "the line went dead." I blew out a sharp breath and met Marcus's gaze.

His cop face returned, eyes dark and hard, expression attentive. "Any background noises?"

I thought for a minute. "Yes, I heard … birds?"

He held out his hand. "May I have your phone?"

I handed it over.

"I'll have to take this with me." He tossed the towel on the kitchen counter and sat beside me. He pulled a notebook and pen from his shirt pocket and wrote down what I said. When he finished, he turned my way. "You okay if I leave? I need to go and get things started with this." He tapped his pen on the notepad and gave a wry grin. "I should've already left."

"Have we told you about meeting with Elizabeth at Derek's office, or what Charlene told us?" Hazel asked.

His mouth quirked up on one side. "Nope." He clicked the pen and opened his notepad to a clean page. "Let me have it."

Hazel filled him in. He asked a few questions for clarification but continued to take notes. When she and I told him everything we could think of, he flipped the pad closed and tucked it into his pocket.

"This gives me a lot to go on. I see where your thoughts are headed." He hugged me, grabbed his crutches, and headed for the front door. "I'll be in touch." He tapped the extra lock on the front door. "Make sure to secure this. Y'all have had enough excitement for one night."

Wasn't that the truth? But what about Shortie?

CHAPTER 21

I SPENT MUCH OF Sunday resting and recuperating—and realizing how often I reached for my phone. Marcus or the tech guys in his department were checking it over. He hadn't told me how long they would need it, and I couldn't call and ask. My fear of what was happening to Shortie, or if he was even alive, ate at me. I couldn't do anything until I heard from Marcus. I hated feeling useless.

After lunch, Cynthia left for the bird sanctuary to help Harry.

"Hang on, I'll grab my purse and join you," Hazel said.

Cynthia plopped beside me on the couch. "I think Grandma's bored."

"She's not used to a lot of downtime." I patted my chest. "I'm holding the investigation back."

"You've had a huge shock, Mom. Take care of yourself. Carter's here if you need anything." She kissed my temple and got up. "Come on, woman," she called to Hazel.

"You might've just lost your favorite grandchild status," I said.

"Nah." She brushed her knuckles on her shoulder. "I'm the oldest. I will always be her favorite."

Hazel chuckled as she entered the room. "Reese may have bumped you down a notch, dear."

They teased each other on their way out to the garage. I sat and stewed as fear bubbled inside my stomach like a two-day-old sandwich.

Late in the afternoon, I insisted Carter accompany me outside. The dogs joined us, and while we dragged the comfy porch chairs into the shade in the yard, they sniffed the fence line. Or CB did. Lucy followed. At least until she got distracted by a butterfly or a bird. Once he'd made his perimeter check, CB flopped down between Carter and me, his tongue out. I switched on the outside faucet for him. Lucy joined us, skipping through the water stream and shaking her drenched fur on all of us. Carter and I laughed at CB's expression.

"He's like this old, grumpy man now." Carter stroked CB's ears.

"I never thought about his age until Lucy came." I turned off the spigot. "Wonder if Grandma knows how old he is?"

Carter stretched. "Probably. She might have his birthday in the notebook she carries around all the time."

A thought hit me. "Can you bring me her notebook and a pen?" If I couldn't help find Shortie, at least I could try to find connections and leads. When he brought them to me, I skimmed through what Hazel had written in the last few days.

Carter rubbed CB's back with his foot, and the dog groaned, shifting his body so Carter could reach his tummy. CB closed his eyes. At the same time, Carter yawned. "I'm going inside, Mom." He toed the dog. "Come on, big guy. Nap time."

I waved and continued reading the notes. Clouds scuttled overhead. A slight breeze ruffled through my hair and cooled the sweat along my hairline.

Lucy finished playing and curled up at my feet. A carpenter bee buzzed by, but I read on. The more I thought about what Hazel had written, the better a picture appeared in my mind. I reached the end of her notes and closed the book, tapping my pen on the cover and thinking through everything I'd read.

All the suspects—Derek, Estelle, and now Finch—and all the questions we'd come up with ran in a loop in my mind. I still believed Estelle was the driving force behind Shortie and Babs's disappearances. And she was somehow involved in Marilyn's murder. It didn't make sense for her to be the mastermind of the other recent killings and not this one. Too many things tied her to Derek, Marilyn, and Babs.

But I couldn't figure out why she'd done any of it.

Finch was a whole other matter. Did Estelle have her thumb on Derek or Finch? Who was his mother? Charlene claimed she didn't know. She only remembered him as a child, not a baby, even though she and Finch were half-siblings. Shouldn't there be a record of his birth, including his parents' names? I opened the notebook and made a note to check for that information.

Derek knew something. He had his hand in everything, from the missing birds to Marilyn's death to his relationship with Babs. I wrote down more questions before sketching out a family tree with Estelle and Roger at the top. Roger fathered Charlene and Finch. Did he have more kids? Estelle didn't have any biological children, to my knowledge. In last month's investigation, we discovered information about her extended family, but no one ever mentioned a daughter or son.

Marilyn was dead. The code enforcement official implied that someone infiltrated their records. We believed Marilyn did it. What else did Derek ask her to do? Had she been part of the group, and were they finished with her? It reminded me of how Estelle killed her husband, Roger, because she grew bored with him.

Those questions joined the others in Hazel's notebook.

An ant crawled across my thigh. I brushed it off and got to my feet. Outside time was over. The breeze had ended long ago. Sweat puddled in the small of my back and trickled down the sides of my face. I scooped up Lucy and took her inside.

"Where's your basket, little girl?" I searched the living room and peeked into Cynthia's bedroom before I remembered it was still in Hazel's Bug. I grabbed her keys and retrieved the basket, setting it in front of the hearth. Lucy snuggled into it and snoozed. As I headed for the bathroom, a thought hit me.

The basket. It'd been in my bedroom when Shortie and I decided to meet for dinner. When Hazel and I planned to go to Babs's, we were in the living room, the basket sitting nearby. It was in the Bug the day before when Hazel and I discussed Finch and Elizabeth and our plan to talk to Charlene, complete with directions to her house.

I moved the puppy to one of CB's extra doggie beds and picked up the basket, holding it away from me.

Could it be bugged?

I knew nothing about bugs. Ones that listened, that is. After searching the basket and finding nothing, I stuck it in the garage to be safe. I knocked on Carter's door, borrowed his cell phone, and called Harry. When he answered, I explained the problem.

He laughed. "You think I know anything about those kinds of bugs? Peg, I can identify almost any bird in the world, as well as ants and beetles. That's about it. Oh, and lovebugs seem to be a thing here. And roaches." He made a gagging noise.

"Funny man. Wait till the no-see-ums come out."

"Yes, but you can't see them, so ..."

"True." I paced the room. Lucy observed me for a minute before her eyes closed, and she continued her nap. "Lucy arrived in the basket."

"On your front porch?"

"Yep." I chewed my thumbnail. "Any idea who I can ask to check this for a bug?"

"Yeah, duh. Marcus." He chuckled. "Hazel and Cynthia were just telling me what happened with Shortie. I'm sorry. Be careful, okay? And, Peg, I'm praying for him."

"Thanks." We hung up. Only God could have created the friendship we now shared. For Harry to say he would pray was a huge step. He didn't know anything about God before we met. I never pushed the subject, but I was thankful to be a part of his faith growth.

I called Marcus, but he didn't answer. With the basket in the garage, no one would listen to my conversations anymore. But, the creep factor didn't stop. The hair on the back of my neck stood at attention, and a heavy dread settled in my stomach. What else had they listened to? And who were they?

Estelle's goons crossed my mind. I struggled to control my breathing. Drawing deep breaths in and out settled me. "Come on, Peg, you can do this." Encouraging myself out loud helped a little, but it took conscious effort to keep my mind off what might have happened to Shortie. I sat and prayed for him and for all of us who searched for him. I pushed myself off the couch to fix dinner, hoping the activity might help distract me.

I pulled out the ingredients for a light summer salad, adding tomatoes, chopped red onion, black olives, sliced cucumbers, crumbled feta, Greek yogurt, and hummus to a multi-sectioned platter. I mixed up a vinaigrette of olive oil, red wine vinegar, and dried oregano.

Hazel and Cynthia returned home as I retrieved toasted slices of sourdough bread from the oven. Lucy scurried to Cynthia, yipping and running in circles.

"Great timing," I said.

"You've been busy." Hazel set her purse on the counter.

"I have." I pulled the salad and platter from the refrigerator. "Did Harry tell you why I called?"

"He did. Where's the basket?"

"I stuck it in the garage," I said as Cynthia and Lucy joined us in the kitchen.

"You really think it's bugged, Mom? Someone has been listening to us?" She wrinkled her nose and snuggled the puppy closer.

"Yes, I think so. At least, it would explain a lot." I carried the salad dressing and toasted bread to the table. "Will you wake Carter? He and CB are napping in his room."

Cynthia tapped on his door, washed her hands, and helped me set bowls and napkins out for everyone. Carter slid into his seat as Hazel asked the blessing. When she finished, I brought him up to speed on the news about the basket.

"I might know someone who can help." Carter dished the toppings he wanted into his bowl.

"Who?" I shook the bottle of homemade dressing before drizzling it over my salad.

"One of my buddies at the restaurant." He set his fork down. "He may not be on the up and up, though." He grimaced.

"I tried to get hold of Marcus, but I haven't heard from him." I pulled Carter's phone from my back pocket. "Give your friend a call. Can't hurt to ask."

Carter stepped into his room. When he returned to the table, he made a face. "I feel like a secret spy. My friend said he'll meet us under the water tower at the beach in an hour. He said he can't promise anything."

I shrugged. "Sounds good."

Hazel's mouth hung open.

"What?" I asked.

"You." She pointed with her fork. "Where is my cautious daughter-in-law? The one who can't decide between two men, both of whom are wonderful men, in my opinion. The one who takes care of all of us and spends time with her sick friend." She narrowed her eyes. "Have the aliens replaced you with a clone?"

I wrinkled my nose. "I have no idea, and I'm not an alien, but something has to give. We have to find Shortie. I have to know if he's okay. Plus, there's Estelle, Babs, locating the egrets, and solving Marilyn's death," I said, counting off each on my fingers. "Figuring out if the basket is bugged is the best next step right now."

Hazel stabbed her salad and took a bite. After she'd chewed and swallowed, she said, "Don't think you're leaving me behind, missy. I'm your wingman, remember? Wingwoman?"

"Sidekick, maybe?" I chuckled. "Sure, you can come. But we can't talk on the way."

She frowned. "Well, you're no fun. How am I going to stay quiet for the whole drive?"

My eyebrow twitched, and I stifled a chuckle. "Good question."

CHAPTER 22

ALL FOUR OF US crowded into my car for the trip to the beach. Before we left, I wrapped the basket inside a comforter, hoping it would muffle any sound we made. But I didn't tell Hazel. I enjoyed watching her attempt to stay quiet for thirty minutes, and it took my mind off Shortie.

At first, she sat on her hands. She always used them when she talked. I pinched my lips together to keep from cracking up. When she began to hum, I assumed words were about to burst out.

"Got another twenty minutes or so," I said. In the rearview mirror, I saw Carter wink.

"We can talk about non-Estelle things, right?" She whispered Estelle's name.

"Sure." If I didn't let her talk, words would burst out of her.

She rambled on about the Center and helping Harry until I crossed the bridge into Gulf Breeze. Then she switched to the weather. She mentioned a tropical storm that the forecasters were keeping an eye on.

"Guess what the name will be if it becomes a hurricane?" she asked.

"Well, it's not Hazel. That was in last year's group of names." Hurricane Hazel had intensified, increased in speed, and changed direction, taking a path straight to Pensacola. It was how my mother-in-law came to live with me.

Carter poked his head between the seats. "I know what it is."

His grandmother tapped him on the head. "What?"

"Chloe." He grinned and sat back. "It'll be a doozy for sure."

Cynthia giggled.

"Carter!" I rolled my eyes. "Sibling rivalry is supposed to end when you grow up." I crossed over to Pensacola Beach, thankful for the bright lights over the road. "Where are we meeting your friend?"

"Park under the water tower. He'll find us. And it's not sibling rivalry. I'm just telling the truth."

I parked where he told me to and turned around in my seat. The sun set, and no moon appeared. "What's your friend's name?" I asked Carter.

"Finch. He's not a friend, really. I work with him." He unbuckled his seatbelt. "I think he is related to the owner of the restaurant. Okay, he's here." He pointed toward the front of the car.

I made eye contact with Hazel. "What in the world?" she mouthed.

What were the chances this Finch was our Finch? I unbuckled and joined Carter and his friend.

I never saw Finch's face when he ran out of Derek's office, so I couldn't identify him for sure. Average height, thin, with dark hair, he wore khaki shorts and a surfing T-shirt. When Carter made the introductions, I interrupted before he mentioned my first name.

"Mrs. Howard." I stuck out my hand. "Nice to meet you."

He shook my hand, dropping it quickly and wiping his palm on his shorts. "Same. Carter said you need my help." He crossed his arms and glanced around the parking lot. A few cars sat parked near the pavilion, but none close to us.

"Yes, I do." I retrieved the basket from the back of my vehicle and uncovered it. "I've checked it over, but can't find anything." I handed it to him.

He stepped under the closest parking lot lamp and checked through the basket weave. He trailed his finger along its edges before pulling a small flashlight from his pocket. "Hold this for me." He passed the basket to Carter.

While Carter held it, Finch inspected the basket. He used a key to separate the weaving. Several times, he returned to one spot.

"What is it? What do you see?" I had no idea what he might find that I'd missed, but I knew nothing about wires or listening devices.

A police car drove up, beeped, and flashed its lights at us. The officer rolled down his window. "Everything okay here, ma'am?" He flashed a bright light over us.

"Yes," I assured him. "This is my son and his friend, who is checking a basket for me." All the truth, but I'm sure we looked sketchy.

"May I have your license?"

I grabbed my purse from the car and pulled out my license. "Here." I stood beside the patrol car door.

He took it and examined both sides. In a quiet voice, he said, "Are you safe, ma'am?"

"Yes." I kept my tone down to match his.

"No drugs?"

"Oh, no, not at all." I waved toward Finch and Carter. "He's truly looking at something for me."

He handed the license back. "Next time, pick a less obvious place than late at night in the beach parking lot. It'll be safer too."

"I will," I said. "Thank you."

He nodded, rolled up his window, and left. My shoulders sagged. I didn't want Marcus to find out what I was doing. Especially now that I'd met Finch. The possibility of two men with that name in the Pensacola area was close to zero.

I returned to the two young men. "Find anything?"

Without a word, Finch drew a knife from his pocket and flipped it open. He wiggled it into the area he'd been studying, and a small, white, button-sized plastic device popped out into his palm. "This is your problem. Want me to destroy it?"

"Yes, please."

He placed the bug on the ground, stuck his knife in the center, and turned. It broke a little. Finch stepped on the device and twisted his foot until it came apart in pieces. "That enough?" he asked.

"Yep, thanks. Do you think it has others in it?" I asked.

"No need. This one would've done the trick."

I held out my hand, and he shook it. "What do I owe you?"

"Nothing, it's all good." He stepped back out of the light.

I had to ask, even though I probably shouldn't. "Finch? What's your last name?"

"Keaton. Why?" He brushed the pieces of the bug into his hand and threw them into a nearby trash can.

"Oh, no reason." I picked up the bug-free basket and headed for my car. "Come on, Carter." I wanted to get as far away from the area as possible. Finch might be Roger's son, but Estelle knew him well. The bug was live until he crunched it beneath his heel. Whoever had been listening in might already be watching us.

We buckled up, and I pulled out of the parking lot, my tires screeching on the pavement.

"Why are you in such a hurry?" Hazel held onto her seat.

"His last name is Keaton. Whoever listened to that bug heard our location before he broke it into pieces. They might come to find us." I checked my rearview mirror.

Hazel watched her side mirror. "Okay, I'll keep an eye out."

"Who are you looking for?" Cynthia asked.

"We'll know when we see 'em," I muttered. "Just watching the traffic, honey," I said louder. "It's busy tonight."

Hazel leaned my way. "Wonder how he knew about bugs?"

I shrugged. "He didn't say."

"Too bad we couldn't ask about the egrets." She sat back and tightened her seatbelt. "Elizabeth said he took them."

I turned onto the interstate. "We could ask Carter to set up another meeting."

"What, Mom?" Carter leaned through the seats again.

"I may need Finch's number," I said.

"No problem. I'll text it to you," he said.

"Hey," Cynthia said. "Saturday is when the Blue Angels fly. I want to go, but I'd have to be out here before sunrise to claim a parking spot."

Her words reminded me of Charlene. She must know more about her half-brother than she let on. We drove by the entrance to her condo, and I tipped my chin toward it. "That's who we're talking to tomorrow," I told Hazel.

She nodded. "Yes." She pumped her fist. "Estelle Keaton, we're on your trail."

Estelle better look out. Finch was the link. I felt sure of it. Time to find out more about him.

No one followed us home. Not that I could tell. In the morning, I rechecked the photo I found in Derek's office. The man standing beside him, holding the other end of the oversized scissors, was, I now realized, Finch. That put him right around Charlene's age. Hazel entered the kitchen as I pondered all the things we'd figured out and everything we still needed to discover.

"You look deep in thought," she said as she poured herself a mug of coffee.

I showed her the picture and explained my questions.

"Call Charlene and set up a meeting," she said. "Finch might be older than her. She said she was about ten when she met him. I don't think she mentioned his age at the time."

"Such a strange family." I searched through my purse. "Wait, Marcus still has my cell. Can you call her?"

Hazel called and made plans with her to meet the next day. I stayed busy working on Mamma Birds. Shortie never left my mind, and I continued to pray for his safety. After scheduling a few posts and answering comments and questions, I borrowed Hazel's phone and called Chloe.

"Hey, Mom, what's up?" she asked.

"Got a minute to talk about the blog?"

"Sure, Reese is napping, and Tom's at work. Let me get my laptop."

"Okay, tell me when you're ready," I said.

Rustling noises sounded in the background on her end. "Got it. I'm ready," she said.

We discussed a few blog post ideas. Knowing I'd already taught her how to upload blog posts, we tossed around ideas for her to write. "Tell me once you've put one up, and I'll do what I need to do on my end," I said.

"I will. Have you seen the weather? If this storm becomes a hurricane, they're naming it after me." She giggled. "Remember how mad Grandma was when they named last year's hurricane Hazel? She was convinced they'd named it after her."

I glanced at the calendar. That had happened almost a year ago. Hazel and I struggled adjusting to living together for the first month or so. We were close friends now. Thinking of friends reminded me of Lauree, so after I finished speaking with Chloe, I called her.

John answered. "I was about to call you," he said. "I need you. It's Lauree."

CHAPTER 23

"What's wrong? Where is she?" I asked. My fingers gripped the phone case.

"The ambulance took her to West Florida Hospital. The kids are at the neighbor's. Can you meet me at the hospital?" His voice broke. "Peg, she is so sick."

"Hang on, I'll be right there. I can pick you up."

"No, meet me there." He sniffled. "I can drive."

I filled Hazel in and rushed out the door. A different kind of fear now filled me. I had imagined receiving this call. Over the last few weeks, I'd watched my friend's situation deteriorate quickly. My prayers were constant pleas to God. I couldn't lose Lauree. John and the kids couldn't lose her.

I sped into the hospital's parking lot and drove into the valet parking area. As soon as I handed them my key, I hurried inside. John leaned against one of the walls, staring out the window. Tears streamed down his cheeks. He didn't hear me approach. I whispered his name.

He startled and scrubbed his face dry. "Hey, thanks for coming."

I was afraid to hug him and set us both to crying. I settled for touching his arm. "What's going on? Where is she?"

I followed him down a hallway. "She's probably still in the ER. Let's go check."

"What is wrong with her?"

"She has cancer, Peg."

"Well, I know that." I pulled him to a stop.

He rubbed his hand over his hair. "I'm sorry. She got dehydrated, I think. This new treatment." He stared at the wall. "I don't think it's helping."

We continued toward the emergency room area and located her in a side room, hooked up to fluids, as pale as the sheets she lay on.

"Hi, friend." I hugged her and stepped back to let John stand by her side.

"Any word yet?" he asked.

"No." The word came out soft and scratchy.

I chewed on my lip, knowing I couldn't fall apart. I pulled up the single chair in the room. "What've they got in the bag?" I pointed to the hanging pole.

She shook her head and shrugged.

How do you cheer someone up in the midst of the most brutal fight of their life? I drew on how she'd been when Zack died, and I kept my mouth shut. Sometimes, sitting in silence with your best friend was all you both needed.

When the doctor came in, I shoved my hands under my legs so Lauree wouldn't see them shaking. His intense body language and the way his brow furrowed didn't bode well.

He introduced himself as her oncologist, shook our hands, and sat on the bed by Lauree's feet. "We have you on fluids and electrolytes and a few other things to help you feel better. We'll get you in a room soon." He turned to John. "I understand that you're worried. This is part of the process."

John's chin quivered. "How long is this part?" he whispered.

I bit the inside of my cheek and fisted my hands. If I cried now, I might never stop. The doctor rose and put his hand on John's shoulder.

"We always said we'd be honest and never leave your wife out of the discussion." He glanced at Lauree. "I think it would be wise to have your kids come up here. They need to spend time with their mom. Today would be good."

Oh, Lord. Oh, no. Please, God, not my friend. I couldn't stop the tears. I tried to swipe them away, but they came faster than I could keep up.

Lauree caught my eye. "Gotta stop that," she rasped.

"Be right back." I darted out of the room, thankful to find an empty bathroom down the hall. Once inside, I locked the door. My breathing came too fast. I leaned over, put my hands on my thighs, closed my eyes, and drew deep breaths. I blew them out forcefully. After a few minutes, I blew my nose and splashed water on my face. I stared at myself in the mirror. "Gotta be strong. It's not the time to break."

When I left the bathroom, John stood alone in the hall. My breath caught.

"Where is she?"

"They took her upstairs to a room." He leaned his head against the wall, his eyes dull and unfocused. Every bit of strength he'd possessed seemed to be gone. "Can you pick up the kids?"

"Of course. I hate to ask, but can my kids and Hazel stop by tonight?"

He straightened up and shoved his hands in his pockets. "Yes." He bit his bottom lip. "The sooner the better."

I'm not sure how I made it to get the twins, or how I maintained a calm façade. Once I dropped them off to John, I drove home, crying the whole way. Hazel waited for me on the front porch. She studied my face and opened her arms.

I held onto her. "It's so bad. She looks so awful."

Hazel stroked my hair. When I calmed down, she led me into the house. "Why don't you sit down for a few minutes? You've been through so much over the last two days. Put your feet up." She brought me a banana and a glass of iced tea.

"Not compared to Shortie or Lauree." Her stern expression pushed me to eat the fruit and sip the tea. I felt a bit better once I finished. "The kids need to go see her."

Hazel texted Chloe, and I called Cynthia and Carter from their rooms. When they were ready, Hazel drove us all to the hospital. Before we went inside, she asked if she could pray.

"Dear Lord, we are heartbroken for our friend and her family right now. I won't ask You to help us not to grieve. But I will ask for the strength to offer comfort and hope. And we still are praying for a miracle. We love you. Amen."

Chloe pulled up through valet parking as we entered the hospital. She hugged each one of us, and we rode the elevator to Lauree's floor. They sat in the family waiting area while I checked with one of the nurses about the number of visitors allowed in Lauree's room.

John peeked his head out of a door while I waited at the nurse's station. "Tell them all to come on in. They already said they could."

The expression on his face broke me. I gathered Hazel and my kids and showed them into Lauree's room. Her twins, Stevie and Suzie, lay one on each side of their mom. When they saw my kids, they scrambled down and climbed up on the girls' laps. Carter teased Stevie and tugged on Suzie's pigtails.

Lauree's face gained a bit of color. I struggled to believe she'd be all right. Hazel talked to Lauree and stepped aside so I could sit by her.

I held her hand. "I don't think this was supposed to happen. You still have work to do on Mamma Birds."

Her mouth twitched. "Ha ha." She tugged my hand, and I leaned over.

"What do you need?" I asked. "What can I do?"

"Remember what I told you." She stopped and paused to catch her breath. "If John remarries or dates, you have to vet those women." Her grin was strained.

Tears filled my eyes, but I chuckled. "I will." I wrapped my arms around her and held her close. "I love you, my friend."

I held her hand, and my kids started telling stories. Cynthia reminded her of the honeysuckle incident.

Lauree's eyes brightened with mirth, her cheeks growing pink. "You're not remembering it quite like I do." She looked at her twins. "Those three ate all of my honeysuckle. Every single one."

Cynthia held up her hand. "I don't think we ate every one of them."

Chloe nudged her. "Pretty sure we did."

"As the youngest,"—Carter held up his hands—"I have immunity. They told me what to do, and I did it." We all laughed.

As the sun set, pink and purple streaking the sky, Lauree's breathing eased. She asked for ice chips, and the nurse came in several times to check her vitals. I didn't know a lot about blood pressure and oxygen levels, but even I could tell they'd improved. I exchanged glances with Hazel, who shrugged.

"God," she mouthed.

CHAPTER 24

We stayed until the nurses shooed us out. Stevie and Suzie could barely keep their eyes open. After I checked with John, we brought them home to Hazel's and made up sleeping pallets for them, Suzie in Cynthia's room, and Stevie in Carter's.

"Sleep well." I hugged them both. "You can play with the puppy in the morning." I turned to my kids. "Wake me if you need me." When everyone settled and only Hazel and I were in the room, I let out a deep sigh of relief.

"I thought this was it. That we were going to lose her." I stretched and snuggled down into the couch. "She looked so different when I first saw her. No color in her face at all."

"They drew more blood. We might have some answers soon," Hazel said.

"I hope so. By the time we left, she was almost back to her old self."

Hazel frowned, her mouth pursed to one side. "The thing you need to remember with cancer is that no matter what, she won't ever be her old self. Cancer is this thing. It's insidious, and it comes from the outside and grabs you. It changes your life in ways people don't understand unless they've experienced it." She shifted on the loveseat. "Don't wait for her to be how she used to be. Love her now. Don't stop."

Her words settled deep into me. She was right. If I waited for Lauree to be in remission, I would miss out on a lot of living and a lot of friendship.

She got up and settled Roscoe for the night, taking time to baby-talk to him. I let CB and Lucy out to potty. The puppy loved to sleep curled up next to Charlie Brown. He'd woof if she needed to go out during the night, and one of us would get up. So far, the system worked.

The twins woke me early the next morning, begging for breakfast and curious for an update on their mom. I called John.

"The twins want to know how their mom is."

"She got a little sleep. Can you keep them longer today?"

"Of course." I ruffled Stevie's hair. "We're going to have some pancakes. I'll text you later, okay?"

We hung up, and before Hazel and I were ready to leave for Gulf Breeze, Cynthia and Carter woke up.

"It's so early," Carter whined. He grabbed a plate and dished pancakes onto it.

"You snore." Stevie stuck a huge bite of pancake in his mouth. When he'd chewed and swallowed, he said, "Next time I'm sleeping in the living room."

I hoped there wasn't a next time as far as Lauree was concerned. I kissed the top of his head. "He's always snored. Even as a little guy."

Suzie giggled.

"Mom, I'll call John and take the kids to him when he's ready," Cynthia said. "But I have class this afternoon."

"Thanks, honey." I told her and Carter the latest update on Lauree.

Carter texted someone and glanced up. "Finch said he'll work for me today, so I'm free until you're home." He patted Stevie's back. "I can hang out with these guys."

"Wonderful. Thanks, you two." Hazel and I said our goodbyes, hugging the twins a little longer than usual.

We were halfway to Gulf Breeze to meet Charlene when Hazel's cell rang. I answered for her. "Hi, Marcus." I hit the speaker button so Hazel, who was driving, could hear too. My stomach flipped, my bagel rebelling against my anxiety. "Any news on Shortie?"

"No, nothing yet. What are you doing today?" In the background, I heard people talking.

I frowned. "Why do you ask?"

He made a humming sound.

"Are you at work?" I asked.

"Yep. And I heard interesting news this morning."

His tone raised my antennas. Had he found out about our meeting with Finch? "Really, what?" I glanced at Hazel and mouthed, "Finch?"

Her eyes widened.

"Peg,"—his voice rose, his tone troubled—"if you and Hazel are going to keep impeding this investigation, well, I ..."

"What are you talking about?" I asked.

"Your name came up in the system Sunday night. You were at the beach? Alone in the dark with two young men?" He ground out the question.

I chuckled. "Marcus, come on."

Hazel covered her mouth, her shoulders shaking. "He's mad," she whispered between her fingers.

"You going to tell me about it?" he asked, no trace of laughter in his voice.

My stomach clenched. This wasn't the first time Marcus's jealousy reared its ugly head. I didn't like it, and I intended to remind him.

"First off," I said, "I don't have to check in with you. And you don't have to keep tabs on me." My relationship with Zack had been one of love and trust. I didn't want to live under someone's thumb or with their jealousy. "Second, how did you find out?"

"My buddy. The one who stopped and talked to you. He recognized your name." His tone turned defensive.

"So, my name didn't really come up in the system?" I asked.

"Well, um, no." He paused. "None of that came out right. I'm sorry."

Hazel's eyes widened again. "He apologizes?" She pulled into the coffee shop parking lot and found a spot to park.

"I have to go, Marcus." I hung up and handed the phone to Hazel. "Might want to turn the ringer off."

She stuck it in the glove box. "This works even better." The phone rang. We exited the car and walked toward the coffee shop. "I thought he'd gotten over all of that."

I did too. He'd acted possessively about me one time, as if he were better than Shortie. His actions cut our budding friendship short. Of late, I considered him more than a friend.

"I'm glad I found out now. I don't want to live with that." I held the store's door for her.

Charlene sat in a corner in a low-back, mock-leather chair. She indicated her drink. "If you want coffee, I'll wait."

Hazel sat with her while I purchased our drinks. When I returned to the small grouping of chairs, I handed Hazel hers. She pointed to my cup.

"Sure it's big enough?"

"I'd take the whole carafe if I could." I settled into my chair and sipped from my ultra-large cup. Anger at Marcus now swirled in my gut alongside my worries about Shortie and Lauree. Coffee might not help, but at this point, I didn't think it would hurt. "What are you talking about?"

"I told Charlene about meeting up with Finch," Hazel said.

Charlene crossed her legs, smoothing her skirt over them. "I looked through some paperwork I have. I haven't found out who his mother is." She raised her coffee cup. "Do you want me to call him and set up a meeting?"

"Sure, please do that," I said. "Can you call him now? We have some questions for him."

I admired the store while she attempted to contact her half-brother. Tucked into the L of a block of businesses, the shop's walls were painted a soothing shade of sage green. Various coffee signs and plaques decorated the wall. I inhaled the aroma of freshly brewed coffee.

Charlene interrupted my musings. "He didn't answer."

"Didn't Carter say Finch would work his shift today?" Hazel asked. She checked her watch.

"Want to go to lunch with us?" I asked Charlene. "We'll go to the restaurant where he works."

She shrugged. "Sure."

We walked to the Bug while Charlene headed for her car. I opened the glove box and checked Hazel's cell.

"Four missed calls, three voicemails, and twenty texts. All from Marcus." I scrolled through the text messages. "He's mad. And he apologizes a lot." I tossed the phone back in the box and slammed the door. "He can stay mad."

"You don't want to listen to his messages?" Hazel asked.

"You can. Not me." I crossed my arms. "We're done."

She snickered. "You say that now."

"Hazel, think about it. Shortie never did this kind of stuff. He wasn't the jealous type." I shifted in my seat, remembering how he'd felt about Harry. I shoved that to the back of my mind. "Zack wasn't either."

"My son was a good man and a good husband." She parked in the restaurant's lot. Charlene parked beside her. "Don't forget, Shortie also never worked you up like this."

I unbuckled and got out of the car. "You're saying I should put up with Marcus's jealousy?"

She hooked her arm through mine. "Not at all. Never, especially if he's cruel or abusive." She pulled me to a stop. "I'm saying don't miss the spark, the way he challenges you. You might reconsider if he's truly sorry and willing to work on it. I never saw you with Shortie the way you are with Marcus."

Before I answered her, Charlene joined us, and we entered the restaurant. A perky blonde showed us to a table and handed out menus. She recited the day's specials and left for our drinks.

I yawned. "I should've ordered more coffee."

Hazel picked up her menu. "What's good here?"

I already knew what I wanted. I had eaten here a few times. "I like their grouper. Or the shrimp po'boy. Anything I've ordered here has been good."

The waitress brought our drinks and took our orders. Before she left, I asked her where we could find Finch.

She glanced around the restaurant. "He does a lot of things, especially at lunchtime. I'll find him and send him over if you'd like."

While we waited, Charlene told us about the upcoming weekend's festivities. The Blue Angels often practiced before their show, and she and some of her neighbors planned to watch. Her face lit up with excitement. I enjoyed seeing her relaxed after the pain she'd been through losing her mom the fall before.

"If y'all want to, you can come to the show Saturday. Sometimes I stand on my deck, but often we all bring camp chairs down to the beach area by the bay. There's plenty of room if your kids want to come," she said.

I thought of the twins and asked if they could come with us.

"Yes, we're not rowdy." She chuckled. "I've never had friends like them before. It's nice." She grimaced. "My dad liked parties. Lots of booze, crazy things. Probably drugs. I didn't see it, but it wouldn't surprise me."

Behind her, Finch approached. I patted her hand. "Your brother is coming." How long had it been since they'd seen each other?

"Really?" She pushed her chair back and rose, turning to face him. "Hey, little brother." She pulled her arm back and punched him in the nose. He fell to the ground, and she leaned over him. "Nice to see you."

CHAPTER 25

NEARBY CUSTOMERS SCATTERED, AND our waitress screamed. Hazel and I stayed rooted to our chairs. Her chest heaving, Charlene remained where she stood, her eyes shooting daggers at Finch, fists clenched as if she were ready to go another round. He shifted on the floor, and she stepped closer, only stopping when he flinched.

"What just happened?" Hazel asked, her eyebrows up under her bangs, hands clutching the arms of her chair.

"Why did she hit him?" I hurried to Charlene and grabbed her arm. "What are you doing?"

She shook off my hand. "Y'all want to ask him questions, fine." She spit out the words. "I had something I've wanted to tell him for years."

I guessed that. She had unresolved anger against her half-brother and decided to act on it today, in public. Finch clasped his hands over his nose before he stood up. Blood dripped between his fingers and dotted his shirt.

"What is wrong with you, Charlene?" His voice sounded funny, and his eyes watered.

I passed him a handful of napkins. "Come sit down, Finch."

He followed me to the table. "Is my crazy sister coming?"

Our waitress brought over a bag of ice. "Y'all want to come in the back?" she asked, her expression anxious.

The four of us followed her to a back office. Finch kicked the door shut, and I jumped at the sound. Within minutes, the waitress returned with our orders, plus a side of fries and a soda for Finch. Hazel and I sat on opposite ends of the couch, with Charlene squished between us. Finch took a seat behind a large, weathered desk. I leaned forward and read the nameplate sitting front and center.

"Manager slash owner? That's you?" I glanced at Hazel. "I thought Carter said you worked with him?"

Finch took the bag of ice from his nose. "I do. But I'm also co-owner and manager." He ate a French fry, grimacing when he chewed. "That hurts. Char, you still pack quite the punch."

"You're welcome." She avoided looking at him.

Hazel shifted forward on the couch cushion, making eye contact with him and Charlene. "What is up with you two? You"—she pointed to Charlene—"said you hadn't seen him in years. Why are you mad at him?"

"Yeah, why are you mad at me, sis?" Finch's eyes gleamed. He enjoyed taunting her, and I got a glimpse of their father, Roger. His tone did not help the situation.

She crossed her arms. "You know why."

I picked up my po'boy and took a bite. The ambiance in this office might not rival that of the restaurant, but I was hungry. After I swallowed and wiped my chin, I said, "Fill us in, Charlene. We want to know too."

She huffed and stood. Finch shrank away from her. She was tall, but thin in a willowy, model-like way. I wondered what kind of sway she had over him.

Charlene narrowed her eyes. "You should've come to my mother's funeral." Hands on her hips, she stomped her foot. "I needed you. Someone. She helped me more than anyone." She thumbed in my direction.

I'd found her in the bathroom before her mother's celebration of life. Her father had run away to Guatemala, but Estelle stayed in town long enough for the service and to irritate Charlene. We discovered someone else killed Sylvia, but Charlene and Finch's stepmother, Estelle, was the mastermind behind it.

"Finch," I interrupted Charlene's tirade, "where's your stepmom?"

"Estelle?" he asked.

"That's the only one, right?" Assumptions hadn't gotten me far in the past, so I thought I needed to make sure.

"Well, yes." He grabbed his soda. "Last I heard, she was hiding in Guatemala with my dad."

My eyebrow twitched. "Yep. Last year. They're back. Well, they were, but she killed your father. As far as anyone knows, she's still in the Pensacola area."

Charlene took a step toward the desk. "You missed our father's funeral too."

He gestured with his cup. "Not true. I was standing in the back. I didn't talk to you." He looked my way, his eyes twinkling. "You can see why. Imagine her punching me at a funeral."

"Seriously." She stomped back to the couch and plopped down between Hazel and me. "You haven't changed a bit."

He held up his hands, wrists together. "Arrest me. I've done nothing wrong, though." He made a loud slurping sound as he finished his drink. "I could bring charges against you, Char, for hitting me."

"Pfft." She narrowed her eyes. "Just like Dad. Always with the lawsuits. Quit calling me Char."

My thoughts exactly. Although I never met Roger in person, his reputation preceded him wherever he went, and it lingered on after his death.

Hazel snapped her fingers. "Charlene, you mentioned having something you wanted to tell Finch for years. After you hit him."

Charlene picked up her plate and ate a bite of her grouper.

"What did you want to tell me?" Finch asked.

She frowned. "You know." She continued eating.

I grew tired of being in the middle of their sibling fight. I finished my sandwich and rose. "Hazel, are you ready?"

She shot me a questioning look before she wiped her mouth and set her plate on the table. "Sure." She pointed at Charlene and Finch. "Work your stuff out. No matter what your dad did or didn't do, he's dead. You only have each other now."

When we left the restaurant, we stopped by the hostess stand and explained who we were to the girl standing behind it. I asked how to pay our bill, but she waved us away.

"Finch will cover it. No problem," she said.

I held the door for Hazel. "We had lunch and a show."

She shaded her eyes with her hand. The sun glared off the white sand beach across the street. "The food tasted good. Not sure about the entertainment."

We climbed into the Bug and rolled down our windows. Hazel turned up the air conditioning to high and backed out of the parking lot.

"Should we have stayed to find out what Charlene's issue is with her brother?" I asked.

"No, I'm tired of their fighting. Seemed silly to me." She turned left to take the bridge over to Gulf Breeze. "Call Chloe and let's go visit the little guy."

I fished her cell phone out of the glove box. "I think Marcus gave up. He only called one more time. No voicemail, though, and no more texts. I have no idea what to do with the man." I called Chloe.

When I explained where we were, she invited us over, and Hazel headed her way.

"I think you should listen to Marcus's voicemails," she said. "What if he has an update on Shortie?"

I started with the last one first. In it, he asked me to call him and hung up. "Okay, next one."

In that one, he asked me to call him. He paused and said, "This is about Shortie, not me. Call me ASAP."

"Hmm." I hit the call back feature and waited while it rang, my hands shaking so hard I had to set the phone on my leg.

"Hazel?" Marcus said.

"It's me. What about Shortie? What have you found out?"

"Hi, Peg. Thanks for calling me back. Finally."

I didn't have time to play games. I could have stayed at the restaurant with Charlene and Finch if I wanted to do that. "Did you find him, Marcus? Is he okay?"

He gave a sharp, humorless laugh. "I haven't found him."

I couldn't believe this man. I dragged a hand down my face, questioning my choices. "Why did you say it was about him?"

"Can I finish?"

His snarky tone irritated me. "Yes. Go ahead."

Hazel pulled into Chloe's driveway. "Want me to wait?" she asked, her brows drawing into a deep *V*.

I shook my head. "I'll be in in a minute. Leave the car on, please." When she got out, I said, "Marcus?"

"I'm here. Ready to listen?"

I understood some of Charlene's anger now. His arrogant tone lit a fire in me. "Yep." That's all I got out without exploding. Shortie was in trouble, and Marcus wanted to one-up me.

"We may have found Estelle's hideout."

My breath whooshed out. "Really?" This was good news. Great news. "Do you think she has Shortie?"

"We're keeping an eye on the place. Several men, similar to what you described, who pulled you out of your car, have been in and out."

"Is her car there? The one with the vanity plate?" I asked.

"Yes, we've seen it." He paused. "I've been a jerk, Peg. I'm sorry. Shortie is a priority right now, for both of us." He drew in a deep breath. "I've always had a jealousy problem. Guess you're aware of that."

I wanted to say, "Duh," but I held back and waited.

"Anyhow, that's the update. I'll call when I find out more," he said.

"Thank you. When can I have my phone back? Has Shortie called it again?"

"I can get it for you. No more calls have come in. Can I stop by this evening?" Marcus asked.

"Sure. I'm at Chloe's, but I'll be home by dinner time." I started to tell him to leave the phone by the front door, but I wanted to see him, spend some time with him. He'd apologized, and not for the first time. We needed to talk.

I stayed in the Bug for a few more minutes, taking the time to pray for Shortie. I wondered if he and Babs were together. We never tried her again and assumed she'd been taken without any proof. Before overthinking it, I dialed High Mountain Realty and asked to speak to Kitty. When she answered, I introduced myself.

"What can I help you with, Mrs. Howard?" Her sweet Southern accent was still in place.

"Do you remember when you said you know Babs? Or knew her?"

"Yes." Her tone grew cautious.

"You said she'd help with the rentals Derek wanted to build. And y'all went to school together. I wondered if you still have some of your yearbooks?" Hazel and I never asked Charlene about them, given that she punched Finch and all.

"I sure do," she said. "Why?"

"Will you mail them to me?"

It took some convincing, but by the end of our conversation, Kitty promised to overnight the yearbooks to Hazel's house. I hoped that by tomorrow, we'd have more answers to our questions. If we waited much longer, Shortie might be in more danger.

CHAPTER 26

I TURNED OFF THE Bug. Playing with my grandson and visiting my daughter was just what I needed. Inside the house, I relayed my conversation with Kitty to Hazel.

"What about Marcus?" she asked.

"The police found Estelle's place. They're watching it." I hugged Chloe and held out my hands to Hazel.

She rubbed Reese's back and pulled back from me. "He's comfy."

"He'll be comfier on me." I lifted him from her arms.

"You've been talking to Marcus too much," she said. "Kinda mean."

"Ha ha." I snuggled the baby close, inhaling his sweet newborn scent.

Chloe watched us go back and forth. "I shouldn't ask, but what's up with Marcus?"

Hazel pointed to me. "I'll let her tell you." She pushed herself off the couch with more ease than the other day. "What can I do to help, Chloe? Laundry, make dinner?"

The two of them went into the kitchen while I sat with Reese, holding him in the crook of my arm, studying his little face.

"I'm your grandma. You have a great-grandma, too, but I'm the funnest." I grinned. "Just kidding. She's the best, but you and I, we're going to have lots of adventures." He studied me with his dark blue eyes. I ruffled his patch of light brown hair. "Your Uncle Carter can teach you how to fish, and your Aunt Cynthia will let you help cook."

He scrunched up his body and released a howl. I propped him on my shoulder and patted his back. After a good-sized burp, he cooed.

"There you go, buddy." I kissed his head and rocked him until he fell asleep.

Chloe and Hazel entered the room, chattering about dinner and laundry. I pointed to Reese, and they quieted. Chloe took a seat on the opposite end of the couch from me, and Hazel sat in the recliner.

"We chatted, he burped, he's sleeping," I said.

"Oh, good," Chloe said. "I couldn't get him to burp earlier." She tucked one leg under her and faced me. "Grandma has been filling me in on all of your recent adventures. Any news on Shortie?"

"Nothing," I hesitated, then plunged in, voicing the fear that had been roiling and burning in my stomach. "I'm afraid for him."

"What else did Marcus say? You were out there a long time." Hazel reclined her chair and yawned.

"I also called Kitty," I said. Reese shifted in his sleep, and I adjusted him. "She's going to overnight the yearbooks she has."

"What will that do?" Chloe asked.

Hazel explained our thoughts and the information we still needed.

Chloe closed her eyes for a minute before saying, "Whoever took the birds used the sticky pads?"

I shrugged, and Hazel said, "Yes, but we don't know where the egrets are."

"Okay." She nodded. "That sounds like the least of your worries, though. Are you sure Babs is missing?"

She had a point about the birds. "I'm not positive on Babs. I've wondered that too. Hazel, we should go by her house again," I said.

Hazel yawned. She seemed very comfy in her reclined position.

"You awake over there?" I called out as loudly as possible without waking Reese.

"Yep." She opened her eyes. "See? Babs's house after we leave here."

Chloe giggled. "The yearbooks will help you spot relationships between Babs and Kitty?"

"And Marilyn and Derek," I said. "Estelle Keaton too."

Her eyes narrowed. "I don't like her."

When Reese was born, either Estelle or someone she hired threatened Chloe in the hospital, and they left a package and a menacing note in her mailbox.

"She's not my favorite, either." I leaned forward, shifting Reese from my shoulder to my arms, and held him out to his mamma. "Here. He's warm and sleepy. Hazel, we need to go."

She stretched and lowered the footrest. We kissed Reese and Chloe goodbye and headed for the Bug.

"I still have your keys. Want me to drive?" I dangled the keyring in front of her. She yawned.

"Maybe you should."

I drove us home in silence, punctuated now and then by Hazel's snoring. A pelican flew beside me as I drove over the bridge from Gulf Breeze to Pensacola. He left when I reached the graffiti bridge. It was a gorgeous late summer afternoon—perfect for taking the scenic route home. When I entered Hazel's neighborhood, I pulled into Babs's driveway. I elbowed Hazel.

"No car out here. Was there one when we came before?"

She stirred and stretched. "I don't think so." She unbuckled. "I'll go check if she's home." She knocked on the door and rang the doorbell. I saw her push her way past the front bushes and peer into Babs's front window.

As she did that, I remembered how heavy drapes had been pulled across the window the last time we were here. Now they were pushed to the sides. I climbed out of the car to tell Hazel, but at the same time, she jumped back, tripped over a bush, and fell to the ground. She screamed, and I rushed to her side.

"Are you okay? What happened?"

She grabbed her hip. "Oh, it hurts. Ouch." She moaned, tears in her eyes. "You'd better call an ambulance, Peg." Her gaze shifted back to the house. "Two, actually. And the police." She lay her head down in the grass and moaned again.

"Police? Why?"

She pointed to Babs's house. "She's in there. On the floor. Dead, I think." She tried to move and cried out in pain.

"Okay, okay. Stay right there." I rushed to the Bug and grabbed her cell. When the 911 operator answered, I explained the situation. I texted Marcus and called Cynthia.

"Hey, Grandma, what's up?"

"It's me." I tried to catch my breath.

"Mom, what's the matter? Where are you?"

"We're at Babs's." I rattled off the address. "Can you come? Grandma Hazel is hurt."

"Hurt? Mom, I'm at school, but I'll be there as soon as I can." A door slammed, and after a minute, her car started. "Tell me the address again. Did you call nine-one-one?"

I recited the address. "Yes. Can you let Carter know?"

After what seemed like a long time, Cynthia pulled up as the ambulances and police arrived. Marcus's cruiser swung around the corner as a young police officer began to question me.

I waved to Marcus. "Hang on," I told the other officer. "The detective is here."

"Detective? Ma'am?" The young woman tipped her head, apprehension filling her eyes. "Why did you call him?"

"He's my friend," I said.

As fast as his crutches would allow, Marcus hurried to me. Cynthia hopped out of her car and rushed to her grandmother. Marcus reached my side and held out his arms. I leaned against him, careful not to knock him off balance.

"I didn't know what happened." He panted. "I thought you were hurt."

"It's Hazel. Her hip." Tears streamed down my face. "And Babs. Hazel thinks she's dead."

"Dead?" His head jerked up, and he studied the situation around us. "Stay right here. I'll be back." He directed his next words to the younger police officer. "Stay with her."

He made his way to Hazel and talked to her for a moment. He patted Cynthia's back and pointed my way. A policewoman saying, "Sir, sir. You can't come up here right now," caught my attention.

I spotted Carter arguing with her. "That's my son. Please let him through."

Carter stopped and checked me over. "You're okay?"

"Yes, it's Grandma, honey. She fell, and she's in a lot of pain."

He leaned over, hands on his thighs, breathing hard. "I was taking a nap until Cynthia called. I thought you were hurt. I'm glad you're okay."

I rubbed his back while he caught his breath. He straightened up and brushed his hair back. "I'm going to check on Grandma."

I followed him to Hazel, who regaled the EMTs with her version of how she tripped over the bushes, complete with hand motions and sound. "I landed and heard a pop in my hip." She imitated the sound. They moved her to a stretcher and started for the ambulance. She moaned in pain.

"Grandma,"—Carter caught her hand as they passed—"I love you."

"I love you, too, dear." She grimaced as the stretcher bumped. "I'll be fine. Don't worry."

Cynthia joined us, and we waited while they loaded her into the truck. Marcus was busy talking to a different officer.

"I'll check in with Marcus, then we'll go to the hospital." I handed Carter the keys to Hazel's Bug. "You can turn on the AC. I'll be right there."

Marcus, deep in conversation with one of the police officers, looked over when I reached his side, his mouth quirking up in a half smile. He held up a finger.

I waited. As soon as he finished, I asked, "Is Babs dead?"

"Yes. How is Hazel?"

"Going to the hospital. She mentioned hearing a pop in her hip. I think she broke it." I made a face.

"Go be with her. I'll catch up to you. Nothing you can do for Babs. Oh, hang on." He dug in his pocket. "Here's your phone."

I turned it over in my hand. "Did you find anything on it?"

"Yep. It helped us locate Estelle's place. We're still watching it."

"Nothing else on Shortie?" I searched his face, hoping for good news, but he just shook his head.

"I'm sorry, Peg. We're not giving up though. We need more evidence before we can search it."

My stomach sank. "Okay." Carter hollered for me. "I gotta go."

Before I left, he reached out and caught my hand. "I'm sorry. About being a possessive jerk. I do trust you, and I'm working on it, okay?"

I had too much else to think about. Hazel might need surgery. Shortie was under Estelle's thumb, enduring who knew what kind of treatment. Babs was dead. Lauree ... I needed to call her. "I know." I tipped up on my toes and kissed his cheek. "I'll be in touch."

CHAPTER 27

CARTER GOT US TO the hospital in record time. On the way, I checked in with John. Lauree was still at the hospital, but he expected her to be released the next day.

"Oh, thank God. I'll be up there in a few minutes, so I'll stop and see her," I said.

"Why are you going to the hospital?" he asked.

I explained about Hazel.

"I'll be up in an hour or so. The twins are spending the night at the neighbor's. I'll find you when I come," he said.

Carter pulled into valet parking. He handed the keys to the young man parking cars, explaining that it was his grandmother's car and it needed to be returned without a scratch. We made our way through the hospital to the emergency room, checked in, and grabbed three seats in a corner to wait for someone to call our name.

A man came through the door carrying a woman with blood streaming down her face, followed by someone holding his arm close to his chest. He'd wrapped a towel around it, but blood dribbled in a path behind him.

Cynthia and I exchanged looks. "Will they be seen before Grandma?"

I shrugged. I didn't know how they decided who took priority. When a skinny woman dressed in multiple layers of clothing sat in front of us, I shifted closer to Carter.

He waved me off him. "Mom, she's just getting out of the heat for a few minutes."

"Wouldn't it make sense if she took some of those clothes off?"

"Where would she keep them?"

He had a point. I never thought I lived under a rock, but apparently, I had been. The woman scratched her arm and muttered to herself. She saw me watching and shot me a mostly toothless grin.

I smiled back.

A mix of people—different colors, clothing, and languages—flowed through the door. The emergency room workers treated all professionally. When one of the staff finally called for the family of Mrs. Howard, I felt like I'd been schooled. I didn't realize how isolated I was in my little corner of Pensacola. Or how hard hospital staff worked.

In Hazel's room, a nurse hooked her up to an IV for pain medication. "We've been busy tonight. They'll bring the portable X-ray in soon and check her hip. The doc will be in after that and talk to you."

"Thank you." I stepped closer. "I appreciate everything you've done."

She tipped her head, a smile lifting her lips. "You're welcome, honey."

Hazel's face reflected her pain. "Why don't y'all go get something to eat. It's going to be a bit, I'm sure."

"I don't want to miss the doctor." I fished my credit card out of my purse and handed it to Cynthia. "Bring me a sandwich, please, and chips if you can find some."

"I'm hungry too," Hazel fussed.

The nurse paused and patted Hazel's arm. "No food for you, dear. Not till the doctor talks to you." She finished with the IV and left the room.

Hazel made a face and imitated her words in a saucy tone, followed by, "She's going to starve me."

"Oh, boy, you're going to be fun, aren't you?" I settled into a hard plastic chair. "Seems like I was just here."

"Oh, Lauree." Hazel's words slurred from the pain medication. "How is she?"

"Still here, but going home tomorrow. I'll check on her in a bit."

She nodded and closed her eyes.

This tiny holding room didn't invite naps, but I was beat. I leaned against the wall and thought back through the day. So many things had happened. How did Finch's nose feel? Did he and Charlene work out their differences? I thought about Marcus and his apology. I yawned and let my eyes drift shut.

"Mom, are you sleeping?"

Carter's question penetrated my brain. I opened my eyes. "Nope, just thinking."

"You and Grandma both snore." Cynthia chuckled. "Here, I got you a ham and cheese." She handed me the sandwich and a bottle of water. "I texted Chloe so she knows how Grandma is."

Poor Chloe. I forgot to tell her. While we ate, techs brought the portable X-ray machine. A nurse pushed more chairs into the room, and we waited for the doctor to arrive. And waited some more. Hazel, relaxed from the pain medication, regaled us with wild stories I had never heard before. When she broke into song—her favorite Broadway tunes—I threatened to smother her.

"I'm tellin' on you." She shook her finger. Or tried to. Her hand got caught in the IV line, and I spent several minutes untangling her. I was bent over getting her situated when someone cleared their throat.

"Hang on." I finished tucking her in.

"Oh, he's a cutie pie." Hazel peered around my shoulder and waved wildly, her hand once again tangling in the line.

"Would you hold still?" I fixed her up and turned to look at the "cutie pie."

The doctor, who appeared too young to shave, smiled. "Hello." He checked Hazel's chart and leaned against the small desk in the room, his arms crossed. "Who is everyone?"

I introduced myself and the kids. Hazel waved again. "I'm Hazel Howard. You can call me Hazel. Or just call me." She batted her eyelashes before glaring at me. "She tried to smother me."

"No, I didn't." I rolled my eyes. "She's enjoying the pain medication."

"I see that. So, here's what we have." He proceeded to bombard us with medical terms and explanations.

Carter held up a hand. "Doc, what does all that mean? Does Grandma need surgery?"

"Yes, sorry." He patted Hazel's leg. "We'll keep you comfortable, Mrs. Howard, and tomorrow we'll fix your hip." He left without a backward glance.

"So, so cute," Hazel said. Her eyes fluttered closed. "Wish he'd call me Hazel though."

After checking with the nurse, I decided to stay with Hazel and sent the kids home. "Tomorrow, when I find out the time of the surgery, I'll call you," I said as Carter and Cynthia got ready to leave. Hazel snored and fidgeted in her sleep. "If I need you before, I'll let you know."

Chloe also called and promised to come out the next day.

John texted me, and I snuck up to Lauree's room to visit, thankful she'd go home soon. When I left her to return to Hazel's, I passed a bank of windows and noticed the sun had set. The dark sky reflected my mood. What a long day. I still didn't know where Shortie was being kept. Surely, he was safe. Babs was dead. I stopped in the nearby family room, sat, and bowed my head.

"I have so much to ask You for, but I also want to thank You. Thank You for Hazel being okay, for getting to visit my grandbaby today, and for my family and friends. Please continue to heal Lauree, and keep Shortie safe, wherever he is. Help Marcus find him. I pray for guidance to live in Your will. Amen."

Someone tapped my shoulder.

"I saw you praying," said an older woman. Wrinkles lined her face, but her eyes twinkled, holding a look of sturdiness and faith. This woman had seen things. She'd lived a life.

"Yes?" I asked.

She held out her hand. "May I pray with you?"

The following morning, the kids returned, and we found our seats in the surgical waiting room. After several hours, the cutie pie doctor approached.

"Your mother-in-law did very well," he said. "She's in recovery, and after that, she'll go to a room. We'll find a skilled nursing facility for her to have rehab." He nodded and left.

"Wait a minute." I hurried to catch him, but he vanished around a corner. I collapsed into the chair that, by now, held an identifiable impression of my backside. "What did he mean by skilled nursing and rehab?"

Cynthia shrugged. "No idea."

Last night's extra prayers with the mysterious woman made Hazel's and my night easier, but hours passed this morning while the kids and I waited for her surgery to take place and for her to get into recovery.

"Want more coffee, Mom?" Carter stood. He rolled his shoulders and stretched. "This waiting is for the birds."

"Birds are what started all of this," I muttered. "I've had enough coffee. I'd like to have some questions answered if the doctor ever comes by."

Cynthia lay her head on my shoulder. "The birds aren't at fault, Mom. Is it time to schedule another outing?"

"I don't know about that." Shortie was MIA, Hazel was laid up in the hospital or skilled nursing for who knew how long, Owen remained in prison for last month's escapades, and Sylvia and Anna were dead. I didn't see any birding trips in my future. What about Carmen? I needed to speak with her and thank her for her help with the code enforcement information. I grabbed my phone.

"Be right back." I walked down the hall to avoid disturbing other family members in the waiting room. Talking with Carmen would be a break from the hospital setting.

"Hi, Peg," she said. "I've been meaning to call you."

"We've been busy." I told her about Hazel and Shortie.

"I'm glad Hazel will be okay, but Shortie? She took him?" Her voice rose. "That Estelle. What a hateful woman." She huffed and fussed about Estelle and her concern for Shortie before she said, "I may have news on those missing egrets for you."

"Really? We spoke with code enforcement. The lady helped us. She thinks someone got into their program and wiped his company clean. Hazel and I believe it was Derek's wife, Marilyn."

"That reinforces what I've learned." She paused. Papers being flipped or shifted came through the line. "Okay, I have friends in all kinds of places, you understand? After working as a real estate agent for so many years, I'm acquainted with a lot of county and city employees. People tell me things."

"Okay?" Where was she going with this?

"One of my friends—I'm using the term in the loosest of ways—told me about a new group of egrets over in Avalon Beach," she said.

"Off the interstate?"

"Yes, near Milton."

"Do they have creeks there?" I couldn't picture what the area looked like.

"It's Florida, Peg. There are creeks, marshes, lakes, you name it, everywhere."

True. "How do we know if these are our egrets?"

"I have no idea. But he did say they weren't there, and then three or four weeks ago, he saw a whole new population," she said.

Interesting. Time-wise, it added up. "What's your friend's name?"

"Finch. He's Roger Keaton's son. But he's not bad like his father. Don't think that," she said.

Finch? His name kept coming up. I suspected him more and more. Was she right about him not being bad like his dad?

CHAPTER 28

I TOOK MY TIME walking back to the waiting room, mentally reviewing everything I knew so far about Finch Keaton. Talking to Charlene might fill in some of the gaps. I checked in with the kids. All three snoozed in the waiting room chairs. When I tapped Chloe's shoulder, she opened her eyes.

"Nothing else has happened." She stretched and winced when her chair squeaked.

"Mind if I make another call?"

"No." She closed her eyes. At least someone could sleep. As a young mom, I'd been just like her, but now, I needed to move around and talk to people, or I'd be down for the count.

When Charlene answered, I asked about her hand and if she and Finch ever solved their problems.

"My hand is fine. I kickbox for fun. And those issues with my brother? They go way back." She chuckled. "He deserved the punch after all these years."

I leaned against a window across from the bank of elevators. "Charlene, who is his mother? You've never said, but I think you know."

She sighed heavily. "Her name is Kitty. Kitty Lynch."

My knees wobbled. "Really?"

"Yes, really." She chuckled again, but this time without mirth. "She always spoke so sweetly. I never trusted her. She struck me as dangerous, if that makes sense. She's right up there with my stepmother. Wouldn't surprise me if the two of them were in cahoots."

"Why didn't you tell me before?" I couldn't depend on Charlene. I knew that now. What else had she withheld from me?

"I'm sick of my father's mistakes, ex-wives, my half-brother. The whole family is a mess," she said.

I understood that. After thanking her for finally telling me what I needed to know, I ended the call. Kitty had overnighted her yearbooks to me. What would I find in them?

After a short time in recovery, Hazel was moved to a room on the third floor. Cynthia mentioned something about her classes, and I sent her and Carter home. Chloe stayed until we realized Hazel planned to sleep for a while. The nurse assured me she wouldn't have a roommate, brought me a pillow and a blanket, and encouraged me to stretch out in the recliner.

"Now, if I could turn off my brain," I said, leaning back and forcing the recliner to balance. As soon as I moved onto my side, the thing flew back to the sitting position and almost tossed me on the floor.

Hazel shifted on the bed. "What? Peg?"

"Shh." I scooted my cranky seat and want-to-be bed closer to her side and reached for her hand. "You're in the hospital. You're safe."

She tugged on my hand, and I leaned over her. "What?"

Her eyes popped open. "Finch. He took the egrets, remember?"

Oh, yeah. I hit myself on the forehead. "Thanks. Go back to sleep." She snuggled into her pillow and snored. "Okay, recliner. One more time." I pushed on the arms, forcing the footrest up. Taking tiny breaths, so as to not upset my balance, I closed my eyes and prayed for rest.

Whoever said hospitals are noisy and you can't get any sleep told the truth. Hazel's nurse came in and out, adjusted things, and noted her vitals. She tried to be quiet, but the little table she dragged around, equipped with her laptop and various devices, squeaked. I heard it coming down the hall and going in and out of the rooms around us.

By the time the morning shift came in, I'd already washed my face and brushed my teeth. I didn't use the little travel toothbrush left for Hazel. My finger and the hospital toothpaste worked fine. Minty fresh.

When physical therapy came to work with Hazel, I used that as an excuse to leave for breakfast. Her mood had gone downhill since the doctor reduced her pain meds. The fact that she'd broken her hip and would need rehab was hitting us both, and we needed a break from each other. I followed my nose to the cafeteria and found the coffee vendor. After ordering, I took my large blueberry muffin to a nearby table. I sat in a sugar daze until someone called my name.

"Peg, did you hear me?" Marcus approached me.

"Mornin.' What are you doing here?" I pushed out a chair with my foot.

He tucked his crutches under the table.

"You're sitting down better," I said.

He grinned, and his dimple popped out. I averted my eyes, thankful to hear the barista calling my name.

"Want anything?" I stood to get my coffee.

He shook his head and waited for my return.

"Long night?" He twirled his finger at my hair.

"Always with the hair." I ran my fingers through the top and sides, fluffing the back. "Better?"

His lips twitched. "I was teasing, Peg." He reached for my coffee and took a gulp. "Wow, that's hot."

"It's fresh, duh." I winked. "Anyhow, why are you here?"

He wiped his mouth with the back of his hand. "I checked on Hazel. She said you ran away, and I followed my nose to the coffee place."

Smart man. He understood me better than I thought he did. "Any news on anything? Shortie, Marilyn, Babs?" I offered him a small chunk of my blueberry muffin.

"Babs is dead." He chewed and swallowed. "Marilyn is too. We think Shortie is alive."

The muffin sat in my stomach like a rock. "Marcus, he has to be alive. Please find him." I told him about the yearbooks and Finch's mother.

He sat back, arms crossed on his chest, nodding at my words. "You're not going to tell me anything else?" Here, I gave him all I knew, and he still wasn't letting me in.

He shifted in his chair and met my gaze, then leaned in. "We've had eyes on Shortie. Estelle is living at some kind of apartment compound kind of place. They've moved him to different buildings twice that we've observed. I promise we're doing everything we can."

"Okay. Will you tell me where he is?"

"I can't endanger you or him," he said.

"I understand." I squeezed his hand. "Thank you."

"You want to get out of here?" His eyes twinkled.

"Yes." I balled up my napkin and muffin wrapper and stuffed them into my empty coffee cup. "Can you take me by Hazel's house? The yearbooks should have arrived yesterday."

He reached for his crutches. "Not exactly what I had in mind, but okay. I'm game." We left the cafeteria. "What do you think you'll find in them?"

"I'm hoping to connect more dots."

He led me to a shiny new red Camaro and opened the passenger door.

"Pretty car." I ran my hand along the side of it before climbing in. He shut the door and got in his side. "I've never seen you in anything besides the cruiser."

"I'm full of surprises." He started the vehicle, the motor purring loudly.

That's for sure. Every time I saw him, I learned new things about him. He told me all the specs about the Camaro on the short drive to Hazel's. I nodded, as if I understood what he said. "Shortie is restoring old cars. He has a Camaro too, I think."

Marcus tapped his fingers on the steering wheel. "Really." He pulled into Hazel's driveway and parked.

"Yeah." I opened my door. "I don't understand anything he tells me either." I winked and closed the door.

He maneuvered his way out of his side and placed his crutches under his arms. "Funny woman. Did you ever talk to him? About the proposal?"

He reached my side as I unlocked the front door. "Nope." I still didn't know what to tell Shortie. Right now, my only concern was for his safety.

Marcus reached for my hand and turned me toward him. He caressed my cheek before leaning forward. A light kiss on my lips, and he straightened up. "Keep me in mind, okay?"

I traced his dimple. "Yep."

Charlie Brown greeted us with a woof. I refilled his food and water and took him outside to do his business. Roscoe chirped happily when I added food to his cage. I joined Marcus at the dining table, where he studied a brown box sealed with packing tape. I found scissors and tore it open. Four yearbooks nestled in brown paper. They ranged from 1975 to 1978. I lifted one out and handed another to Marcus.

He laid it on the table and took a seat. "What am I looking for?"

I pulled out the chair opposite him. "Marilyn, Derek, Estelle, Sylvia Newman, Roger. They all went to school together at Woodham High School. Babs and Marla Braden too."

"Really? I may hire you when this case is over." He thumbed through the book. "Kitty sent these?"

I explained my conversation with her. "She said she was friends with Babs and the Crofts. Remember the picture I found of Estelle and Derek at prom?"

"Yeah." He pulled out his notebook and wrote the list of names. "Anyone else? Estelle kept her high school circle close."

"Now that I think about it,"—I propped my elbow on the table—"Babs never told me she went to high school with Derek. She said she had an affair with him. Interesting."

"Not to be morbid, but we can't ask her now. Does it even apply to our case?"

"No idea." I waved him back to his book and continued to study mine. I finished flipping through 1975 and pulled out 1977. "This was the year Estelle went to prom with Derek." I found the picture and turned the yearbook around to show it to him. "I'm not sure who the other couple is standing with them in the second picture, but this is the one I found at the library."

He ran his finger under the words beneath the picture. "This one is Kitty." He tapped the woman's face. "We've seen her at the compound with Estelle. My men have sent me pictures of her."

"Really?" I pulled the book back to me, stood, and checked the top of the box. "She mailed this from Pensacola, not overnight from Colorado. She told me she lived in Colorado and how much she missed Florida." I plopped onto my seat. "That little liar."

CHAPTER 29

Discovering Kitty's lies astonished me. After I repeated, "She's a liar," several times, Marcus interrupted me.

"You have to stop," he said. "She's a criminal. She's in cahoots with Estelle Keaton. You can't trust her." He flipped through the final yearbook before stuffing them all back in the box. "I'm taking these. Now that we have our fingerprints all over them."

I leaned back in my chair, arms crossed, my mind whirring—Finch, Kitty, Estelle—and everything I'd learned. "I'm forgetting something." I tapped the side of my head. "Can I see the ones from '77 and '78 again?"

He handed them over and propped his chin on his hand. "What are you looking for?"

"I'll know it when I see it." I flipped through the pages to the back of the yearbook, where pictures were sorted in a semi-logical order. "Okay, here we go. I'm in the 'most likely' categories." I ran my finger over the photos. "Right here." I tapped the page. "Derek Croft and Estelle Keaton, most likely to marry."

Marcus grunted. "That didn't happen. Good thing for him, or he might be dead."

"You do have a sense of humor. I've always wondered." I winked to soften my sarcasm.

"Funny woman. You almost finished? I do have a job."

"Not yet. None of the others are in these." The following section featured sports. "Roger was a big-time football player. No surprise there," I said.

"He probably used that to sharpen his intimidation skills." Marcus yawned. "I'm going to make some coffee. Where are the kids?" He shuffled into the kitchen.

"Where are your crutches?" I rushed them to him. "You need these. Even in the house."

"Yes, doc." He placed one under each arm, and I smoothed the wrinkles on his forehead with my thumb.

"I'll make the coffee. Go sit on the couch and put your leg up." Carter's and Cynthia's doors were both shut. "I assume the kids are asleep. We'll know when Cynthia gets up because Lucy will bark."

I added bread to the toaster and started the coffeepot. After slathering butter and grape jelly on the toast, I poured two mugs of coffee and carefully carried them into the living room. CB scooted up beside Marcus's feet and did his best impression of a starving dog.

"Hey, buddy," Marcus crooned. "Here you go." He tossed him half his crust. CB caught it mid-air and gulped. "Good boy!" CB wagged his tail.

"He shouldn't be begging. Hazel will be mad if we undo her years of training in one morning."

"Hazel trained him?" He sent another bite of toast the dog's way.

"I don't think so. He's a sweet fellow, though. She's going to miss him when she's in rehab. I spent some time in there. It's tough."

"Someone in the waiting room mentioned therapy dogs. That would cheer her up." I set my mug on the coffee table. "I'll miss her too. More than the dog and the bird."

He smiled.

"What?"

"You two weren't, well, let's just say you didn't seem to be the best of friends when I first met you. It would be hard to live with your mother-in-law."

"We grew on each other." I munched on my toast. "I want to look at more of the yearbook pictures." I carried both books back to the couch. "Derek and Estelle must have been close if they labeled them most likely to marry."

"Silly teenage stuff." He repositioned his leg on the coffee table. "Being a teenager was the worst. How did you raise three of them and have them turn out to be good people?"

I studied him.

"What?" He rubbed his jaw. "Jelly?"

"No, I'm wondering something, but I'm not sure how to ask."

He shrugged. "Ask. I won't answer if I can't. You know that."

"This has nothing to do with the case. I wondered ..." I fiddled with the page. "Well, I wondered if you still want kids." The words came out in a rush, and I held my breath while waiting for his answer.

He sat back, head tipped, no dimple in sight. "No. Not really."

"Okay. You're sure?"

He reached over and tugged one of my curls. "My wife was younger than I by about ten years. I loved my daughter very much, don't get me wrong. But I'm kind of old to go through all of it again."

That answered my question. I glanced through the remainder of the yearbook and flipped to the other one. "Here's a picture of Kitty, and I think Marilyn and Babs. Hard to tell. Possibly some kind of court or homecoming."

The tiny print under the picture confirmed the women's identities. I flipped to another page. "Look. Kitty and Roger, king and queen of homecoming. The little liar."

Marcus pushed himself off the couch. "I need to go. Do you want a ride to the hospital?"

"No, I've got my car here."

He dropped a kiss on my forehead. "Bring the box, will you? I can't carry it and use these." He pointed to his crutches.

I followed him to the Camaro and dropped the box into his trunk. "Where's this all leading?" I leaned against the side of his car.

He put his forearm on the doorframe next to me. "You and me?" He trailed his finger down my cheek. Warmth flooded my chest.

"No. Yes, but no. The case. The birds, Finch, Derek, Estelle. Too many moving parts."

He opened his door and got in. "Not your moving parts to worry about, remember?" He revved the engine and left me standing, hand shading my eyes against the mid-morning sun.

The birds. I knew where they were. Carmen had told me.

I never saw the egrets when they lived in the creek in Hazel's neighborhood. But I'd seen pictures and knew what to look for. Adult snowy egrets were white with black bills and black stick-thin legs. Their yellow feet would be hard to spot in marshy areas.

Finch told Carmen about a new egret colony at Avalon Beach. I left the kids a note explaining I would return soon, texted Hazel to check on her, and set out on the less-than-twenty-minute drive. When I left the interstate, I only made it a few miles before spotting the area. I pulled to the side of the road and parked.

My cell phone rang before I got out of the car. "Hey, Harry."

"What are you up to today?"

"I think I've found our missing egrets." I explained about Finch and Carmen.

Harry whistled. "Interesting. Take a few pictures of them and send them to me."

"Okay." I did what he asked and waited.

"From what I can tell, they appear healthy. I don't think the sticky substance hurt them."

"According to Derek's receptionist, Finch moved the egrets for Derek." Although he couldn't see me, I shook my head. "You would not believe the tangled web these people have weaved."

"Woven?"

"Harry, that's not the point. The point is, the birds are safe. Derek wanted them out of the way so he could build his little rental houses. After I bring the issue to the code enforcement lady's attention, he can't go forward with his plans."

"Do you think this Finch killed Marilyn?" In the background, birds squawked.

"Maybe," I paused. "I'm saying that a lot with this investigation."

"You are. How is Hazel? Cynthia texted me about her hip."

I grimaced, sorry I hadn't thought to let him know. I filled him in on the latest and explained what I found in the yearbooks. He started laughing before I finished the story.

"What's so funny?" I asked.

"You. You say you don't want to investigate or be involved, but you, my friend, are quite involved."

I wrinkled my nose. "You called me, remember?"

"Oh, yeah." He cleared his throat. "I was thinking about Carmen."

"Oh?" Where was he going with this?

"Yes." He gave a nervous laugh. "I might ask her out on a date, er … to dinner or a movie?"

Hmm, I never pictured the two of them together before. "She might like that." I grinned.

"Ha ha. Can I have her number?"

"I don't give out women's numbers. Even to you. I will text her yours, though." Out of the corner of my eye, I spotted a speck of white flapping in the breeze, tucked under some leaves about five feet in front of my car. "I need to go, but I'll let her know you're interested."

I hung up and texted Carmen explaining Harry's request before getting out of my car. "Please don't be a dead bird." I approached slowly. As I drew closer, I saw a notebook. "Why's that out here?" I pulled it out from under the leaves and brushed dirt off it. A closer inspection of the pages answered many of my questions and created lots of others.

"Hmm, I need to call Harry again." I pulled out my phone, but before I placed the call, someone jerked a hood over my head and muscled arms wrapped around my waist.

CHAPTER 30

I KICKED AND SCREAMED and struggled until whoever captured me wrapped tape around my legs and upper body and stuffed me inside a vehicle. They didn't tape my mouth, thankfully, but hollering in a moving car driven by some bad guy wouldn't help me anyway. I needed to think.

After wiggling and rolling as much as possible, I figured out they'd tossed me into the back of an SUV. I went still. Movement exhausted me. The hood restricted my breathing. I didn't know what to do next.

The notebook I'd found in the grass was a ledger that, to my eyes, indicated a smuggling ring. Someone—Estelle, I assumed—was stealing birds and trafficking them into and out of the country. Some of the birds originated in Central and South America, while others were taken from the United States and transported to other countries. From what I knew about the listed birds, they seemed rare. Parrots and Macaws were endangered. The ledger included them, as well as Myna birds and Cockatoos.

The egrets were safe, though. I'd seen them with my own eyes. I couldn't make the necessary connections between them and the smugglers. I whispered a prayer for wisdom and understanding and waited. Whatever these people had in mind for me, I wouldn't go down without a fight.

I couldn't tell how long or far the car traveled before it came to a stop. My stomach crumpled into knots, and I struggled to control my breathing. If Estelle was behind my kidnapping, I knew she didn't mind killing.

The back of the SUV opened, and a little slice of sunlight filtered through the hood's material.

"What do we do with her now?" a deep voice asked.

"Let's put her with the guy 'till the boss gets back," another man said. One of them grabbed my ankles and pulled. The other got me under my arms, and they swung me out of the vehicle.

Were they talking about Shortie? Where had they taken me? Besides sunshine, I heard waves, and it sounded like the two men walked on gravel. Something crunchy and uneven, judging by how hard of a time they had carrying me. Instead of holding my body stiffly, I let myself go limp—anything to make them work harder and possibly make a mistake.

Something squealed open and slammed closed, the sun disappeared, and the men set me on my feet.

"I'm gonna cut the tape around your ankles so you can walk up the steps. Behave, and don't forget I have a knife."

The man's nasty breath reached my nose, and I turned my head. I almost fell over when the tape loosened before strong hands held me upright. Climbing stairs would be easier if I could also use my hands, but I didn't want to ask. Not yet. Adrenaline shot through me. Harry had an idea of where I'd been with the egrets, but no one would be looking for me anytime soon. Marcus was at work, Hazel was in the hospital, and my kids were sleeping when I left.

All I had were my wits, such as they were. I stomped up the stairs, hoping noise might alert someone. One of the men nudged me.

"No reason to do that. No one's around who cares. But hey, knock yourself out."

So, I did. I continued clomping as hard as possible, letting them see some of my anger. We reached a landing, and someone knocked on a door. It opened, and a woman said, "Finally. I didn't think we'd ever catch her."

I knew the voice. One of my captors removed my hood, and my mouth dropped open. "Charlene?"

She swept her hand toward the inside of her condo. "Please, come in and join us."

I stepped back. Was her condo the compound Marcus talked about? None of this made sense, and I didn't want to enter her lair. Especially now that I knew she was involved with Shortie's disappearance, judging by what the men said. One of them pushed me forward, and I stumbled into the room. I looked up and had the third—or maybe the fourth—revelation for the day. "Estelle Keaton? And you must be Kitty."

Both women sat on the couch that Hazel and I had occupied only days before. One of them rose and offered her hand. "Yes, Kitty Lynch. It's wonderful to meet you, Ms. Howard."

My hands were still taped to my side. I fluttered my fingertips as an icy feeling spread throughout my body. The room spun, and my eyes closed.

Someone grabbed my upper arms. "Take this tape off her." Charlene ground out the words and shook me, whispering in my ear, "Now is not the time. Hold it together."

Once they freed me from the tape, Charlene shoved me onto a chair. One of the men stood beside me, his hand resting on the butt of his gun. The other stood in front of the door, an automatic rifle strapped across his chest.

"Do we have to be so uncouth?" Kitty asked, her southern-belle accent on full display. She sat beside Estelle and crossed her skinny legs, the red sole of her shoe showing as she swung her foot back and forth like a metronome. She leaned toward me. "Now, Ms. Howard ..."

"Mrs." I spat the word at her. "It's Mrs. Howard."

She sat back. I waited for her to pull out a fan, flip it open, and clutch her pearls. Instead, her eyes narrowed, and her lip curled. "Should we just throw her in with him?" Her accent vanished.

By my calculations, Shortie had been missing for a week. "What have you done to him?"

"Why do you care?" Estelle spoke up. "We've seen you gallivanting around with that handsome detective of yours. Love the dimple, by the way."

I studied her. My nemesis. The bane of my existence for the last eight months. Some might say that if I had never started the Empty Nesters Birding Group, no one would have died, but I didn't think it was true. Estelle Keaton was a killer at heart.

I needed to be careful.

"Thank you, he is handsome. Quite smart also." I turned to Charlene, who sat apart from the two women. "I never thought you'd be mixed up with your stepmother. You were so intimidated by her, as I remember from your mother's funeral."

Charlene's nostrils flared. "That happened months ago." She stared at her hands, twisting the rings on her fingers.

Estelle stood and approached her stepdaughter. Afternoon sunlight streamed through the sliding glass doors, highlighting the dangerous glint in her eyes. She set her hand on Charlene's shoulder, long red nails digging in. Charlene winced. "I had to find"—she dug in again—"the right motivation." The corners of Estelle's mouth tipped up. "Everyone has something that motivates them."

I knew that was true. "Sylvia found the hummingbird first, didn't she? Not you." I studied Kitty. "Did you know? She killed Sylvia, your old school pal, out of pride. She wanted bragging rights, but Sylvia claimed them."

"It was *my* rufous hummingbird." Estelle let go of Charlene and pointed a thin finger at me. "You're wrong."

Kitty's eyebrow twitched. Should I keep poking the bear? I crossed my legs, imitating her. I may not have on fancy shoes, but I knew something they didn't. I pressed on.

"She got our former mayor to do the dirty deed, but she masterminded everything. Did your friend tell you that? Then,"—I cleared my throat—"she brought quetzals into the country."

Kitty nodded. "She told me."

"That's where you came in?" I asked, observing the silent exchange between her and Estelle. "Huh. It was, wasn't it? I didn't know." I pretended to be disappointed.

Estelle sat on the couch and waved a hand. "You don't know anything, Ms. Howard." She emphasized "Ms."

"Well, those quetzals are in a better place now. They're even making more little quetzals. Harry made sure."

"You've made friends, I see. That's different." She sneered.

My weak point. At least it used to be. Once, I thought I could make it on my own, with a bit of help from Lauree. Now I had a larger circle of family and friends to draw from.

Outside, two blue jets flew over the bay. A loud roaring sound filled the room, and we all paused to watch them.

"Do you know why you hear the sound after seeing the jets?" I asked. "Sound travels slower than they do. Kind of like when you hear thunder after seeing lightning." I thought of Owen and remembered how lightning shattered the glass doors he stood by, and how a large chunk of glass pinned him to the wall, keeping him prisoner until the police arrived.

I didn't see that happening this time.

"Enough talk," Estelle said. "Put her with her friend." She gestured to the two men.

The one closest to me reached out. I jerked away from him. They hadn't taped me up or handcuffed me. I had to get away. The other man swung his gun around. Going through the front door wasn't an option. I eyed the glass door.

CHAPTER 31

BEFORE I COULD MAKE my move, the front door burst open and a man stumbled inside, knocking the armed guard out of the way.

Kitty jumped up. "Finch, dear, what's wrong?" She ran her hands down his arms until he pulled away from her.

Finch? What was he doing here? I glanced from him to the three women. I remembered what one of my kidnappers had said. "*You're the boss?*" I asked.

He ignored my incredulous tone, leaned over, hands on his thighs, panting. "They're onto us." He looked at Estelle. "I don't know how, but they are."

My pulse raced. Marcus was coming. I knew it.

"How?" Estelle roared.

"Who?" Kitty asked.

Charlene stood and approached her half-brother. "Calm down. No one knows where we are."

"Yes, they"—the words left my mouth without any thought—"do." I whispered the last word.

Estelle took a step toward me. "How?"

I bit my lips together.

Her jaw tightened, her lips pulled thin, and her eyes went blank. She snapped her fingers in my face. "Tell me." She held my gaze until I couldn't stand it any longer.

"Marcus said you have a compound. He's seen you and Kitty. And Shortie."

Then the three women all laughed in that genteel way snooty women sometimes do.

"You are a darling." Kitty's accent reappeared. "Isn't she?" She patted Estelle's arm. "Just a hoot. But I do have a question?" Her eyes glinted with glee.

I regretted my outburst. I hadn't helped myself or Shortie by giving them information. "What?"

"Why do you think we've done all this?" She fluttered her fingers and sat back, a satisfied expression on her face.

"Pride, greed," I said. "Lust of the flesh, lust of the eyes, and the pride of life."

"Huh?" Finch's brows drew together. "What are you talking about?"

He didn't know I quoted part of First John chapter two. "Estelle, your pride over the hummingbird is what got Sylvia killed."

"Well, and she slept with my husband." Estelle wrinkled her nose, her tone and face filled with disgust.

Charlene flinched. I imagined Estelle's words hurt, as Charlene was the product of their union.

I pointed to Kitty. "You and Roger were homecoming king and queen."

She nodded. "We sure were. He was so handsome. A great kisser too." A dreamy look crossed her face.

Estelle snapped her fingers. "Focus. Finch, we were about to put Peg here with her old boyfriend. Does that sound like a plan?"

What hold did he have over these three women? Estelle acted as if he were in charge.

He shrugged. "I don't care what you do with her, but you have to believe me. They know where we are." He crossed his arms and leaned against the door.

"Duh." I clamped my hands over my mouth. I had to stop letting every thought that flew through my brain escape my mouth.

He cocked his head. "What do you know?" He pulled up a chair beside me and sat.

Another pair of jets shrieked by, startling me. Traffic was bumper-to-bumper on the bridge from Gulf Breeze to Pensacola Beach. Even this late in the day, tourists and die-hard Blue Angels fans wanted to enjoy the show. Boats of all makes dotted the bay. I remembered what Charlene said about how the traffic backed up on Blue Angel weekend, and how hard it was to get in and out of her place.

What about the police? Could they get through? *Hurry Marcus.*

Finch patted my leg. "They're practicing today. The real show is on Saturday."

I pulled away from his touch. "Yes, I know."

He scooted his chair closer so our legs touched. "Tell me what else you know. The bug we planted helped, but you made me remove it." He grinned.

It took everything in me not to smack his smarmy face.

He crossed his arms over his chest. "Explain what you meant about lust of the flesh and eyes. I'm curious."

When I didn't respond, his eyes darkened. "Now."

I shifted on my chair, trying to put more space between our bodies. "Like I said, your stepmother's pride led to her killing one of her friends. She wanted the fame and notoriety that came with claiming the hummingbird. Sylvia took it from her."

"Okay, and ..." He motioned with his hand for me to continue.

"Lust of the flesh is fairly simple, Finch."

"Sex, food, that kind of thing?"

I glanced around the room. Roger used these women. He'd cheated on his wife with Sylvia, resulting in Charlene's birth, and with Kitty, ending in Finch being born. A tiny part of me felt sorry for Estelle—an itsy, bitsy tiny part.

"What about lust of the eyes?" he asked.

I moved again but couldn't inch any further away from him. My left side was almost flush against the wall beside the sliding door's handle. He elbowed me, and I jumped.

"Material possessions. Like smuggling rare and endangered birds. Greed." The words burst out. I focused on him while I reached up with my left hand and nudged the handle to test how easily the door would open. It slid just a smidge without making a sound before sticking. It wouldn't budge anymore.

"Enough!" Estelle stood and clapped her hands. "We don't need your input." She pointed to the armed men. "Take her. Throw her in with that man. Maybe when she sees him, she'll shut up."

They grabbed me again, one under my arms and one holding my ankles. I kicked and yelled until one of my legs got loose and encountered a wall. My knee buckled, and my scream of anger turned into one of agony.

"Quit moving." The guard holding my ankles grunted. He got a firmer grip, and I whimpered against the pain. "Serves you right," he hissed.

They took me through one room and into another. It seemed as if two condos were connected. This had to be what Marcus meant by a compound.

I continued to holler until a door opened and the guards tossed me into a room. I landed with a thud, my knee crunching under me and heard the door close.

"Ow, ow, ow." I rolled onto my side, holding my leg, tears streaming down my face.

"Who's there?"

I froze at the voice. "Shortie? Is that you?"

"Peg? What are you doing here?"

I collapsed on my back, pain soaring up my leg. "Where have you been?" I panted through the nausea.

A raw chuckle came, followed by his raspy voice. "Here."

I swept my hands to each side of me. "Where are you?"

"Hang on. Keep talking."

He followed my voice and reached my side. "You're hurt?" He held my hand.

I squeezed his fingers. "My knee. I kicked the wall when they brought me in."

Another chuckle. "Not surprised."

I pushed myself to a sitting position and took deep breaths to control my rolling stomach. I leaned against him. "How are you? What did they do to you?"

He shifted and held me closer. "The day I was supposed to pick you up? I went out to my Jeep, and I guess the guy had hidden in the back seat. I started the car, and the next thing I knew, I woke up in this room. How long have I been here?"

"It's been a week. We've been so worried."

"Kim? Does she know I'm missing?"

I patted his leg. "Yes, Cynthia talked to her. Marcus has been searching for you. He told me the police found a compound. That's what he called it." My knee turned, and I gritted my teeth against the pain. "He said they spotted you, Estelle, and Kitty."

"Yeah, they took me outside and into another building a few times. I got the impression none of them know who's in charge." He ran his hand through his hair. "I think it might be some guy? Who's Kitty?"

I explained what happened in the week he'd been gone, as well as Kitty's role in the whole thing.

"Hazel?" Sadness filled his voice. "She's okay?"

"Yes, she had surgery and was her old ornery self when I left the hospital." Tears welled up and spilled over. Would I see her again? What about my kids and grandbaby? And Marcus?

Shortie wrapped his arms around me. "I never thought I'd see you again." He leaned his head against mine.

I wiped my face with the backs of my hands. "How do we get out?"

He grunted. "I've tried. Many times."

My eyes slowly adjusted to the dark. On one wall were slits of light. "What is this room?"

"It's a living room, I think. You can't tell right now, but there's a blanket in the corner." He drew in a slow breath, then released it. "They let me out to use the bathroom. Craziest hostage situation I've ever heard of."

I didn't think they were professionals except for Estelle. I hung my head. "If I'd never started the birding group, none of this would have happened. Anna, Sylvia, and Kurt would still be alive. Even Marilyn and Babs."

"None of this is your fault, Peg." He jiggled my shoulder. "None. Never think that. These people are bad."

I sniffled. "Finch seems to be the boss, but it doesn't make sense." I explained his relationship to Kitty and Estelle.

"He must have something over them."

But what? My brain, functional on a good day, now only told me how much my knee hurt. I ran my hands over the swollen joint. "Doesn't feel like anything's broken."

"You're a doctor now?" he asked, a smile in his voice.

"Mhm." I leaned against him, and we were quiet for several minutes. Outside, more jets roared past, and an idea came to me.

"You said this is a living room?"

"Yeah." He straightened his legs. "There are blackout curtains over the glass. But they're inside it. Blackout blinds, I guess." His stomach growled.

"Do they feed you?"

"Usually. I think it's dinnertime."

"Is it lighter in here in the morning? There's no light switch?" I scooted closer to the window, grimacing at the pain in my leg.

"Yeah, no switch. There's more light in the morning around the edges, but not a lot." He stood and followed me. "Here, give me your hand."

He pulled me up to stand, and I leaned against him, allowing him to take the weight of my bad leg. I searched the edges of the window frame for the lever that controlled the blinds.

"I tried that," he said.

"Yeah, but it can't hurt to try again." I felt underneath the window ledge. "Over in Charlene's place, this was a sliding glass door."

"They must have changed it when they connected the rooms."

"I think so." A small piece of wood protruded in one area. I reached for his hand. "Feel this?"

He leaned forward, and at the same time, the door behind us opened.

"What are you two doing?" One of the guards slammed the door shut and clicked on a high-beam flashlight. "Get away from the window. Now!"

I blinked away the bright spots from the sudden light and glanced around the room. A couple of blankets were bundled up on one side, but I didn't see anything else. Nothing useful to help us anyhow. Shortie put his arms around me.

"We need to sit down. Ready?"

I nodded and attempted to keep my leg straight when I sat. Pain shot up from my knee, and I gasped.

"I got you." He tightened his grip.

The guard came closer. "Dinnertime." He whistled, and another guard holding two paper bags came inside. He held both above us and shook them.

"Time to eat," he said in a sing-song cartoony voice. He dropped the bags, cackling with glee. "Might be a bit mushy. Oops."

They left, and we tore open the bags to find two small bowls of soup—the covers survived the fall—plus one spoon, a chunk of bread, and half a cookie. The other half was more crumbs than cookie. One of the bags held a mini bottle of water.

"This will be fun," Shortie said. He brushed the crumbs into his hand and popped them in his mouth before he handed me the half cookie.

The light coming through the gaps in the blinds continued to fade. As we ate our tiny meal, I prayed for help to come. Surely Marcus would find me.

CHAPTER 32

AFTER DINNER, SHORTIE CONVINCED me to lie down. My knee swelled to what I hoped was its max. The pain became more than I could handle. I dozed off once I found a comfortable position. When I woke up, I heard a scratching noise.

"Shortie? Is that you?" Please, Lord, don't let there be mice in here.

"Yep. It's me. Why are you awake?" His voice came from across the room.

"What are you doing?" My throat and mouth were dry. The tiny sip of water we shared hadn't gone far.

"I think," he grunted, "the slide for the blinds used to be," another grunt, "under here. Ouch." He groaned. "Splinter number four hundred."

Darkness shrouded the room. "Keep talking." I scooted toward his voice, my uninjured leg extended before me. My foot hit the wall, and Shortie touched my shoulder.

"Over here," he said.

I angled myself, and he guided my hand to where he'd been searching. "Why would it be under here?"

"Not sure," he said. "When they redid this wall, I'm assuming they put in a way to open the window. I don't know. It's a single pane. There's no way to open it now."

"Double-paned if the blinds are inside it." I felt the area again and the knot in the wood where the old slide had once been.

A weary sigh escaped him. "Yeah, true."

"I'm sorry. I didn't mean to discourage you."

"You're fine." He scratched at what sounded like the scruff on his face. "If I wrap my arm in the blanket, I think I can hit the glass hard enough to crack it."

"Have you tried before now?"

"No." He shifted his legs. "I kept thinking someone would come for me. The couple of times I went outside, I looked for a chance to escape, but they held guns on me the whole time."

"I would've been terrified."

He nudged my shoulder. "You're brave, Peg. I think you'd have been home by now, a large cup of coffee in hand.

I smiled. "Extra-large. With whipped cream to celebrate."

He chuckled. "Go back and rest. Nothing else we can do in this dark."

In the morning, light filtered into the room through the edges of the blinds. Shortie slept, using the window ledge as a pillow. I rolled to my side and pushed up to sit. Getting my hurt leg into a decent position took a minute, and I couldn't stifle a yelp.

"Peg?" He yawned. "What are you doing?"

"Sitting up." I studied him. His usually trim beard was scruffy, and he'd lost weight. His shorts hung off his hips. "When's breakfast?"

"There's no coffee, I can tell you that." He stood and stretched before reaching down to help me up.

One of the guards entered. "Bathroom break." He pointed to me. "You first."

I steadied myself and hopped the short distance to the bathroom. Every landing sent a jolt of pain through my body. The guard let me shut the door to the small room. The doorknob didn't have a lock. I did what I needed to do and washed my face and hands in cold water before running my fingers through my hair—anything to help me wake up and be alert. He jerked the door open as I slurped water from my cupped hand.

"You're done. Come on." He waved his rifle.

Once Shortie took his turn, the guard handed us a single paper bag and locked the door. Outside, several boat motors started, and people talked and laughed.

"Another day of Blue Angel practice." A peek inside the bag revealed two small, powdered donuts and two water bottles. I handed Shortie his rations. "Those people have no idea what Estelle is up to in here."

He unscrewed his water and took a long gulp. "Before you showed up yesterday, I heard one guy say a bad storm is coming, and they might move the Blue Angels show to today."

"Hurricane Chloe."

He cocked an eyebrow.

"That's what the name will be if it turns into a hurricane. Chloe, like my daughter's name." I nibbled on my donut.

"Let's hope it doesn't do that." He popped his donut in his mouth and rubbed his stomach. "Yum. If only we had another dozen."

I closed my eyes. "Some glazed and some filled with raspberry."

"And chocolate icing." Shortie licked his fingers. "How's the beard?"

In the dim light, I spotted powder in several spots and pointed to them. "Now I know what you'll look like when you're old and gray."

"Ha. I have gray." He ran his fingers through his hair. "Some of it came from you."

"Funny man." I sat beside him. "Shortie?" I held out my hand, and he wrapped his larger one around it.

"Yeah."

"If I have to be kidnapped, I'm glad it's with you."

"Right back at you." He covered our hands with his other hand. "Peg?"

"Yep."

"I'm sorry. About proposing." He shook his head. "I already knew we weren't marriage material." He blew out a breath. "I was just mad."

I chuckled. "Mad? So you proposed?"

"You're not going to make this easy, are you?"

I grinned. "Nope." Jets blew past the condo. They squealed away, and I pictured them flying over the Gulf. "The sound of freedom."

"Yep." He squeezed my hand. "For the record, I do love you and your kids. And Hazel."

"I love you too." I leaned my head on his shoulder. "We are good friends."

He grunted. "Friends. Yep."

We spent the morning listening to the Blue Angels practicing. I tried to peek through the cracks in the blinds, but I couldn't see anything. When I leaned my ear against the glass, though, I heard people talking.

I waved Shortie over. "Listen. I think it's Finch and Kitty."

He pressed his ear up to the window. "How do you know it's them?"

"The Southern accent. That's Kitty. Finch is younger. I'm pretty sure it's him. Doesn't sound like one of the guards." I closed my eyes to concentrate. "Their deck must be right next to this one."

He started to speak, and I held up a finger. "Hang on. Finch said his dad left everything to him." I stared at Shortie. "Do you know what that means?"

"Who is Finch's dad?"

"Roger Keaton. Keep up here. If Roger willed his estate to Finch, that's why he's the boss. Estelle must have found out. Otherwise, there's no way she would be under Finch's thumb."

"Makes sense," he said. "After everything she's done—killing Sylvia and even Anna—she's used to being in charge." The voices next door went up a notch. "When did Roger die?"

"Estelle killed him a month or so ago. I assume she's who killed Marilyn and Babs."

"Probably. Or got Finch to do her dirty work. They must have just read the will. Kitty sounds mad." He backed away from the window. "You think there's a deck outside of this window?"

I thought back to Hazel and my first visit. "I think so. If I remember correctly."

He nodded and continued to study the area. "If that's true, and I can break the window, we might be able to get down from the deck."

We discussed different options for breaking the glass. Shortie wanted to use the blanket over his elbow. I wondered if he could kick through it. I suggested we do it at night when everyone was asleep.

An expression crossed his face. One I hadn't seen before. "This is our only chance. And what I do will be noisy. What about when the jets are flying? The roaring noise should cover any I make."

"In broad daylight?"

"Late in the afternoon. They do a finale, remember?"

"The sun's still up then." I ran my hand over my knee. "I won't be able to run."

"I'm not leaving you behind." His brows drew low. "We go together or not at all."

"Now I feel like we're in a war."

His smile didn't reach his eyes. "We are."

After a small lunch consisting of one apple and two protein bars, I dozed off. Someone entered our room, and I woke up.

"Charlene?"

"Hi, you two." She wore a cardigan, and from its large pockets, she pulled out two bottles of water and two bananas. "I snuck these out for y'all. Here, let me look at your knee."

Shortie and I made quick work of the bananas. When he finished his water, he asked, "Why are you here?"

She poked and prodded my knee. "I wanted to wrap this to keep it steady. I'm sorry I couldn't do it until now."

Charlene had done a one-eighty again. "What's going on? What do they plan to do with us?" I asked.

She met my gaze. "You have to escape, okay? Y'all are in danger." She searched the room. "There's nothing here to help you. I'll try to have you moved. Somewhere you have a better chance. Everyone's gone, but they'll be back soon. I'll ask Kitty. She'll be more likely to help."

I caught her hand. "Why are you helping us? Why are you helping Finch?"

"Finch." She spat his name. "What a joke. Dad left everything to him. What am I? Nothing, I guess." She turned away, but not before I saw the tears in her eyes.

"Your dad didn't value women, did he?" I asked. He'd proved that in the way he treated his wife.

"I don't want to be here either. But ..." She looked over her shoulder.

"Can you help us get out?" Shortie asked. "Now?"

"No." She wrapped my knee and stood. "They'll be back soon. Wait, okay? Trust me." She put her finger to her lips and backed out of the door.

Not long after, the two guards came in.

"Up," one said.

Shortie helped me hop down the hallway. Between his height and my injured knee, we wobbled a lot.

"Where are we going?" he asked the guard in front of us.

"Be quiet." The one behind us poked me with his gun.

Shortie and I exchanged looks. We wove back through the original condo, Charlene's place. Sunlight streamed down a hallway, catching my attention. At the end was the room where Hazel and I visited Charlene a few days before. I glanced down the hall and saw her and Kitty talking. The front door opened, and two men walked inside. Finch faced me, and when the man by his side turned, I gasped.

"Harry?" His name burst out before I could stop myself.

He saw me, and his face lost all color. He mouthed my name. The guards hurried us through another room and into yet another.

Shortie bent close to my ear. "What's Harry doing here?"

"I don't know." My lips trembled, and tears streamed down my cheeks. Harry, a traitor like Owen? How did it happen? I thought I knew him better than any of the birders besides Shortie.

"Hang in there, Peg." Shortie squeezed me closer. "We'll find a way out."

"Stop talking." The guard poked me again.

The other guard stopped and opened a door. "In here."

We shuffled into a room that must have been a child's bedroom at one time. Sailboat wallpaper covered three of the walls, with the third painted a navy blue. Sunlight streamed through the window. I tipped my face to it, but said nothing. It would be better for us if no one thought to cover it.

The guards left, being sure to lock us inside. Shortie helped me sit in a corner while he inspected the window. "This one has a slide." He slid the blinds closed.

"Sunshine, please." I fiddled with the wrap on my knee.

"But if we leave these closed when they're not in here, they might forget about it."

"Maybe they'll forget to lock the door."

He sat beside me. "Someone's grumpy."

"Why is Harry helping them?" I wailed, unable to stop more tears from rolling down my face. "I understand you don't like him, but he's a really good person. At least, I thought so."

Shortie gave me a questioning glance, one brow raised in silent inquiry. "I thought you were interested in him."

"Harry?" I wiped my cheeks with the backs of my hands. "He's like one of my kids."

"I know. Now." He dropped his head in his hands. "Relationships aren't my strong suit. Just ask my ex-wife."

I peeled his fingers away from his face. "You're a great guy."

He groaned. "Death knell."

"Let me finish." I scooted back, trying to find a better position. "I think our problem was me." He started to protest, and I held up my hand. "I hadn't dated since Zack died. I got a bit carried away. I really liked you. I still do. Really. But I don't think I was ready."

He studied my face. "And Marcus?"

My cheeks burned. "Maybe Marcus," I whispered.

He cracked his knuckles. "He hurts you, and I'll find him."

"I'll let him know." If we ever got out of here.

Chapter 33

Harry's duplicity wrecked me. My heart hurt, and my knee hurt, and I couldn't stop crying. After Owen, I didn't think anyone could betray me quite like that again. Shortie tried to talk me out of it, but I knew what I'd seen. Harry with Finch. How did they know each other? When Harry saw me, he said nothing. Did nothing.

I thought of all the times he'd eaten dinner with us and how Cynthia worked with him—all the conversations we'd enjoyed over the last couple of months.

"Such a rotten man," I said. After I repeated the words several times, Shortie gave up trying to change my mind.

The Blue Angels stopped flying late in the afternoon. We watched the tail end of their practice, standing to the sides of the window to keep from being spotted.

"Are we still going to break out?" I asked. The deck beyond the window lacked several boards. The few remaining ones appeared less than sturdy. "I guess they didn't maintain this deck since there's no access to it."

"If we stick to the cross beams, we might be okay . We won't know how rotten it is until we get out there. We'll have to move quickly, no matter what." He turned to me. "We'll know when it's time to go."

When the light grew dim, Shortie stood in front of the window, hands on his hips. "What do you think Finch plans to do with all the money?"

"Huh?" I sat curled up in a corner.

He turned to me. "Estelle smuggled rare birds, right?"

I nodded. "Endangered ones too."

"Think Finch will continue in the business?"

I shrugged. "I don't know. Does it matter?"

"No idea. They've had me for a week, and this is your second day here." He sat beside me. "They won't keep us around for long if they plan to continue to smuggle." He leaned against the wall and pulled me closer so I could prop against him. "How's the knee?"

"No better, no worse. I think the wrap helped." I fiddled with the edge of it. "Weird how Charlene helped, isn't it?"

"Very."

We fell silent, and I slept. In my dream, I talked to Lauree. She lay on a bed, and I held her hand, her skin translucent. She bowed her head and prayed, "God, You're good and faithful. You're with Peg right now. Give her wisdom and peace." She squeezed my hand. Her eyes were so big in her thin face. "I'm with you through this. Whatever happens, I'm here. He's here. We're going to cling to that."

I awoke with a gasp. I remembered the prayer. I once prayed those words for her. "Thank you, thank you," I whispered. God used my best friend through a dream to comfort me and pray for me. I spent time praying for her and Hazel, my kids, and my grandson, and finally for Shortie and me to know what to do to break out.

Morning brought another paper bag, this time containing four donuts and a banana. We split the fruit and gobbled down the sweet treats.

"Today's the show." I uncapped my water bottle. "What's the plan?"

Shortie wiped his hands on his shorts. "We have to get out. The guards are only coming at mealtime now."

"Thank God they're still feeding us." The sugar from the donuts and banana was kicking in.

"Yep." He brushed off his beard and stood. "What if we use the blinds for an SOS?"

"Do you know Morse code?"

"I learned it way back when I joined the Navy. One of those things you don't pay much attention to. Hopefully, I remember a little." He fiddled with the lever for the blinds. They didn't move side to side. They only opened and shut. "Worth a try." He slid the handle several times, using both short and long motions.

"What if you spelled out hello?" I attempted a grin.

He frowned. "Do you have any better ideas?"

"Nope, sorry." We fell quiet.

After several minutes, Shortie stuck his nose against the glass. "Peg? Come here. I think I see a policeman."

I pushed myself up, gripping his hand to stand. All the blood rushed to my knee, and it throbbed. "Distract me." I leaned against him for support. "Ow, ow, ow."

"Check him out. Over there." He pointed to the beach area nearest the marina. "Isn't that guy in a uniform?"

"I think so." I squinted, trying to spot who he was showing me. The man walked closer to the condos. "Would they have police in this area for the show? It might be a security guy."

"I don't think so. Police are at the beach, but why waste manpower out here?" He slid the lever several times. "There, did he look at us?" He waved, making big motions with his long arms. I knocked on the window and hollered.

"Wait!" I called as the man turned back toward the boats.

Behind us, the door slammed open. "What are you two doing?" Charlene entered the room. "Stop it!" She shut the door. "Are you crazy?" she asked, her voice lowered to a whisper. "You can't call attention to yourselves."

"Whose side are you on?" Her words and actions confused me.

"Yours," she hissed. In a loud, commanding voice, she said, "Go sit down and be quiet. Or I'll send the guards down here." She turned to leave.

"Wait." I grabbed the back of her shirt. "What's going on?"

She shook me off. "Be patient. For once."

She sounded like Marcus.

Shortie and I took up our positions on either side of the window again. Being seen might be dangerous, but at the same time, we wanted to be rescued. The pain in my knee kept me from standing for long.

"Who would have thought missing egrets would lead to this?" I sat and rewrapped my leg, attempting to support the joint as much as possible.

Shortie chuckled. "I hate to tell you, Peg, but I'm not super surprised."

"Pfft. That's not nice." He had a point. Since I'd formed the birding group, things kept happening, like people dying or being killed. "Maybe I need a new hobby."

Our banter continued—anything to distract us from where we were and the danger we faced. The truth was, I assumed Marcus would have rescued me by now. When I looked through the window,

I expected to see him riding in—not on a white horse, but on a police boat—saving the day.

The sun was high in the sky, the Blue Angels doing their daring loop-de-loops, when the door to our room burst open again.

"Now, now, now," Charlene yelled. She swept her hands as if to scoop us up and throw us from the room. "Come on," she groaned. "Finch left for the beach, and the others are watching the show. Let's go. Let's go."

Shortie grabbed me around the waist and hopped me down the hallway. He lifted me into his arms when we reached the stairs. "This will be faster."

I ignored the little grunts he made with each step. He set me down when we reached the ground. We exited out at the back of the condos, onto the grassy yard that led to the water.

Charlene hurried in front of us. "This way." She ran to the left, away from the marina, and we followed. At the corner of the next set of buildings, she peeked around the edge. "It's clear. Let's go."

Over the bay, the jets roared by in formation. Applause and shouts rang out. In front of us, Charlene fell to the ground.

Shortie turned, then jerked me around the corner of the closest condo. "It's Estelle." He peeked around the building.

"What happened to Charlene? Did she shoot her?" I couldn't catch my breath. How did I get involved in all of this? I wanted to make friends and learn about birds—seagulls, pelicans, blue jays—not run away from bad guys.

"We gotta go." He wrapped his arm around my waist, and we took off. He ran one way and then the other. My knee screamed in agony.

"Where are we going?" I asked between each breath. I couldn't keep this up. My leg felt like it would come apart into two pieces.

We turned a corner and ran smack into Harry. I stepped away from him.

"Thank God, I didn't think I'd ever find you." He started running, waving for us to follow him.

I dug my toes in the grass and pulled Shortie to a stop. "I'm not going with him."

Harry trotted back. "Peg, please believe me. I'm not with them. Come with me, and I'll prove it."

"Estelle is back there." I jerked my thumb behind me.

"I know, I saw her. She shot Charlene." He tipped his head. "Don't write me off," he said. "I'm not Owen, I promise." He peered over my shoulder. "We've got to go. Now."

He took off, and after a glance behind us, Shortie picked me up again.

"I can walk," I shouted.

"This is quicker." He threw me over his shoulder like a sack of potatoes and followed Harry.

"What if he's taking us to Kitty or Finch?" I asked, each word coming out one at a time.

A shot rang out. Shortie tripped and tossed me behind him as he went down. Harry stumbled and fell. The next thing I knew, the world went dark.

My eyes snapped open, pain encompassing my body. My head hurt, my leg throbbed. "Where am I?" I attempted to roll onto my side and found my ankles and wrists were zip-tied. "What in the world?"

A tall pine tree soared above me. A glance to the side showed the water. In the distance, blue jets soared away from me. "No, come back." The words came out raspy.

"Ah, you're awake." A woman leaned over me, blocking out the sunshine.

"Estelle?" I squeezed my eyes shut and opened them again. "But … what?"

"Yes, it's me." She motioned with her hand, and one of my former guards scooted me back against the base of the tree.

I couldn't control my cries of pain. Tears streamed down my cheeks. Overhead, seagulls squawked, oblivious to what went on below them.

"Stop it," the guard said, jerking my wrists.

"It's okay," Estelle crooned. "No one can hear her. You can go now." She flicked her fingers as if he were a piece of dirt.

Confusion showed in his eyes. "You sure?"

"Yes." She spat the word. "Go."

The man walked away before picking up his pace and trotting toward the marina.

"What's your plan?" I asked Estelle.

She gestured to my right, away from the bay. "Your friends are out."

Shortie lay in a crumpled heap near me, his legs sprawled, one shoe missing. Several feet away, Harry sat propped underneath another tree, his head slumped to the side.

"You shot him." How badly was Harry injured? I couldn't tell if he was breathing.

She shook her head, her mouth pulled back in a grimace. "Silly boy."

"Harry?"

"No, Finch. He thought he had me under his thumb." Disgust crossed her face. "No one controls me." She swept back her hair.

"Harry's on your side, though," I said.

"No, I'm not," Harry mumbled.

Estelle laughed. "No, Peg. Silly woman. He buddied up to Finch, but I saw through it."

"Told ya," Harry said, his words slurred.

More tears fell. I misjudged everything. "I'm so sorry, Harry."

"I was trying"—he drew a deep breath—"to save you ..." He coughed and went quiet.

I wigged myself into a sitting position. "Please help him. Let him go." Guilt pierced me. Harry wasn't a bad guy. "You get away every time. I'm sure you have a plan."

"It's over, Peg. You lost. I won. I don't have to escape anything." She grinned, all of her teeth showing, like a satisfied cat who'd just eaten a mouse.

"You killed Marilyn? And Babs?" I needed to confirm that.

She frowned. "Derek. He did it. Both of them."

"Really?"

She crossed her arms. "You don't think for a minute I would kill someone, do you?"

"You killed Roger." I knew that for sure.

She huffed. "That man. Such a bother."

Behind her, I spotted Finch walking our way. His determined expression scared me.

"What did you win?" I asked. "You killed Sylvia—your friend. You killed your own husband. But you're still a fugitive, Estelle. That's *all* you are." Her body jerked. My words hit their mark.

She drew a deep breath and laughed. "You came in here sputtering your useless Scriptures."

"They're true. Not useless." My head pounded. Dizziness overcame me, nausea roiling in my stomach. "You don't know the power God has."

"What is that?" Contempt filled her face. "Look at you. You can't do anything."

Finch stopped behind Estelle and tapped her on the shoulder. "She might not be able to, but I can."

She turned, hands on her hips. "What do you want now?"

He flipped open his wallet. She leaned in, squinting her eyes. "U. S. Fish and Wildlife? What's that?"

He pulled handcuffs from his pocket. From behind me, I heard feet pounding the ground. A deep voice, one I knew well, said, "You're under arrest, Estelle Keaton. For murder, attempted murder, kidnapping, and smuggling endangered birds." Marcus stopped next to me. "I'm sure we'll find other things as well."

CHAPTER 34

SHORTIE, HARRY, AND I went by ambulance to the hospital. Marcus stopped by my room for a minute, kissed my forehead, and said he'd be back later. All three of my kids showed up and fussed over me. The nurse shooed them out when visiting hours ended. I asked them not to tell Hazel what happened, afraid it would delay her own recovery.

The next morning, breakfast time came and went, and no Marcus in sight. When someone knocked on my door, I perked up and ran my hands through my hair.

"Come in," I called.

Shortie peeked around the door. "You decent?"

"Hey, kidnap buddy. I'm good. Come on in." I raised the head of my bed.

He entered and turned in a circle, showing off his two hospital gowns. "The latest in patient wear, and they keep me warm in all the right places." He pulled the recliner closer to my bed. "I was unconscious yesterday. Why are you still in bed?"

"Dehydration. They want me to keep resting."

He made a face. "I'm sure you were. They've loaded me down with liquids since I've been here." He crossed his legs, tucking the gown down for modesty. "Has anyone been by to visit you?"

"My kids came by last night. Marcus peeked in for a second, but that's all. Have you seen anyone? Harry?"

He shook his head. "Kim came by for a bit. How's your knee? Do you need surgery?"

"No, I'm getting a brace. I'll have another 'appliance' to add to my boot." "Did you find out what happened?"

He stretched out in the recliner, putting his hands behind his head. He had no trouble keeping it in position. "I've gotten bits and pieces. A police officer interviewed me this morning." He yawned.

"Don't you go to sleep. Tell me everything."

His eyebrow twitched. "From what I gathered, Finch works for Fish and Wildlife. He really is Roger's son, but he chose to work on the right side of the law. I guess he went undercover and infiltrated Estelle's group."

"Wow. I wouldn't have guessed that in a million years." I readjusted my knee. "He did an excellent job impersonating a bad guy." I thought about his interactions with Elizabeth and wondered how much of it he made up.

"Apparently. That's all the information the officer would tell me."

"Hmm. Sure wish Marcus would show up." I pushed my nurse button.

"Yes," someone answered.

"I need help getting to the bathroom."

"We'll send someone right down," they said.

Shortie chuckled. "You can't go potty by yourself?"

"Thanks." I crossed my arms. "And, no. They say I'm a fall risk."

"They've got your number," he mumbled.

A CNA entered, whistling cheerfully. "It's a beautiful day! What's wrong, dear?" She opened the blinds, sunshine piercing every corner of the room.

"I need help to go ... you know."

"I've got you." She giggled. When she saw Shortie, she did a double-take. "You didn't want this strong young man to help?"

I scooted to the edge of the bed, and she helped me stand. I bit back a grunt. "Don't call him young. It'll go to his head."

When I finished, she helped me back into bed. "Anything else you need?"

"When do I get to go home?" I pulled the sheet and blanket up over my legs.

"She's grumpy." Shortie thumbed my way.

"Aren't visiting hours over?" I glared at him.

"I sure hope they're not." Charlene entered, a basket hooked over her arm. The CNA waved and left the room.

"Charlene, I'm glad you're here. Are you all right? I thought Estelle shot you?"

She showed a bandage on her upper arm. "Only a graze. I'm okay." She set the basket on the bed. "They let me go home last night."

"Lucky you." I raised my hands. "Sorry, you got shot, so not lucky you. I just want to go home."

Shortie pawed through the basket, picked out an apple and a granola bar, and stretched out again. "She's kind of grouchy." He chomped into the apple.

"She has every right to be." Charlene pulled up another chair. "I imagine you have questions."

"I do. Shortie told me about Finch. I thought you were on Estelle's side."

"Never. That woman. Ugh." A look of disgust covered her face.

I put my hand on her arm. "Thank you. If it hadn't been for you, we might not be here."

"Hey, what about me?" Shortie grinned. "I carried you down the stairs. And I ran with you."

"Eat your apple." I turned back to Charlene. "Did the police capture Estelle's men?"

"Yes, we did," Marcus said as he entered the room. "We got Kitty too. Okay if I come in?"

"The more the merrier," I said. He greeted Charlene and Shortie. With no other chairs available, he leaned against the wall.

"Hey, man," Shortie rose. "Take this seat. I need to head back to my room. They said I might get to go home today." He grabbed an orange from the basket, told Charlene goodbye, and pinched my toes. "I'll talk to you soon."

"Thanks." Tears filled my eyes.

"No crying or they won't let you leave," he teased. He leaned toward Marcus and muttered something I couldn't hear.

Charlene stood and made excuses to leave. Finally, only Marcus and I remained. He settled into the recliner and studied me.

"What?" I ran my fingers through my hair. "What have I done now?"

"What did you tell Shortie?" His dark eyes burned into mine.

"About ..."

"He just threatened me." He shifted on the chair, pushing it back so he could stretch out. "Within an inch of my life, I believe. I'm actually a little scared, and I carry a gun."

My face heated. "Well, I, oh, my." I didn't know how to explain the conversation Shortie and I had. "We were kidnapped together. We talked about a lot of things."

His eyebrow twitched.

"Anyhow," I smoothed my blanket. "How's the paperwork?"

"Peg, if you keep having these escapades, I'll end up with carpal tunnel."

"I'm finished, trust me. Hazel has a broken hip, Harry got shot, and Shortie ended up unconscious after being held hostage for days. The only positive thing is that you arrested Estelle."

"Finally. We found Derek too." He yawned. "He confessed to trapping the birds with those sticky pads you found."

"That'll stop his construction of tiny homes over the creek." Derek's greed caused it all. His desire to make more money led him to get rid of the egrets, kill his wife, and be Estelle's bad guy. It all snowballed into something even he never imagined. Warmth spread through my body. "A job well done," I whispered.

A nurse entered the room. "Time for meds." She spotted Marcus. "Your CNA told me you had a handsome man in here."

Marcus laughed. "Don't look at me. I just got here."

The nurse batted her eyelashes. "You have two male friends?" She winked.

"Sorta." I swallowed the capsules she gave me. "Thanks. Any idea when I can leave?"

"The doctor will make rounds in the morning." She fiddled with my IV and left.

"Morning? I want to go home now," I whined.

Marcus yawned again. "Close your eyes. Get some rest."

I'd dozed off when someone else knocked on the door. "Come in." Marcus looked over at me, a question in his eyes. I shrugged.

"Peg?" Harry entered, a worried expression on his face, and a vase filled with pink roses in his hand.

"Harry!" I held out my arms for a hug.

He set the flowers on the window ledge and hugged me. "I thought you'd still be mad." He squeezed me tighter.

"No, you said you weren't on their side. The only reason I thought you were was because of Owen." I kissed his cheek.

"I know." He straightened up and shook Marcus's hand. "Finch told me his real identity. He wanted me to help you. He's the one who left Lucy, by the way."

"He forgot to tell us any of that," Marcus said.

"Yep." Harry pulled up the other chair. "I'm not sure I helped, except for finding out about the puppy."

"Didn't you get shot?" I asked.

"Just a graze." He patted his side. "I played it off as worse to keep Estelle talking."

Marcus let out a soft whistle. "If you ever get tired of birds, you can come work for me."

"No, thank you." Harry grinned. "I'll stick with the birds."

"I don't know how safe birds are," I said. "Everything that's happened has been because of them. Have they already released you too?"

Harry nodded. "I stopped by to visit you before I went home."

I pouted. "Why does everyone go home but me?"

Marcus and Harry exchanged glances.

"It's really hot out today," Harry said.

"It was when I came in. Figured it would still be." Marcus smirked.

"I see what you two are doing. You can't get me off topic like that."

Both of them stood. Harry handed Marcus his crutches.

"I love you, Peg. See you soon." Harry kissed my cheek and left.

Marcus leaned down and kissed me. "I love you, too, Peg." He winked and left.

"Wait. He loves me?" I touched my lips and stared at the door. "He didn't really say that, did he? He repeated what Harry said, and Harry thinks of me like a sister." I crossed my arms. My stomach did flips and loop-de-loops like the Blue Angels. My head kept telling me it wasn't really love Marcus felt, just friendship.

My CNA entered carrying white towels over her arm. "Time for a shower."

Hoping the shower would help settle me, I limped my way into the bathroom, accepting help with the shampoo and soap. I dried off, and the CNA draped a clean gown over my head. I perched on the side of my bed. "Do I have to get back in the bed? Can I sit in the recliner?"

She helped me over to it. "Where did your handsome man go?"

"The first one or the second?" I laughed at her expression. "The one you saw proposed to me not too long ago."

"You said yes, didn't you?" She fanned her face. "That's one tall, handsome man." She handed me the remote for the television.

"No, I shut the door in his face. We got kidnapped together, though, and we talked it out. The other guy the nurse saw? That's the one. I'm sure of it."

"Kidnapped?" Her eye widened. "Were you the lady on the news?"

I palmed my forehead. In the news again. "Yes, probably. Oh, before you leave, do you know where my phone is?"

She pulled it from her pocket. "Yes, a good-looking detective gave it to me for you. I forgot."

I nodded. "That one. He's the one."

Cynthia picked me up the following day. The doctor released me with strict orders to rest and follow up with the orthopedic doctor. Once I got in her car, I told her to go park it.

"Why? Mom, you just got out of the hospital."

"I know. But I want to visit your grandmother." It felt like I hadn't seen her in months instead of only days. I had so much to tell her.

Cynthia stayed in the valet lane and rolled down her window. "Can you take care of my car, please? My mother needs a wheelchair too."

Before we went to Hazel's room, we stopped at the hospital gift shop where I bought a teddy bear.

"Hey!" Hazel's face brightened when she saw her granddaughter. She spotted me in the wheelchair. "What have you done now, Peg?"

I couldn't help laughing. Cynthia pushed me up beside the bed, and I took Hazel's hand. "I've missed you so much."

"I've missed you too." She squeezed my hand. "Why are you in a wheelchair?" she repeated.

I told her everything that had gone on while she'd been in the hospital. Her mouth dropped open and stayed that way through my story.

"I wondered why you didn't come see me." She shifted in her bed and groaned. "This hip stuff is for the birds."

I waved my hand. "I don't want to talk about birds for a while. If ever. Except for Roscoe. What did they say about your hip?"

"I have to go to rehab." She pouted.

"We'll come visit. I'll sneak CB in if I have to," I said. "We'll make it work."

Cynthia nodded. "I can smuggle Lucy in my purse."

"No more baskets with bugs," I said. We all shared a laugh.

Hazel leaned back on her pillow. "I can't believe you finally got her. Estelle."

"Me too." I held up my thumb. "Estelle is in jail." My pointer finger went up. "And Derek killed Marilyn. He's in jail too. We found the egrets." That was for my middle finger. For my ring finger, I said, "And Lauree's okay. For now."

She reached out and raised my pinky. "God has her in the palm of His hand." She wrapped my hand in hers. "I'm so glad you solved all of it. But boy, am I mad at you."

"Why?" I couldn't think of any reason for her to be angry.

"You did all of it without me," she said, patting her hair. "I could've been on the news. And shown off my new haircut."

I smiled through my tears. "Never change, Hazel. Okay? Never change."

Epilogue

"Are you sure this dress works? I don't look too young?" I fiddled with my pearl earrings—a gift from Hazel for my something old. I told her I counted as the something old, but she swatted my words aside.

"Mom," Cynthia said as she smoothed the buttons on the back of my sundress, "you look beautiful. The blue brings out your eyes." She turned me toward the mirror. "Look at yourself."

I smiled, appreciating her compliments. I looked exactly as I wanted-ed. My dress counted as something new and blue. I tapped my watch, the one Lauree let me borrow for this special day. "It's almost time." My stomach fluttered. "Will you pray for me, Hazel?"

My mother-in-law, dressed in a peach-colored sundress, sat in the corner of the room. She stood and took our hands. "Father God, we ask Your blessing on this day. Calm any worries." She squeezed my hand, and I squeezed back. "Thank you for what you've done in our lives. Thank you that Lauree is here today to celebrate with us."

My nose began to run. "I can't cry now."

She shot me the stink eye. "I'm praying."

I bowed my head, sniffling through the rest of the prayer. When she said, "Amen," I rushed for the box of tissues.

"They sure have cleaned up the meeting room since the time we came for the neighborhood association fiasco." I blew my nose. "Did you have anything to do with that?"

Hazel grinned. "Possibly. I am the one who makes all of those decisions now, you know. Since Babs and the Crofts are gone." She whispered the last sentence.

I stifled a shiver. I couldn't believe a year had passed since the egrets went missing and I found them. I'd been kidnapped and held with Shortie. And Finch, Harry, and Marcus rescued us.

Repairs on my house were finished a few months afterward, and I moved back in. Carter would be home between semesters, and Hazel often stayed over. She still talked about selling her house, but so far she hadn't made the leap. Recently, Cynthia told me she was thinking about renting her own apartment. I didn't care as long as my family and friends were nearby.

Cynthia touched up her makeup and headed for the door. "Couldn't you have gotten married in December when we have a chance of it being cold? I'm going to check and make sure the reception food is all on ice."

"We're going to Bermuda for our honeymoon, though. What better time than in July?" I called as she left the "bride's room."

Chloe came in as she left. "You ready? Oh, Mom, you look beautiful." Tears welled in her eyes.

"No tears, dear, even if you are pregnant again." Hazel patted her back.

Chloe fanned her face. "Barely pregnant, but yeah, the hormones are on high."

I hooked my arms in Hazel's and Chloe's, and we left the small room for the main one. I wanted the ceremony to be only for our family and wedding party, with the reception open to all of our friends. Even Shortie would be there. "Where is Carter?"

He tapped my shoulder. "Right here."

I turned and straightened his tie. When I reached out to fix his hair, he stepped back.

"Mom, I'm fine." His grin was lopsided. "You'll never stop momming me, will you?"

"Never, and you love it." I grinned at his pretend pained expression.

Lauree entered the back of the room and clapped her hands. Dressed in a flowy, pale blue peasant dress that hid her thin figure, her hair in a cute short pixie cut, she looked the picture of health. Hazel's words from the year before came to my mind. I worked hard to make the most of every moment I had with Lauree. Some days were better than others. Today was a good day.

"Take your places," she called. "Carter, Peg, back here with me." She stood us in front of her and placed my hand on Carter's arm. Chloe and Cynthia stood up front, Suzie beside them as a junior bridesmaid. All three wore white sundresses, complete with flip-flops. Hazel argued against them, but when I showed her my footwear, she gave up.

"Groomsmen and groom up front. That goes for you, Mr. Junior Groomsman." Stevie joined the other men, all of whom wore khaki shorts and blue-patterned Hawaiian shirts. Lauree looked around. "Where's Reese?"

"Tom should be here any moment. He didn't think Reese would last long," I said. I didn't care how long he lasted or how he behaved. I only wanted all of my family here. "Oh, but where is Harry?"

The front door opened. "I'm here," Harry said as he strolled in, Carmen on his arm. "Let's get this party started." He kissed my cheek before they sat up front beside Hazel. "Tom's on his way in."

The door opened again, and Tom entered with Reese in his arms. He set the toddler down, and Reese turned around and clung to my legs, stomping on my fresh pedicure. He offered up the sweetest grin. I shifted my sparkly blue sandals away from his bare feet.

"Don't you look handsome, big guy?" I admired his shorts and shirt that matched the groomsmen's.

Tom sat beside John in the row behind Hazel. He clapped his hands. Reese turned and saw his daddy and the stuffed bear he held out.

"Cue the music," Lauree called.

"It's all in the timing." I chuckled. At the rehearsal, Tom used a different stuffed animal, saving Reese's favorite bear for the real deal. Reese toddled down the aisle, the wedding rings safely stuffed inside his tiny Hawaiian shirt pocket.

"Everyone's here," I whispered.

"Except the groom. Where's the groom?" Lauree hollered over the music. Another door opened, and I looked up. Marcus made his way toward the front of the room. Dressed in blue Hawaiian shorts and a white T-shirt, he walked with only a slight limp.

He reached the front and turned. Catching my eye, he grinned. There it was. The dimple I'd get to see and trace for the rest of my life.

"Everyone's here now," I said as Carter and I made our way down the aisle.

The End

I so appreciate my friend, Dani Wade, and my sister, Debbie Williams, for taking the time to read *No Egrets* before I sent it to my publisher. They provided valuable feedback and made the story stronger. Thanks to you both!

About the Author

Jen Dodrill is married and is the mother of five adult children and grandmother of three, two girls and a boy. She homeschooled for thirteen years, taught Oral Communication for her local community college, and is a 'retired' Navy wife. After her youngest graduated high school, Jen started writing her first book. Her inspiration comes in many forms, and she loves incorporating humor and personal experiences into her stories.

Jen is an avid fiction reader with an eclectic collection of novels, many of which sit in an old embalming fluids box belonging to her great-grandfather, Captain Alfred, MD.

When she's not writing, you'll find her spending time with her family or curled up on the couch with her favorite black cat, reading and drinking a mug of dark roast coffee.

To learn more, visit —https://jendodrillwrites.com

Find all of Jen Dodrill's books at:

https://jendodrillwrites.com/books-by-jen-dodrill/

Birds Alive! – An Empty-nesters Cozy Mystery, Book 1

A clean, humorous cozy mystery featuring a midlife, amateur sleuth, small-town secrets, and a deadly birding group.

Peg Howard—widow, mom blogger, and brand-new empty nester—is desperate for a fresh start. When a late-night post sends her loyal *Mamma Birds* readers into a panic, Peg takes a follower's advice and launches the Empty Nesters Birding Group in sunny Pensacola, Florida.

But their first outing turns deadly.

A fellow birder collapses after handling birdseed contaminated with peanuts—seed that should have been safe. As a hurricane barrels toward the Gulf Coast and Peg's overbearing (and animal-loving) mother-in-law invades her newly quiet home, Peg hopes the chaos will pass.

But the real danger is just beginning.

After the storm, Peg discovers one of her new friends has been attacked, and the killer is still on the scene. A fall down a staircase leaves Peg injured, shaken, and more determined than ever to uncover the truth.

With a broken foot, a stubborn streak, and help from her unlikely allies—including her meddling mother-in-law and a charming detective whose dimples are dangerously distracting—Peg dives into a murder investigation that proves retirement from motherhood doesn't mean a quiet life.

Where's the Quetzal? – An Empty-nesters Cozy Mystery, Book 2

Still settling into life as an empty nester in Pensacola, Peg has found purpose leading her birding group and building new friendships. But just as life begins to feel steady, danger returns. News that Estelle and Roger Keaton—linked to the deaths of two birders—are back in town sends unease through the group. At the same time, the discovery of a historic shipwreck and a rare quetzal feather at Fort Pickens raises troubling questions no one can answer.

Then Roger Keaton turns up dead—and another birder is attacked. What begins as curiosity quickly becomes a dangerous investigation as Peg uncovers clues tied to stolen artifacts, secret research, and rare quetzals that don't belong anywhere near Florida's Gulf Coast. With her sharp eye for detail and growing confidence as an amateur sleuth, Peg teams up with her loyal friends—and a familiar detective—to piece together the truth.

But when an anonymous caller targets her family and Peg herself becomes a suspect, the stakes turn personal.

As the danger escalates, Peg must balance the joy of becoming a grandmother with the fear that solving this mystery may cost her everything.

Finding Ginny

A heartwarming multigenerational drama about addiction, forgiveness, and a grandmother's fight for custody.

Kat Johnson is a widowed elementary school teacher living a quiet life in Virginia Beach—until her estranged daughter returns after eight years, leaves behind a six-year-old granddaughter Kat never knew existed, and disappears.

Ginny is frightened, vulnerable, and desperate for stability. Kat opens her home and her heart, knowing Becky is still battling drug addiction and could come back for Ginny at any time. As summers pass and Ginny keeps returning, their bond grows stronger—but Becky's relapses grow more dangerous.

When Becky vanishes, and Ginny is taken across state lines, Kat must fight for custody of the child who has become her world. Facing a failing heart, a painful family history, and impossible legal odds, Kat turns to her faith, her friends, and a strength she never knew she had.

In a battle between addiction and love, only one can win.

Trinity Sands Beach Club – Second Chances: Romance & Mysteries

What do a widow, a newly divorced woman, and a retired professor of art history have in common?
They all came to Trinity Sands Island to find a simple life without any entanglements. But instead, they are each confronted with a mystery and another chance at romance. Will they be brave enough to face the possible dangers of solving a mystery and losing their hearts?

This collection includes three novellas:

"SeaBreeze Obsession" by Jen Dodrill—Newly single Karah Halyard returns to her beach cottage and starts "SeaBreeze Designs," a business specializing in beach decor. But beneath the tentative peace of her life, unresolved feelings stir as she considers reconciling with her ex-husband, Gage, who is in town doing research. When a secret admirer confronts her on the beach, Karah defends herself and runs. That night, he's found dead. As she and Gage face a murder investigation, they must confront their past and unravel the mystery of the real killer.

Can they solve the crime and reconcile their fractured relationship?

"Trinity Sands Treasure Hunt" by Sharon Carpenter—Retired art professor Claire Anderson inherited all of her uncle's worldly goods. Arriving at his Trinity Sands Beach Club bungalow, she faces the daunting task of sorting through the boxes and bags that he left behind. When someone tries to break in and steal seemingly worthless items, Claire calls Chief of Security, Ben Hastings and sparks fly. Claire and Ben realize all is not as it seems when they set out to discover who is targeting the house.

In their search for answers, will the attraction between Claire and Ben deepen into real treasure?

"Searching for Serenity" by Deborah Sprinkle—Grace Caldwell hasn't been to their beach house since her husband passed away three years ago. Her grief has kept her from moving forward with her life.

But, when a letter arrives from her friend, Serenity James, saying something strange is going on at the Beach Club, Grace decides it's time to head south. However, when she arrives, Serenity has disappeared, and no one knows where she is. Detective Peter Young gets involved and, as Grace and he work together, a mutual attraction blossoms—one that takes Grace by surprise.

Will Grace find love again while solving the mystery behind Serenity's disappearance?

Stay up-to-date on my books by subscribing to my free newsletter: https://jendodrill writes.com/sign-up-for-newsletter/